PRAISE FOR
THE BOOK CLUB MYSTERIES

"Smart, fast-paced, and fun . . . [an] appealingly clever protagonist and her witty group of Readaholics, who dissect great books while solving an intricately plotted murder that kept me turning pages late into the night."
—*New York Times* bestselling author Kate Carlisle

"Laura DiSilverio hits it out of the park . . . engaging characters. Beautiful setting. Readers will be enchanted."
—*New York Times* bestselling author Carolyn Hart

"Witty, fresh, and thoroughly engaging, Amy-Faye Johnson and her Readaholic friends will leave you wanting more in this engaging new mystery series."
—national bestselling author Sally Goldenbaum

"A very enjoyable debut . . . [an] evenly paced mystery that quickly became a page-turner, as the unfolding drama was hard to put down." —Dru's Book Musings

"[DiSilverio] shows a masterful grasp of detail. . . . The mystery unfolds at the perfect pace and has a climactic and satisfying ending." —The Qwillery

"Mystery lovers of both classic and current cozies will love this. . . . It is fast-paced, witty, and intelligent, with likable characters and a lovable, loyal protagonist, Amy-Faye." —Open Book Society

"An enticing plot with an eccentric cast of characters that is sure to please the reader . . . fantastically written."
—A Cozy Girl Reads

P9-CNB-428

Chapter 1

Normally, when I'm surrounded by books, I'm in a state of bliss. Today, I could feel a headache coming on. That wasn't the books' fault; no, it was a by-product of dealing with the people who wrote them. I'd never had much contact with writers. Barring the one signing I went to some years ago in Boulder, where the author entertained the small audience with humorous stories about writing his police procedurals and life in Wyoming, I didn't think I'd ever met a writer. I'd blithely assumed they'd all be something like the Boulder author—affable, entertaining, happy to interact with fans. First wrong assumption . . .

I'd discovered the hard way that attending an author signing bore no resemblance to organizing a multiple-author event. When Gemma Frant, owner of Heaven's only bookstore, Book Bliss, had hired me to put together a "Celebration of Gothic Novels" to coincide with the September birthdays of her favorite twentieth-century gothic authors, I'd jumped at the chance. What could be more fun than organizing an event focused on books? After all, I'd grown up in a house with more books than dust mites, with a mother who was a librarian. I had read voraciously since sounding out my first

2 / Laura DiSilverio

Dr. Seuss book, and would just as soon have gotten on a plane or gone to a doctor's waiting room naked as without a book. Five years ago, I'd started the Readaholics, the book club currently reading du Maurier's *Rebecca* in honor of this event. It's one of the most widely read gothic novels of all time, after all. So, I'd figured any event that revolved around books had to be fun, right? Second off base assumption . . .

I'd had fun decorating Book Bliss for today's activities and I smiled with satisfaction as I scanned the effect I'd created. Thinking "gothic," I'd borrowed the Heaven High School theater department's backdrops from last year's production of *Dracula*. They depicted a spooky stone castle, complete with painted bats and sickle moon. Arranged in a semicircle behind the signing table, the flats gave the bookstore an appropriately eerie air, I thought. I'd added to it by having my friend Lola Paget, who owns Bloomin' Wonderful, the best nursery in a five-county area, rent me some potted trees, which I'd clumped together near the door to make it feel like customers were entering a forest. Once the signing was over, Lola and her crew would relocate the trees to the Rocky Peaks Golf and Country Club, which was hosting tonight's gothic-themed costume party. My assistant, Al Frink, had put together a sound track for the event, downloading music from the sound tracks of *Dracula*, *The Phantom of the Opera*, some Hitchcock flicks, and *Sweeney Todd*. It was all gothic and atmospheric and I was hugely pleased with myself and Al. Gemma was oohing and aahing, while the photographer I'd hired was taking dozens of photos that would go on the store's and my Web site and Facebook page.

Gemma wanted a full day of activities, starting with a birthday party and an author panel this morning and culminating in the costume party with all the guests dressing as their favorite gothic characters from books, TV, or movies. She thought it was wonderfully appropriate because there was that disastrous costume party sequence in *Rebecca*, and costumes play a large role in many gothic works. Think of the masquerade scene in *The Phantom of the Opera*, and the protagonist's mask, for that matter. Since Heaven, Colorado (population 10,096, according to the sign as you drive into town), was, sadly, devoid of gothic castles, we were holding it at the Club tonight.

The birthday party was because all of Gemma's favorite gothic authors were born in September. They included Victoria Holt (September 1), Joan Aiken (September 4), Phyllis Whitney (September 9), Mary Stewart (September 17), and Barbara Michaels (September 29). I had to admit it was almost eerie how many of them were born in the same month. To top it off, this September would have been Mary Stewart's one hundredth birthday, so my go-to baker had constructed a cake decorated with icing replicas of some of the birthday authors' covers, and crowned it with a hundred candles.

Following the birthday party and the panel, we had media interviews for the visiting authors, a high school writing contest for the authors to judge, and an auction of donated merchandise, including a collection of first-edition books by the birthday novelists. The auction was to fund a scholarship for a Heaven High School student to attend the Pikes Peak Writers Conference in Colorado Springs. Gemma had proposed naming the scholarship after du Maurier, but when the high school administrators found out that she was apparently bi-sexual and had had an affair with the novelist Gertrude Lawrence, they put the kibosh on naming it after her. They'd christened it simply the Book Bliss Scholarship for Creative Writing Students.

Even though gothic novels weren't my reading ma-terial of choice, I'd heard of all of the event's headliners: Constance Aldringham, writer of perennially bestsell-ing gothic romances; Francesca Bugle, the midlister rumored to have a hit and a major studio movie deal on her hands with her forthcoming novel; and Mary Stew-art, the much ballyhooed debut novelist. Apparently, the latter's birth certificate name was actually Mary Stewart, although she was no relation of the gothic romance author of the same name who had been big in the genre in the 1950s and '60s. It made me wonder if names were destiny. Were all Mary Stewarts fated to become gothic novelists? If so, what did being named Amy-Faye Johnson portend?

Aggravation.

"I simply must be seated in the middle," Constance Aldringham was telling my assistant, Al Frink. She re-arranged the nameplates he had set on the table for the author panel that would start in half an hour. "And don't forget to have a bottle of Perrier and fresh sliced limes at my place. Talking to fans parches me, simply parches me, and I must rehydrate. I count on you to attend to these details for me. I cannot, simply cannot, waste my creative energies on such mundane matters." This last was apparently directed at her mousy-looking assistant, who quailed at the sharp note in her boss's voice. Or it might have been meant for her husband, a bearded man with stooped shoulders, who had made his way to the bookshelf with World War II histories immediately upon entering the shop, and was now hiding behind a study of tank warfare tactics.

The acknowledged grande dame of modern gothic romances, Constance Aldringham was a well-preserved sixty-something who had wisely let her hair go white. Smoothed back from a wide forehead and caught up in a low chignon, it emphasized her pale skin, which was minimally lined for a woman her age. Her brows were darker, peaked instead of arched, framing skillfully made-up light blue eyes. She affected clothes in dark hues that set off her hair. Today's dress was navy blue, sweeping almost to her ankles, and accented with a paisley silk scarf, chosen, I suspected, to obscure the slightest hint of jowls and a crepey neck.

Al gave me a "What do I do?" look, and I signed for him to let it be. We had intended to have the authors sit in alphabetical order, but if no one else complained, it didn't make much difference if Constance sat in the middle. On the short side, wearing a sweater-vest and bow tie, and with his sandy hair recently buzz-cut, Al looked like a refugee from the 1950s, the "good kid" Mrs. Cleaver and her ilk would have trusted without hesitation. In truth, he'd been a bit of a troublemaker in high school and it had taken him a couple of years to straighten up and enroll in college. The university had matched him with me as an intern for my event-organizing business—Eventful!—a couple of years ago and it had worked out great. I'd recently asked him to come on board full-time when he graduated, and he was still thinking about the offer.

Now he straightened Constance's name tent, gave the table skirt a twitch, and disappeared into Gemma's stockroom, where we had parked the refreshments for the signing. I was about to follow him to set out the cake decorated with images of covers from the birthday authors' most famous novels, when there was a knock on the still-locked front door. Gemma hurried to let in a stocky woman I recognized from book jackets as Francesca Bugle. She wore a red jacket with wide lapels that did not flatter her top-heavy figure, and a felt hat decked with red poppies.

A man followed her, his attire making it plain he wasn't from around here. I'd bet tonight's paycheck he was from L.A. He wore a black linen blazer over a black silk T-shirt, slacks, and loafers without socks. Facial hair that was several days past "forgot to shave" but not quite up to "mustache and goatee" framed his mouth. I figured he worked hard to keep it at that exact in-between stage. Maybe ten years older than me—in his early forties—he had a round bald spot on the crown of his head and kept the rest of his hair cut short. A pair of trendy glasses was shoved up on his head and I wondered if they were meant to hide the bald spot.

"Gemma! Hon!" Francesca threw her arms around slim Gemma and squeezed so hard she knocked Gemma's glasses askew. "Nice to meet you finally."

"Thank you for joining us for our Celebration of Gothic Novels," Gemma said in her fluttery way. She smoothed the ruffle at her neckline. "I enjoy your books so much."

"Especially the naughty bits, hey?" Francesca winked, then drew the man forward. "This is Cosmo Zeller, president of Zeller Productions. That's the company that's turning *Barbary Close* into a blockbuster. Right, Cos?"

Cosmo slouched forward and pulled one hand out of his pocket to shake hands with Gemma. "Spot-on, Frannie. It's going to be big. Bigger than big. Huge. I think the opening-weekend gross will beat the numbers *Fifty Shades* put up." His gaze went to the smartphone in his other hand.

"He's scouting locations, since a large part of the book takes place in a small town in the mountains. It's really in Oregon, but Cosmo says Colorado's been offering filmmakers a lot of incentives. We're staying the whole week—I'm fascinated by everything that goes into making a movie."

The photographer approached and took a photo of the duo. Francesca smiled for the camera, stood beside Gemma for another photo, and then looked around the store. Spotting Constance and her entourage, she called, "Hey, Connie, Merle, Allyson. Good to see you."

Constance dipped her head like a queen recognizing a peasant. "Francesca." Her husband and assistant copied her, their nods tentative, as if Constance might divorce or fire them for acknowledging Francesca.

"A little bird told me sales of your latest are way down," Francesca said, her mobile mouth puckering into a moue of seeming concern. "Is it true Oubliette Press isn't picking up the option on your next book?"

Constance sent her an icy look from narrowed eyes. Before she could reply, Francesca laughed heartily, and sailed toward me, hand out. "I'm Francesca Bugle. And you are?"

"Amy-Faye Johnson. I'm the event organizer."

We shook and my fingers tingled when she released her grip.

"Bang-up job you've done," she said with a decisive nod that set the poppies on her hat bobbing. "Love the castle." She gestured toward the painted flats. "I've never been to Heaven before, but it's a nice-looking little town you've got here. Love that B and B, the Columbine."

I'd managed to get all the writers and their various relatives and hangers-on into Heaven's most exclusive B and B, the Columbine. In fact, they'd taken over the whole house for the week. Francesca and Cosmo were staying to scout for movie locations, Constance Aldringham and her family were taking advantage of the free accommodations and lovely surroundings to have their first vacation in eight years (or so Constance had told Gemma), and Mary Stewart was using the charming inn as a writing retreat.

"I'm ready for a change of pace," Francesca said. "Just turned in a manuscript, so I'm in no hurry to get back to Winnetka. It was twenty-two degrees there when I left yesterday. Felt more like December than September. *Brrr.*" She gave an exaggerated shiver. "Scouting for movie locations will be fun."

"I hope you enjoy—" But before I could finish, she was turning away, introducing herself to Al as he came out of the stockroom bearing the birthday cake decorated with frosting replicas of some of the birthday authors' books.

"That is the most beautiful thing I've ever seen," Francesca exclaimed. "Who is the genius that did that? I've got to get a cake like that for my next book launch. I can just see the cover of *Never Again, My Lovely* done up in buttercream and fondant. The mist, the seascape—it'll be gorgeous."

I gave her one of the baker's cards. She was tucking it into the structured purse hanging from her elbow when there was another knock, Gemma unlocked the door, and a light voice said, "I'm not late, am I?"

We all turned to look at the willowy young woman glowing on the threshold. The sun shone through her white dress—my mother would have insisted on a slip—and set her red hair on fire. Pleased that we had been struck dumb by her entrance, Mary Stewart the Living (which is how I differentiated between her and the author of *Madam, Will You Talk?*, the Merlin trilogy, and other books I'd enjoyed when I stumbled on them as a college freshman) glided into the room and shook hands with Gemma. Behind her, one of the most handsome men I'd ever seen carried in a box and set it on a table. I couldn't help but think that he was a gothic hero come to life, tall, dark, and brooding, with full lips that would have landed him a men's cologne commercial if he was an actor, and springy black hair that I knew would feel crisp if I ran my fingers through it.

What was I thinking? I was happily involved with Lindell Hart, Heaven's chief of detectives. I didn't need to be fantasizing about a man who hadn't yet hit thirty and who looked like he might be the model for the vampire on the cover of Mary's book, *Blood Will Out*. He politely backed out of the frame when the photographer came forward to take a photo of Mary Stewart.

Mary hugged Francesca and told Constance, "*Simply* lovely to see you again."

While I was wondering if her emphasis on "simply" was a sly dig at Constance or if that was how all authors talked, she took the gorgeous man's hand and said, "Everybody, this is my brother Lucas."

We all chorused, "Hi, Lucas," as if we were at an AA meeting.

He flashed a brilliant smile that dispelled the broodiness. "Nice to meet you all."

"There's quite a crowd out there already," Mary said, apparently delighted. She had a way of talking that made every sentence sound like it ended with an exclamation point. "Scads of people waiting to meet us and hear about our books. This is going to be such *fun!*"

Strike three . . .

Chapter 2

Gemma propped open the doors on the stroke of ten o'clock. As excited book lovers poured in, the three authors took their seats at the panel table. The photographer snapped photos nonstop, first of the authors and then of the surging crowd. The fans were primarily women, but there was a sprinkling of men among them. Husbands, mostly, I thought. They settled into the folding metal chairs Al and I had set up earlier, with help from the rental company owner. Gemma, fairly vibrating with excitement, welcomed everyone and launched into a description of the Celebration of Gothic Novels and the day's events. She thanked me for organizing the day, and insisted I come forward to take a bow. When I did, I noticed my Readaholics friends sitting together in the back row. Kerry Sanderson, the town's part-time mayor, patted the empty chair beside her, making it clear they'd saved it for me.

When I tuned back in to Gemma, she had finished talking about Victoria Holt's eight different pen names, and was reminding everyone that Mary Stewart had been born Mary Florence Elinor Rainbow and allegedly started writing stories at the age of three. So much for my ruminations about names being fate. Someone named "Rainbow" should have been writing children's lit or New Agey stuff. Gemma went on a bit too long with the biographies for my taste, but the audience seemed interested in details about the original Mary Stewart's degrees and ectopic pregnancy; Phyllis Whitney's birth in Japan, early life in Asia, prolific writing career, and death at 104; and Joan Aiken's work as a librarian for the United Nations. I noticed that the panelists seemed less so, with Francesca Bugle fidgeting with her pen and Mary Stewart the Living surreptitiously checking her phone under the table.

"And now it's time to introduce our panelists, who really need no introduction," Gemma said, pushing her glasses up her nose. "It is my very great privilege, my honor, to introduce three of the—no, *the* three most exciting authors of gothic novels working today." She read each author's biography, mentioning Constance's Berkeley education and early writing success, Francesca's hardscrabble childhood, and Mary's stint as an international-caliber junior tennis player. She then led the audience in a round of applause. Constance Aldringham inclined her head graciously, Mary Stewart twiddled her fingers in a little wave, and Francesca Bugle said, "Glad to be here."

During the clapping, I sidled around the standing-room-only crowd and slid into the chair Kerry was saving for me.

"Nice turnout," Kerry whispered with an approving nod. She sat erect, back not touching the chair, her short brown hair recently trimmed, low-heeled pumps planted on the floor. She wore a mulberry-colored suit, so I knew she considered herself to be here in an official capacity as Heaven's mayor. "Wish I could get this many people to come to my town hall meetings, but I guess city ordinances about roosters, and tweaks to the town's IT contract, aren't nearly as interesting."

I grinned. From Kerry's other side, my best friend, Brooke Widefield, leaned forward, her mink-dark hair spilling over her shoulders, and said in a low voice, "Speaking of interesting, who is *that*?" She gave a discreet nod of her head.

Without even looking, I knew she was motioning toward Lucas Stewart. "Mary Stewart's brother," I whispered back.

"Yummy."

A woman in the row ahead of us turned and frowned, so we guiltily shut up. I contented myself with waving to Lola Paget, who sat on Brooke's right. She pushed wire-rimmed glasses up her nose and smiled at me, before giving her attention to the panel.

"As the panel's facilitator," Gemma said, half-turning to look at the authors, "I wonder if you could explain the elements of a gothic novel to our audience. Mary, would you like to start?"

"Of course, Gemma. There's pretty much nothing I'd rather talk about than gothic novels." Her voice had a little-girl quality I thought would get irritating if I had to listen to it for long. "Gothics are a cross between mystery and horror, but horror in the psychological sense, or the supernatural sense, usually, not the blood and gore horror of a chain-saw-wielding psychopath. Some early examples of gothic literature include *The*

Castle of Otranto, Austen's *Northanger Abbey*, the Brontë sisters' books, *The Turn of the Screw*, Poe, *The Hound of the Baskervilles*, and, of course, *Dracula* and *Frankenstein*. Oh, and a lot of you have probably seen *The Phantom of the Opera*, right, at least the musical?" She got some head nods. "Young, virginal opera singer, tragic 'monster' in love with her, crumbling old opera house with a lake beneath it . . . gothic, gothic, gothic!"

Francesca Bugle leaned in to the mic. "If a story's got a governess or another young woman who for some reason or other has to put up with a tyrannical and/or tortured hero, ghosts, maybe a nun or monk, spooky houses you just know have plumbing problems, sinister servants, maybe an at-risk kid or two, and a lot of really bad weather, it's probably a gothic." The audience chuckled.

Mary added, "There are subsets of gothic called Southern gothic—think Faulkner—where the 'horror' is more about a decaying culture and really dysfunctional families haunted by old secrets, incest, alcoholism . . . you name it."

I was reluctantly impressed by her answers and had to admit she knew her field, even if she sounded like Betty Boop.

Before Gemma could direct a question to one of the other panelists, a woman's voice asked from the other side of the room, "Is it true you're involved in a lawsuit over *Blood Will Out*, that someone is suing you, saying you stole the manuscript?"

Assorted gasps rose up and people craned their necks to see the speaker. I knew I recognized the voice, but couldn't place it. Half-standing, I caught a glimpse of the questioner. I should have known: Flavia Dunbarton, a reporter for the *Grand Junction Gabbler.* I'd met her while investigating Ivy's death. One of the Readaholics, Ivy had been poisoned in May.

Gemma Frant opened and closed her mouth without making a sound, obviously appalled by the question. Mary Stewart, however, handled it calmly. "Yes, there is a lawsuit. But, no, I didn't steal poor Eloise's manuscript, if that's your next question." She gave a little laugh. "My lawyers have advised me not to discuss the case, but I will tell you I've never even met Eloise Hufnagle."

Gemma fluttered her hands at chest height, and tried to regain control, leaning too close to the microphone so her words boomed out and she took a startled step back. "Ms. Aldringham, you have been writing gothic novels for a very long time, even while the book world was saying gothics were out of fashion. Do you feel vindicated now that they are enjoying a resurgence?"

"I'd like to think I had a little something to do with gothics regaining popularity," Constance said coyly. "I've had a book on the *New York Times* list nonstop for thirty-one years, except for the year I had Allyson."

While the crowd clapped for her accomplishment, I studied the mousy girl I had thought was her assistant. Allyson was her daughter? She scrunched down in her chair, as if in guilt over having broken her mother's streak of bestsellers. She was seated at the end of a row and Lucas Stewart stood only feet away. As I watched, he put a hand on her shoulder and leaned down to whisper in her ear. Something close to a smile trembled on her lips, and she sat up straighter. As he stepped back, her gaze followed him.

A draft brought my attention to the door, where I noticed a newcomer slip in and sidle to his right. I didn't recognize him. With crew-cut hair, pasty skin, and a burly build, and wearing jeans that were none too clean, he didn't fit my idea of a gothic-novel lover. Military, maybe? A sailor, I thought doubtfully, eyeing the short hair and the forearms and knuckles covered with tattoos. After a furtive glance around the crowded room, like a fox wanting to be sure he couldn't be cornered, he focused on the authors up front.

Constance had wrapped up her comments and Francesca Bugle was speaking about the movie being made from *Barbary Close*. "It's not a done deal, yet," she said, "but I understand the producers are talking to Jennifer Lawrence."

Pleased oohs and aahs rose from the crowd. Francesca's books featured what I thought of as the classic gothic heroine, the Jane Eyre type, a virginal young woman at the mercy of an employer or relative who looked a lot like Lucas Stewart, only older. Her books had spooky castles and isolated manor homes, disturbed children, sinister servants, and mysterious disappearances of the heroes' wives. Her protagonists were extremely well drawn—emotionally vulnerable, but with a reservoir of spunk. In a definitely unclassic twist, their relationships with the brooding heroes usually took a bondage-related turn. Her books had been gaining in popularity with readers looking for a more literary and suspenseful *Fifty Shades of Grey*.

After another twenty minutes of back-and-forth with the panel, Gemma turned to the audience and said, "And now our authors will be happy to take questions. Anyone?" She craned her neck and swiveled her head before pointing to a woman two rows ahead of me who wanted to know where the authors got their ideas.

I stood and hustled over to where Al Frink was keeping an eye on the refreshments, knife ready for cake slicing when the panel wrapped up. One hundred candles ringed its perimeter. The three authors were jointly supposed to blow them out when I rolled the cake on its mobile cart into the center of the room. "Let's start lighting," I told Al.

As a flame sprouted from the lighter's tip, a man's voice asked, "How do you all choose your pen names? Why use pen names, anyway?"

Glancing up, I saw that the question came from the jeans-clad latecomer. A sharp intake of breath from the panel table made me turn my head, but I couldn't tell who had reacted to the man's presence.

"I'll take this, shall I?" Mary said with a bright smile, pulling the table mic closer. "'Mary Stewart' is not a pen name. It is the name given to me by my parents. I've been asked about it so often, I should carry a copy of my birth certificate with me." Laughter from the audience rewarded her droll remark.

"Sometimes an author's real name is simply too hard to pronounce, or too common," Constance offered, "so the author uses a pen name."

"Or the real name doesn't fit the genre," Francesca

said. "I mean, who's going to read a romance written by someone named Ralph Mudd?"

Amid more laughter, Al and I hastily lit all hundred candles. "I hope this doesn't cause a conflagration, boss," he said in a low voice.

"A bonfire," I countered, "and don't call me 'boss.'" I had once helped him study for a vocabulary test and now we one-upped each other routinely with vocabulary words.

"An inferno," he said, just as Gemma called for a final round of applause. During the hubbub, Al and I rolled the cake into position in front of the panelists' table. Gemma, face pink with excitement, reminded everyone of the auction at two o'clock, the writing contest winner announcement at three, and the costume party at six, and led a rousing chorus of the birthday song. The three guest authors circled the cake and blew out the candles with loud whooshes. Al started slicing as audience members got to their feet, stretched, and began milling around, some descending on the authors and others forming a straggly line to get cake and punch.

I helped Nate, the audio guy, coil up the cords from the microphones and put them in a box. "Two o'clock at the high school," I reminded him.

He merely nodded, hefted the box, and left, leaving me to ponder yet again the irony of a man who spoke as little as possible being in the business of amplifying and recording others' words. Turning, I bumped into Merle Aldringham, who had exchanged his tank book for one on the effect of airpower in the Vietnam War. Up close, he was taller than he'd seemed, at least six feet two, and smelled pleasantly of bay rum. I said, "Excuse me," and got a surprisingly nice smile in return, half-hidden behind a mustache and beard, both showing more silver than the dark blond hair on his head.

"Don't worry about it," he said in a soft voice. "It's—oh, my God."

For a moment, I thought I'd crushed his toe or something, but from the way he was staring over my shoulder, I realized he wasn't reacting to my klutziness. I turned to see what had caught his attention as he exclaimed, "Maudie!" and elbowed me out of the way to sweep my friend and fellow Readaholic Maud Bell into a bear hug.

"When I saw Connie was coming, I wondered if you'd be here," she said, planting a kiss on his lips while I watched in astonishment. Goofy little smiles played around both their mouths and they gazed into each other's eyes in a way that told me they had History with a capital *H*. I cleared my throat.

Maud laughed, crinkling the skin around her eyes, and reached out a hand to draw me closer. She was only a couple of inches shorter than Merle Aldringham and in her early sixties, like him. Wearing her usual henley shirt and multipocketed camouflage pants, she exuded health and vigor; no one would have been surprised to learn she made her living as a hunting and fishing guide during the good weather.

"Amy-Faye Johnson, Merle Aldringham. We go way back."

"I got that impression," I said drily.

Maud laughed, completely unembarrassed, but Merle looked around and I suspected he was checking to see if his wife was within earshot. "Connie and Merle and I were quite the threesome during our Berkeley days," she said.

I squelched the urge to wonder what kind of threesome.

"We met in a class on the politics of revolution. Remember, Merle? The teacher—what was his name?"

"Professor Kendrick—'Call me Kenny.'"

"Oh, heavens, yes. Kenny! I always thought he looked a little bit like Castro. How long has it been? We haven't seen each other in—oh, what? A couple of decades."

"Twenty-nine years," Merle said, looking nostalgic. "Remember? We had dinner at that Italian place in D.C. when we bumped into each other after the hearing on acid rain."

"You're right! How did we let it get to be so long? How long are you in town? You and Connie have got to come over for a drink or dinner before you leave. Joe would love to meet you."

"Joe? I thought you and Robert—"

"Divorced not long after our D.C. dinner," Maud said.

"I'm sorry."

Maud shrugged. "It was a long time ago."

"Doesn't mean it doesn't still hurt," Merle said in a way that made me think he had something other than Maud's divorce in mind.

"Let's go say hi to Connie," Maud said. She grabbed Merle's hand and plunged into the crowd.

This I had to see. I followed in their wake.

The crowd parted before the force of Maud's will (or the jab of her elbows), and in moments she was face-to-face with Constance Aldringham. The fan who was fawning over her gave way, and Maud swooped in to plant air-kisses on either side of Constance's face. "Connie! It's been a long time."

Constance pulled away, inclined to be startled and offended, but her eyes widened as she recognized Maud. "Maud Bell. In Heaven, Colorado. Who would have thought—?"

"'Of all the gin joints in all the world,' right?" Maud grinned.

"What have you been doing with yourself? You're so brown." Constance put a hand to her own cheek, as if to assure herself that it was still smooth as a baby's butt.

"This and that," Maud said. "Hunting, fishing, building Web sites, blogging. I have a conspiracy blog called Out to Get You dot com. At Berkeley, we used to see conspiracies behind every tree, under every rock. Remember?"

"Some of us outgrew that," Constance said. "Although"— her voice turned waspish—"if you want an industry simply rife with conspiracies, you should look into publishing. I could tell you stories. . . ."

"I want to hear all of them," Maud said. "Drinks at my house tonight? Before the ball?"

"We'd love to," Merle put in before Constance could respond.

She shot him a speculative look, but nodded. "I've

got to get back to my fans," Constance said, gesturing to the line of people waiting to get books signed. "Merle, it's chilly in here and I left my pashmina at the B and B. Fetch it for me, would you?"

"We'll catch up later." Maud smiled, and scribbled her address on a bookmark before handing it to Merle. As he took it, I noticed their daughter, Allyson, staring at her parents and Maud from across the room, a plate of cake in her hand. As her gaze went from her father to Maud, her expression went from confused to hostile.

As we moved away, Maud murmured, "Constance Jakes hasn't changed a whit. She's still the same stick-up-her-butt, self-centered prima donna she always was, even at twenty-two. I never did see what Merle saw in her. She treats him like a dog." There was a wistful note in her voice.

"Joe's a great guy," I reminded her.

"The love of my life," she affirmed with no self-consciousness. "But that doesn't mean I purged all my memories, like deleting photos off my computer. The glorious Maud you see before you"—she stopped and swept a mocking hand the length of her torso—"is the sum total of many experiences and adventures: good, bad, stupid, embarrassing, courageous, ill-advised, scary, wonderful, felonious, and more. Joe likes the me that my past has made me. He loves the real me. When you find a man who can say that he knows and loves the true you, the deep-down you with the bits even you don't like, hold on to him. I need a piece of cake." She headed toward the refreshment table, where I imagined she would take pleasure in plunging the knife into the heart of the cake.

Did Hart love the real me? I put a hand to my mouth, as if I'd said the *L* word instead of merely thinking it. Hart and I had certainly not said it to each other. It was too soon. We'd known each other only since the spring, and been dating for only about six weeks. We were a long way from even thinking about thinking about saying the *L* word. A long way.

A touch on my shoulder made me start. "Miss, can you tell me where the bathrooms are?"

I spun to find myself facing the man who'd come in late. Up close, I could see scalp through his close-shorn hair, and he exuded an odor of stale alcohol. His brown eyes were bloodshot, but his tone was polite. Despite that, he had an air of menace, or maybe desperation, that made me uncomfortable. He clutched an expanding file folder to his chest, twanging the cord that held it closed.

"In the back left corner over there." I pointed. "Past the self-help books." Maybe he'd pick one up on the way.

"Thank you."

I watched as he threaded his way toward the restrooms, wondering again why he was here. Maybe he was homeless and was here for the free cake. I put him out of my mind and moved toward Gemma, who stood surveying the long line of people waiting to get books signed. Her expression was a perfect blend of pride and happiness.

"It's going so well, Amy-Faye," she said when I came up to her. "Thank you!"

"It was your vision," I reminded her. "And you convinced the authors to come."

"I'd met them all before, you know. At Gothicon in San Francisco. It's a convention of all things gothic for people who are into that. It attracts readers, fans of shows like *Sleepy Hollow,* historians . . . all sorts. There are panels, costumes. . . . Tim Burton gave the most amazing speech. He has such a gothic sensibility." She sighed ecstatically.

"Sounds like fun. Look, I'm going to leave Al in charge here and go over to the high school to make sure things are set up for the auction and writing contest, okay?"

"I'll see you over there in a couple of hours," Gemma said, turning away to answer a question from a customer.

Snagging a piece of cake on my way, I slipped out Book Bliss's back door to where I'd left my van in the small lot behind the store. It was a perfect fall day with the sky so blue and sharp it felt like I could cut myself on it, and the sunshine warm on my bare arms. It was going down into the thirties at night, but today was a glorious sixty degrees. *This is why I live in Colorado,* I thought, unlocking the van. Earlier I'd loaded the boxes from Gemma's stockroom that contained the auction items, and I peeked in to make sure they were still there. Yep. With the cake balanced on my lap, I was cranking the ignition when someone pulled the passenger-side door open and I jumped.

Chapter 3

Brooke Widefield hopped onto the seat. "Can I come with?"

Grabbing for the cake plate, which had slipped when I jumped, I got frosting on my fingers. I licked them. "You scared me, leaping in the van like that. I thought I was being carjacked."

"Riiight. Like any self-respecting thief would want a van that said 'Eventful!' in big green letters on the side."

She had a point. My wheels weren't exactly inconspicuous. Nor were they the sexy sports car I would have preferred. However, the van was reliable and utilitarian. In my biz, it was more important to be able to cram sixty boxes of giveaway T-shirts, eight folding tables, two dinosaur-shaped piñatas, and a partridge in a pear tree into my vehicle than it was to go from zero to sixty in less than five seconds. I chuckled at the thought of my van getting to sixty in much under a minute and a half. Putting the van in gear, I rumbled out of the lot and turned onto Paradise Boulevard, the main drag through Heaven.

"What's so funny?" Brooke asked, pulling down the visor to check her mascara in the mirror. She removed a smudge.

"Nothing. What did you think of the event?"

"Went great. Your usual bang-up job." She snitched the cake plate off my lap and broke off a bite and ate it.

"Hey!"

"You said you were on a diet. I'm saving you from yourself. It's what good friends do for each other." She put on a saintly expression.

"Wow, what a pal."

"Did you see Lo chatting with that man-god? What did you say his name was, the one who came with Mary Stewart?"

"Lucas. Her brother. No, I didn't notice Lola." Our friend Lola Paget was a serious woman who'd been a year ahead of Brooke and me in high school, then had studied chemistry at Texas A&M before coming home to Heaven to turn the failing family farm into a profitable nursery. She supported her grandma and her much younger sister, Axie, who worked for me a few hours a week; in fact, she was scheduled to help with the auction setup. It had been a couple of years, at least, since I'd seen Lola show interest in a guy. She always said she was too busy.

"Yeah, it looked like they were having a real heart-to-heart."

"Well, good for her," I said, "although if he's only here for a week . . ."

I pulled into the Heaven High School lot, beneath a sign proclaiming that the Heaven Avengers were the 3A state champs in track and field. There were a smattering of cars in the lot, and I remembered the assistant principal telling me we wouldn't be the only ones using the high school on a Saturday. The basketball team had a practice scheduled in the gym, a robotics group was using a lab to build their entry for a contest, and a Destination Imagination team was rehearsing in a classroom.

"Grab a box," I told Brooke, opening the van's back doors. I had parked up against the door closest to the auditorium, where we were holding the auction. The sounds of bouncing basketballs greeted us when we entered, even though the gym was two halls over. The auditorium was a chilly, cavernous space, dark until I located a switch that turned on one tiny light, with a stage at the front, sloping aisles, and seats for about four hundred. I noted with approval that the tables and the podium I'd asked for were on the stage.

As we tramped back and forth, carting in the boxes of merchandise for the auction, the decorations for the tables the items would be displayed on, and my other paraphernalia, Brooke said, "Troy and I are meeting another mom-to-be on Tuesday evening."

Her voice was carefully neutral, the product of two other attempts to arrange a private adoption that had fallen through. She and Troy Widefield Jr., heir to a local auto dealership, and scion of the richest family in Heaven, had married straight out of college. They'd been trying to have a baby for more than five years now, and had recently decided to try to adopt one, much against the wishes of her in-laws, who wanted only blue Widefield blood flowing through the veins of their grandchildren.

"I'll keep my fingers crossed," I told her. "Is she another teenager?"

Brooke shook her head. "No, she's married with a couple of toddlers. Her husband ran out on her, though, and she can't afford another baby, so she's giving this one up for adoption."

"How sad."

"Yeah, it weighs on me some that our joy might come from someone else's misfortune. Anyway," she continued, in the voice of someone who wants to change the subject, "I told Troy I'm planning to buy something at the auction, something expensive. I think the scholarship is a great cause."

"What are you going to bid on?"

"I don't know what all's up for sale. That's why I wanted to ride along with you—so I could get a sneak preview." She grinned.

Light footsteps jogged down the aisle and I looked down from the stage to see a figure trotting toward us. It was too dark to make out who it was until she spoke.

"Hi, Miss Amy-Faye!"

"Am I glad to see you, Axie," I greeted the girl, Lola's much younger sister. Her real name was Violet, but she professed to hate that and prefer Axie, which was short for "the accident." She had Lola's features, but none of Lola's solemnity. Her cocoa-colored skin was a couple of shades lighter than Lola's, and her hair corkscrewed to jaw-length, where Lola kept hers shorter. They had the same smile, though, and the dark auditorium felt brighter when Axie beamed at me. "I don't suppose you know how to work the lighting in this place?" I pointed vaguely upward to where I figured the spotlights might be.

"Sure do," she said. "I took tech theater last semester."

"Great. We need some light on the stage."

"Not a prob." She disappeared up a side aisle and soon the muted clangs of sneakers on metal drifted down. Moments later, three spotlights illuminated the stage, and the floodlights beamed on, as well, blinding me. I blinked my eyes rapidly until they adjusted. Then, the three of us draped the display tables in the dark blue cloths I'd brought, and arranged the auction items upon them. The visiting authors had donated copies of their books, and each offered the opportunity for a winning bidder to name a character in her next book. Gemma had put together baskets with six or eight gothic-themed books, the local movie theater had donated a popcorn bucket that they would fill for a year, and the closest winery had supplied a bottle of Cabernet. Other Heaven merchants had donated auction items, as well. Pride of place went to the three first-edition books, which I propped up on display easels. One was Victoria Holt's *Mistress of Mellyn*, the second was Phyllis Whitney's *The Moonflower*, and the third was by Mary Stewart.

"I'm going to buy this," Brooke said decisively, running a finger down the spine of *Nine Coaches Waiting*. "I loved Mary Stewart and Victoria Holt and Phyllis Whitney when I was in high school. Loved them! It'll be fun to have a first edition. Maybe I'll become a serious book collector. Have you finished *Rebecca*?"

"I'm two chapters from the end. I'll be done before we meet tomorrow. I'm a little weirded out that the heroine doesn't even have a name. What's up with that?"

"I want the new Mary Stewart to use my name for a character in her next book," Axie said. She held the certificate that announced that opportunity. "Maybe she'd make me a vampire. That would be sick. I've got forty-three dollars saved from babysitting. Do you think that will be enough?"

"I have no idea," I said truthfully. I wouldn't pay twenty cents to have my name in a book, but I remembered reading somewhere that people paid a lot (usually in auctions, like this one, that benefited a cause) to have a famous author use their names.

"Did you enter the writing contest, Axie?" Brooke asked.

The girl shook her head. "Nah. Lo wanted me to—she said it would look good on my college applications—but I don't much like creative writing. A friend of mine, Thea, did, though, and she's a finalist!"

Entries for the short story contest had been due two weeks ago and had undergone a preliminary judging by Gemma and my mother, who was not only a former librarian but also a prolific book reviewer. They had whittled the entries down to three, which a local actor would read aloud this afternoon. The guest authors, who had been e-mailed copies of the finalists' stories to select the best one, would announce the winner and award him or her a gift certificate to Book Bliss. I had the finalists' stories in a file folder and I placed it inside the podium's cubby.

"I'm starving," Brooke announced. "Do your indentured servants get lunch?" She slung an arm around Axie's shoulders.

"Sure," I said, taking a twenty out of my wallet. "You fly, I'll buy. I don't want to leave this stuff unattended now that it's set up. And I've got to put up the signs." I pointed to a stack of signs I'd had made, directing people from the high school's front doors to the auditorium.

"I'll stay," Axie volunteered. "I can put up the signs and then do some homework if you'll bring me back a sandwich."

"Homework?" I said suspiciously. "On a Saturday afternoon?"

She grinned sheepishly. "Well, there's this guy I like, Josh, and he's on the robotics team, and he said he would help me with my physics assignment. When I told him I'd be here today, he suggested we study together when the robotics guys break for lunch."

Something about her airy delivery made me ask, "Do you actually need help with physics?"

"Nah. It's pretty easy. But Josh doesn't need to know that." She kept her mouth primmed, but her eyes danced with mischief.

"That's a good lesson to learn early," Brooke said, laughing. "The men in your life don't always need to know everything." She high-fived Axie and we left.

Brooke and I returned half an hour later, coming in through the high school's front doors, where Al was now seated at a small table, prepared to register bidders and hand out paddles. He was chatting with two high school girls, friends that Axie had recruited, who were ready to hand out the auction sheets I'd made up and had printed.

"All set?" I asked him.

"Good to go, boss."

"Can I register now?" Brooke asked, printing her name on the clipboarded form and taking the paddle with the numeral 1 on it that Al handed her. "I'm number one," she clowned, waving the paddle in the air.

"*El supremo,*" Al confirmed.

"No fair using foreign words," I said. People were trekking in from the parking lot, so I told him to holler if he needed me for anything, and Brooke and I headed to the auditorium. We found Axie and a geeky guy seated decorously in the front row of auditorium chairs, poring over a physics book. Axie introduced us, and the boy shook our hands before making a hasty exit, telling Axie he'd text her later.

"He's cute," Brooke told Axie.

We didn't have time for a more in-depth assessment of Josh's charms because a voice twanged, "We about ready to get this show on the road?"

Cletis Perry came down the aisle toward us with his bowlegged gait, grin splitting his seamed face, which was the color and texture of a well-used saddle. A white Stetson sat back on his head, showing a shock of white hair tinged with yellow, and a bolo tie dangled from around the neck of his checked shirt. "Dang, it's good to see you again, Amy-Faye. And who are your pretty friends?"

"Brooke, Axie, this is Cletis Perry, auctioneer extraordinaire and the biggest flirt this side of the Colorado. Don't be fooled by his age."

"Eighty-two and still goin' strong," Cletis said, hugging me hard enough to prove the "strong" part. "Let me see what I'm selling. We're going to raise some money today, yes, sirree." Climbing the steps to reach the stage, he took out a notepad and began examining the items set out on the table.

Before he finished, people started to trickle in. When the clock rolled around to two o'clock, the auditorium was full. Gemma and the authors arrived last, seating themselves in the places I'd reserved for them in the front row. I saw quite a few people from the morning's event, plus my mom, who waved to me from the last row, and my brother, Derek, whose brewpub had donated a beer-tasting party for a group of eight. Kerry and Maud arrived together and joined Brooke, who was standing in the front left corner; they had all volunteered to serve as spotters to figure out where bids were coming from. I was just wondering if Lola was going to make it when she came in, trailing Lucas Stewart and Allyson Aldringham, who were chatting away like they'd known each other for years. *Huh.* Mary Stewart turned and waved to her brother, pointing to the open seat right beside her, but he opted to follow Lola and Allyson to where the rest of the Readaholics stood, and gave his sister a casual wave back. Mary tightened her lips as she faced forward again. The two open seats beside Constance remained unfilled, as well, when Merle didn't appear.

"Are we ready to spend some money, ever'body?"

Cletis shouted into the microphone. He got a loud chorus of *yay*s and *you bet*s in response. Reminding the crowd that they were spending money for a good cause, he opened the bidding on the opportunity to name a character in Constance Aldringham's next book. When the bids reached five hundred dollars in a couple of seconds, I noticed Axie's shoulders slump.

"What's your name, sir?" Cletis asked the winning bidder after bringing down his gavel with a resounding *whack*.

"Nestor Niedernecker," a rotund man shouted from midway back. "That's a great name for a hero, right?"

The crowd roared with laughter. Constance paled and I could see her planning to make Nestor Niedernecker the smallest of bit characters.

Cletis kept the auction moving as efficiently as he always did, and the Readaholics did a great job as spotters, marking down the winning bidders' numbers. Brooke got the book she wanted, and my mom bid on a basket of books but didn't win it. Only two or three items from the end, Cletis held up a fat manila envelope. He opened it and peered inside. "This item doesn't appear to have a lot number, but there's a note here that says it's an original manuscript of *Never Again, My Lovely*, donated by the author, Fran—"

Francesca Bugle leaped up. "It's a mistake. That's not for sale," she said, striding toward Cletis, poppies bobbing with each step. "I don't know how that got mixed up with the sale items." She held out a hand, clearly expecting Cletis to hand it over.

He peered down at her with a puckish grin. "Not so

fast, little lady. This auction is for a good cause—you can't just change your mind about donations. Perhaps you'd like to make a bid?" He held up the envelope and waggled it.

Francesca forced a smile. "Five thousand dollars," she said. In the stunned silence that followed, she added, "I'm happy to support the scholarship fund. I wouldn't be a writer today if I hadn't gone to college on a scholarship."

Cletis brought his gavel down. "Sold, to the lady with the flowery hat." He handed the envelope to her with a courtly bow, and she returned to her seat. The crowd applauded her generosity and she acknowledged them with a wave and a more natural smile. From my vantage point, standing near the stage, I could see her furrowed brow when she sat. She removed her hat, scratched her head, and riffled through the envelope's contents. I knew she was trying to figure out, just as I was, how the manuscript had ended up on the auctioneer's table.

Chapter 4

During the intermission between the auction's end and the story contest, Francesca bulled her way through the crowd to me, expression ominous.

I forestalled her with upraised hands. "I have no idea how that got into the auction, Ms. Bugle," I said. "I've never seen it before. If you didn't put it up there . . ."

"It's my latest manuscript," she said. "My publisher would kill me if it got out before publication day, which isn't until next year. They'd probably void my contract and make me give back my advance, which was what we call in the biz a 'significant deal,' the most I've ever gotten."

No wonder she was willing to cough up five grand to get the manuscript back. "I'm so very sorry. Do you want me to ask Cletis—"

She interrupted me with an impatient wave. "That old coot won't know."

"Who had access to it?" I asked, unable to help probing the mystery.

She shot me a look. "You're a sharp one, aren't you? My assistant, of course, and my researcher. Then there's my agent—she had a copy—and the folks at the publishing house. . . ."

"A long list, in other words."

"True. But how many of them are here?" She left me, craning her neck and swiveling her head, as if trying to spot the traitor in the crowd coming back from the bathrooms.

I let out a long *phew* as she bustled away. I looked around for Shannon Vela, the actor I'd hired to read the short stories. The original plan was to have the kids read their own stories, but one of the finalists was a boy with a painful stutter, and the principal had asked if, in fairness, we could find someone to read all the stories. Shannon, a decade older than me, had recently returned to Heaven from New York City, where she'd made a living as an actor, even having a Tony-nominated supporting role in a Broadway play.

She hurried in now, svelte in slim black slacks and a matching cropped jacket over a gray cami. Black was a habit she'd picked up in Manhattan, she said, and she couldn't afford to toss her whole wardrobe just because she'd moved back to Heaven. Her husband had gotten her a red plaid lumberjack shirt for her last birthday (I knew because I'd organized the party and been highly entertained by her expression when she unwrapped the shirt), but I had yet to see her wear it.

"Sorry I'm late, Amy-Faye," Shannon said, her voice low-pitched and as smooth as molasses. "Jack picked today of all days to upchuck on the living room carpet. I had to do something about the stain before it set."

I couldn't remember if Jack was her terrier or her son, so I merely said, "Yuck. Glad you made it. Are you ready?"

She nodded, and lifted the slim blue folder she carried. "Printed out the stories this morning. My, those kids are talented, aren't they? That vampire one—"

I hadn't read the stories, but I nodded, and urged her toward the stage as Gemma went to the podium to welcome the audience to the story contest. She'd be introducing Shannon in a second, using the biographical notes I'd written for her. It constantly surprised me how many people wanted the event organizer to write remarks, toasts, or introductions for them. I joked sometimes that if I ever put together a conference on weapons of mass destruction, someone would expect me to come up with a few words about anthrax and nukes. The crowd had shrunk a bit—only to be expected—but it was still a respectable gathering. I spotted the jeans-clad guy with the crew cut from Book Bliss sitting alone in the second to last row, flipping through a book's pages. He must really be a fan of gothics. The three finalists sat at the end of the front row, two girls and a boy, the former in their Sunday best, the latter in jeans and a hoodie. They all looked nervous, with one girl clutching the armrests of her chair so hard her knuckles gleamed, the boy chewing on a hangnail, and Axie's friend Thea swinging her foot so hard her shoe was in danger of sailing onto the stage.

The stories were all five hundred words or less, so it didn't take Shannon long to read the first one and then introduce its author. The teen rose, flushing, and acknowledged the applause with an embarrassed wave. Shannon embarked on the second story and I knew it was the boy's by the way he leaned forward, elbows on his knees, and mouthed the words along with her. He raised his hands over his head like Rocky when introduced, and the crowd laughed. When Shannon started in on the third story, I noticed Thea frown and say something to the boy. He shrugged in response.

Before I could puzzle out what was bothering her, Mary Stewart the Living stood up, arms straight down at her sides and hands fisted, and said, "Is this some kind of joke?"

Shannon stopped speaking and peered down at Mary over the top of stylish reading glasses. "I'm sorry?"

"That's not my story," Thea said softly. Getting braver, she said more loudly, "That's not my story."

Uh-oh.

"So sorry—there must be some mistake. . . ." Gemma fluttered, looking to me for help.

The crowd began to murmur and shift restlessly in their chairs. I climbed the four stairs to the stage and pulled Shannon away from the microphone. "The last story should be by Thea Jensen," I said, checking my list, "and it should be called 'A Night in Amarantha.'"

"Well, this is the one I got last night, and it's by someone called Eloise Hufnagle," Shannon whispered.

Not good. That was the woman Mary Stewart had mentioned at Book Bliss, the one who was suing her. How had Shannon gotten—? That could wait. Right now, we needed to get the show back on the road. "Do you have Thea's story?"

"Sure. It's the last one."

"There were only supposed to be three. We'll straighten this out after. Just read Thea's story and let's get through this."

With a smile, I stepped to the mic and said, "I apologize for the delay. Just a mix-up, folks. Shannon will now read Thea's story, 'A Night in Amarantha.'"

Mary and Thea subsided into their seats, Shannon read beautifully, and the three authors came onstage to proclaim the boy's story the winner. He bounded up the stairs to accept his prize, doing the Rocky thing again to the crowd's amusement. Gemma closed by thanking the judges and reminding folks about the costume ball, and the audience began to drift out. I wished I could leave, too, but with Mary Stewart and her brother bearing down on me, along with Shannon and Gemma, I wasn't going to be able to escape.

They all talked at once. "My sister's book—" "—e-mail last night—" "—don't understand why—"

I held up a hand, trying to convey a calm I wasn't really feeling. "Shannon, you said you got the story last night. How was that?"

Pushing her reading glasses atop her head, she said, "I got an e-mail, like with the others, saying it was a late finalist. I didn't think anything of it."

"Was the mail from my mom, like the others?" I knew my mom, as one of the judges, had been in charge of forwarding the finalists' stories to Shannon; I'd given her the e-mail address myself.

"Now that you mention it," Shannon said, brows drawing together, "I think it was from the kid, that Eloise."

"She's not a kid," Lucas said. He ran a hand through his thick black hair and it fell back perfectly into place.

"This is all about embarrassing me," Mary put in, tears making her eyes glitter. "That woman—" She stopped and her eyes widened. "She's here, isn't she? She's here to cause trouble." She looked over her shoulder as if expecting to see Eloise Hufnagle creeping up on her.

Lucas slung an arm around her shoulders. "I told you we should have gotten a restraining order after what happened in Birmingham."

"What happened in Birmingham?"

Lucas gave me a brooding look. "That woman accosted Mary in the street and flung a jar of blood on her."

Gemma gasped and put a hand to her mouth.

"It turned out it wasn't real blood," Mary said. "It was an ooky stage blood, but it still ruined my dress."

"And it's a gross thing to do," I added.

"We should call the police," Gemma said, more decisively than usual.

"And tell them what?" Lucas rounded on her. "That someone mailed a story to Shannon here and lied about it being a contest finalist? Ooh, scary. They're not going to give a damn about that."

Taken aback by his scathing tone, Gemma looked like she might cry. Lucas seemed much less attractive all of a sudden, gorgeous hair and dark blue eyes notwithstanding. "It's a good idea, Gemma," I said. "I know someone at the police department and I can talk to him, let him know what the situation is. Maybe he'll have an idea."

"Thank you," Mary said, throwing her shoulders back. Clearly, she was ready to move on. She managed a brave smile. "I'm not going to let this poor, deluded woman ruin my experience here in Heaven. Where's that young man whose story won? I'll take a photo with him and his family. They'd probably like that."

Lucas rolled his eyes. "You won't need me for that," he said. "I'll bring the car around." He followed his sister out of the auditorium toward the hall, where the babble of voices suggested there were still a few people hanging around.

Shannon put a hand on my arm. "I'm sorry if I—"

"Not your fault," I assured her. "And it's no big deal. You did great."

She flashed a smile. "Thanks. If you don't need me for anything else, I've got an appointment with my Bissell steam cleaner. Mitch and I are coming tonight, so maybe I'll see you. I'm coming as Morticia Addams. Remember *The Addams Family*?"

Before my time, but I'd seen a couple of episodes in reruns. With her long dark hair, she would make a great Morticia. "I'll look for you. Can I have those?" I gestured to her file folder with the stories.

She handed it over. "All yours."

I flipped through the folder after she left, not sure why I'd even asked for it. I'd look at it later. Right now, I needed to dash home and put on my costume before driving to the Club to make sure everything was in train for the ball. I wanted nothing more than to kick my shoes off, relax in a bubble bath, and spend the evening watching anything as long as it didn't have a gothic vibe—*Big Bang Theory*, maybe—but that wasn't an option. Reminding myself that my paycheck for organizing all of today's events would pay my office rent for next month, I exited the auditorium, stopping to thank Cletis on the way and remind him that we were working together again on Friday for an event at the First Baptist Church of Heaven. I'd always thought that churches that could say they were located in Heaven had a leg up on other churches.

On my way to the main doors, I spotted Axie commiserating with a glum Thea, who was gnawing on a red spiral of licorice. I detoured toward them. "Great story, Thea," I said. "Sorry it didn't win."

"Yeah," she said. "Catch you later, Ax." She drifted away, shoulders slumped.

"Axie," I started, "were you and Josh in the auditorium the whole time I was gone?"

Giving me an anxious look, she asked, "Uh-uh. Was I supposed to be? I was mostly in the auditorium, but I put up the signs." She pointed to a neatly lettered placard that read, "Auction and Story Contest This Way!" with an arrow. She crinkled her brow in thought. "And I went to the drinking fountain to fill up my water bottle." She jiggled the half-empty disposable bottle.

"Did anyone come in the auditorium while you were there?"

"Just the janitor."

"What did he look like?"

She shrugged. "I didn't really notice. Josh and I—I'm sorry if I screwed up, Miss Amy-Faye."

I hugged her. "You didn't screw up, Axie. I'm just trying to figure out how Francesca Bugle's manuscript got mixed up in the items for sale. It could have happened at Book Bliss, too. I don't know how long Gemma had the auction items boxed up in her stockroom. No biggie. Don't worry about it."

Her face lit up with a thought. "Maybe I could help you find out. I could track down the janitor and ask him—"

I was shaking my head before she finished. Lola would not thank me for encouraging Axie to neglect her studies in order to play Nancy Drew. "It's really no big deal. Concentrate on making Thea feel better."

"Nothing but Twizzlers will make Thea feel better," she said, "and I had a bag on hand to give her, just in case. She's convinced herself that licorice has some sort of mood-elevating property. I think she's doing something for the science fair with Twizzlers."

I had a feeling Thea wasn't going to win any prizes at the science fair, either.

At the front door, Al Frink was snapping the legs down on the folding table he'd used for the auction registrations. "That Cletis is a hoot, isn't he?" Al said. "He looks like he walked out of one of those old Western movies. I'm betting that 'gosh darn, pardner' routine of his is an act," he added shrewdly. "He took one look at the sales list and added up the total in his head. And he rode out of here on a Mercedes, not a horse. I was loading stuff up and I saw him get into a navy blue S-class with tinted windows. Sweet ride."

"Did we make a lot?"

"Seven thousand four hundred and two dollars," Al said.

I whistled. "That's a lot."

"Yep. Gemma Frant was floating six inches off the ground when she left here. Of course, she's so hippie-dippie she practically needs a tether anyway."

Al was not known for censoring his opinions of people, including important clients. Before I could tell him for the pazillionth time to be more discreet, he handed me a flowered hat.

"Someone turned this in. I think it's Miss Bugle's."

"I'll drop it at the Columbine on my way home," I said, sighing. My hot bath was beginning to look like an unattainable fantasy. "Good work today, Al. Just the costume ball to get through now. What are you coming as?"

"Poe. Did you know he went to West Point before he started writing and got all creepy? One of my friends from high school got an appointment to West Point. He gave it up after a year, like Poe, but he kept his uniforms. He couldn't stand all the rules—rules for what to wear, rules for how to fold your socks, rules for how to eat. We all tried to tell him he wouldn't like it, but he was all about being an army officer. Watched *Taps* too many times. Anyway, he's letting me borrow one of his uniforms. And I've got a stuffed raven that says 'Nevermore.' It's proximity activated, like those Santas that go 'ho-ho-ho' if you walk past them in department stores near Christmastime? 'Nevermore, nevermore,'" he croaked, beaming. "Maybe I'll bring it to the office and keep it on my desk."

"Don't you dare," I said, tucking Francesca's hat under my arm and making my escape.

Chapter 5

The Columbine is Heaven's nicest B and B. The building dates from the late 1880s, when the town was incorporated as Walter's Ford, and Sandy Milliken and her husband, transplants from the East Coast, spent beaucoup bucks fixing it up. It sits on a quiet, treelined street a block from downtown, and it isn't hard for tourists to locate—its pale tangerine paint with the carnation pink gingerbread makes it visible for miles. In the spring, hanging baskets of pink and orange petunias, pansies, marigolds, and other flowers add to the colorful effect. At this time of year, with the nights already dipping below freezing, Sandy had replaced the hanging baskets with potted mums in bronzes and creams that sat on either side of each of the six stone steps leading to the Victorian B and B's double oak doors.

I nudged one door open and entered. The foyer, graced with wide-plank oak floors, Laura Ashley fabrics, and a Tiffany chandelier, murmured of history and the expensive restoration. It smelled like lemon furniture polish. It was quiet at this time of day with most guests dressing for the costume ball, I guessed, and Sandy and her husband working on their never-ending to-do list of repairs, modernizations, and routine maintenance. She'd told me once that they'd had no idea what they were getting into when they left their Madison Avenue jobs to take on the B and B.

"I imagined that my having a background in advertising and Dave being in finance would be useful when we bought this place," Sandy had said. "We'd have been better off with a plumbing certificate and a high school class in woodworking!" Her droll expression made me grin.

I could just leave Francesca's hat on the registration counter, but I was reluctant to do that. Before I could call out for Sandy or Dave, I heard voices from the room ahead of me on the left. It was a small parlor, decked out with reproduction Victorian furnishings, where Sandy kept hot coffee and tea going all day. I walked toward the room, but something about the intensity of the voices, lowered but intermittently audible, made me hesitate.

"—told you I will not tolerate—" It sounded like Constance Aldringham, but I couldn't be sure. "—playing you for a—"

Was she haranguing Merle, annoyed by his evident pleasure in meeting Maud again? The voice that replied to her was female. Allyson.

"I'm an adult and I'll do what I want to." Fury thrummed in her voice and she was making no effort to be discreet. "I don't need a keeper! You treat me like I'm too stupid to be let out alone. Well, I'm done with this, with only being the daughter of the bestselling Constance Aldringham. I need to be me—I need to listen to my inner goddess."

I almost gagged. Allyson Aldringham was a *Fifty*

Shades fan. I knew that only because, for a joke, the Readaholics had read the book last year. It had been vaguely titillating, but I gave up on it after about the twelfth reference to the heroine's—no, *stooge's*—"inner goddess." Maud had posted a very funny essay on her blog about how the book was really written by a committee of men conspiring to convince young girls that they should continue to accept lower wages and glass ceilings. She suggested, tongue in cheek (I think), that the book was about economic bondage, but Kerry told her it was just smut.

"You don't really need a secretary," Allyson went on. "You only talked me into coming on this book tour because you wanted to keep an eye on me. Well, I'm going back to California. He said he's going to be out there next week, and I'm going to see him."

Allyson didn't add "So there!" but I could hear it on the air. I wondered who the mysterious "he" was that had mother and daughter fighting like, well, mother and daughter. Cats and dogs have nothing on mothers and daughters when it comes to fighting.

Suddenly feeling guilty about eavesdropping, I retreated a couple of steps and called out, "Sandy? Dave? Anyone here?"

"In the kitchen." Sandy's voice floated to me. I followed it, peeking casually into the parlor as I passed it. Constance and Allyson stood three feet apart from each other, stiffer than waxworks, cheeks flushed, eyes turned to the door.

"Oh, hi," I said in a voice that clearly implied, "I didn't know you were here and I certainly wasn't listening to your argument." I waved the hat. "Francesca left this at the school." Without waiting for a reply, I navigated the maze of hallways to the kitchen (where I had supervised many a party) and gave the hat into Sandy's keeping, regretfully declining the opportunity to sample her new currant and rosemary scone recipe on the grounds that I needed to head out to the Club.

The parlor was empty when I passed it. I heard footsteps on the stairs, but when I arrived in the foyer, no one was in sight. A door closed on the floor above me as I let myself out of the B and B. When I got back in the van and pulled away from the curb, movement in my peripheral vision made me look to my right. Slightly ahead of me, a man emerged from the alley formed by two rows of evergreens that led to the rear of the Columbine. He brushed a twig from his arm and set a brisk pace walking west.

As I passed him, I recognized the stranger with the crew cut from the panel discussion and the auction. What was he doing at the Columbine? I wondered, keeping an eye on him in the rearview mirror. He couldn't be staying there, because all of Sandy's rooms were taken by the gothic guests of honor and their families. Maybe he'd stopped by to see if a room was available and was now searching for alternate accommodations. His presence felt suspicious. He didn't look like he could afford the Columbine's rates, but that didn't prove anything. Could he be casing the inn? Mentally chastising myself for thinking ill of the man because he looked a bit down and out, I lost sight of him and determinedly put him out of my mind.

* * *

At home in my two-bedroom bungalow, which I'd bought with Kerry's help (she was a Realtor in addition to being the mayor) only seven months ago, I took a quick shower and eyed the Catwoman costume hanging in my closet. Hart, who was taking me to the ball, had turned out to be surprisingly enthusiastic about a costume party. Most men I know duck out of costume parties whenever possible, and if they have to go, they make their wives or girlfriends choose their costumes, or they insist on going as something totally simple, like a football player (which requires only a jersey they already have hanging in their closet) or a surfer (if they have abs they want to show off). Not Hart.

No sooner had I mentioned the ball to Hart than he announced, "Batman and Catwoman."

We were at a barbecue place outside Grand Junction, broiling on the patio, and I licked sauce off my fingers before asking, "What?"

"We can go as Batman and Catwoman." His lean face lit up with enthusiasm. "Think about it. . . . There's no superhero more gothic than Batman. Even the city he lives in is called Gotham. And the new show—not that Batman or Catwoman are really in it—it oozes 'gothic' with all the smog and darkness, and Arkham Asylum."

"I didn't know you were so into comic books." I looked at him with new eyes, worried that he'd gone all Leonard or Sheldon on me. But no. He still had ever-so-slightly receding curly brown hair, a nose that had clearly been broken at least once, and tanned skin that said he spent time fishing or golfing or playing league softball. He was almost a foot taller than me, maybe six-four, and had a subtle air of command, which I figured came from more than a decade as a police officer, including time as an Atlanta detective. Nothing about him said "geek."

"Please," he said with mock affront. "Graphic novels." He bit into his pulled pork sandwich, which leaked. He swabbed barbecue sauce off his chin.

"Don't tell me you own a Batman costume." My tone said I was prepared to reevaluate the nature of our relationship—not that I knew what that was yet— if he said yes.

He grinned. "No, but I know where I can rent one. Come on, it'll be fun. What did you want to go as?"

"Jane Eyre." Going as the governess felt more literary, and her long skirts would hide my thighs much better than a Catwoman outfit would. Comic book heroines and villainesses never needed to lose a few pounds. Frankly, most of them were so top-heavy, I was surprised they could stand upright. A car blew past, sending a swirl of exhaust and grit onto the patio. I coughed.

Hart chewed and swallowed before saying, "I'd have to be Heathcliff, right? He's the *Jane Eyre* guy, isn't he, or is he the *Wuthering Heights* guy?" Without waiting for an answer, he gave me a coaxing smile. "C'mon. There'll be fourteen Jane Eyres at the party. I bet you'll be the only Catwoman. And Catwoman is a hundred times hotter than Jane Eyre." He waggled his brows and I laughed, conceding defeat by toasting him with my sweating iced-tea cup.

Now I removed the black catsuit from the hanger and unzipped it. The fabric—some sort of rubberized latex that, thankfully, had a bit of stretch—felt slick. Wriggling into the suit, I sucked in my tummy and zipped it up, checking my rear view in the mirror. Not as . . . prominent as I'd thought it might be. In fact, not bad at all. I pulled on the black boots that had come with the costume rental, and twisted my coppery hair up before sliding on the cat ears attached to a headband. A strip mask across my face—very Lone Ranger, I thought—completed my costume. "Meow," I said to the mirror, making a scratching motion with one hand.

Laughing at myself, I gathered my purse and keys and headed for the Club. I was driving myself, since I needed to be there so early. Hart would arrive with the rest of the guests. He'd warned me that he was on call tonight, and might get called away by police business. I almost hoped it happened, because I couldn't think of anything much funnier than him showing up at a crime scene dressed as Batman.

Chapter 6

I stood beside the Caped Crusader on the landing overlooking the lobby of the Club, watching the guests swirl and laugh and mingle. There was really no way to "gothicize" the lobby, which screamed "hunting lodge" with its massive deer antler chandeliers and the roaring grizzly head mounted over the main doors, but Lola and her crew had transported the potted forest from Book Bliss, and the guests had entered through an alley of trees just inside the doors. The fog machines I'd rented added to the atmosphere, too, spewing fog that refracted the light in interesting ways, cloaking or revealing guests as it massed and dispersed. It didn't seem to bother the guests, a mix of vampires, brooding Heathcliff types, cowled monks, sinister housekeepers, Elviras, and the like. Hart was right in saying that I'd be the only Catwoman, although I did spot another Batman—a paunchy superhero several inches too short for the costume, since his cape trailed the floor behind him.

"Seems to be going well," Hart said. His tight-fitting Batman costume showed off muscles in his thighs I hadn't known were there, and outlined biceps I'd appreciated whenever he wore a short-sleeved shirt. He'd taken off his mask, saying it itched, and his gaze roved over the crowd in that policeman way I was growing accustomed to. He was never completely off duty.

"*Sh.* You'll jinx it." It did seem to be going well, though, with music and laughter mingling in the way that indicated a good time was being had by all. I took pride in that, since I'd coordinated everything from the ticket sales (the tickets were bat-shaped pieces of thin cardboard), to the food and drink (carried off to perfection, as always, by Wallace Pinnecoose and his staff), to the looping video in the ballroom showing scenes from classic gothic films and TV shows, interspersed with still images of gothic-novel book covers. It had been a while since I'd had this much fun putting an event together; I almost felt guilty charging Gemma for my services. Almost.

From my vantage point, I spotted Maud Bell as a svelte Emma Peel, in a catsuit not too different from my Catwoman attire. She might be in her sixties, but she was still slim and sexy in a Helen Mirren–ish sort of way, her silver and iron hair curled into a flip. If Francesca's producer, Cosmo Zeller, spotted her, he might try to rope her into a new version of *The Avengers: The Golden Years.* Joe Wrobleski, her partner, made a suave John Steed, wearing a bowler hat and twirling an umbrella. I almost didn't recognize him—he'd shaved off his beard. I wasn't sure *The Avengers* really qualified as "gothic," but I wasn't the costume police. A cowled monk hovered near them, and from the way his head inclined toward Maud, I suspected it was Merle Aldringham. I didn't see Constance nearby, and I wondered how their little get-together for preparty cocktails had gone.

"Amy-Faye!"

I tracked the voice and saw Brooke and Lola waving at me. Brooke was beautiful as Rebecca from du Maurier's classic novel. The period costume suited her and her white dress with the puff sleeves swished as she came up the stairs toward us. She looked just the way I imagined the character. My days as an English undergrad came back to me, and I couldn't help pondering the fact that she was at a costume party, dressed as a character in a book going to a costume party, who dressed like a woman in a painting. It was all too meta for me to get my mind around. I planned to finish the book when I got home tonight. Lola wore what looked like a man's garb from the eighteen hundreds, complete with eye patch under her glasses, and a sword swinging at her hip. A ruffled white shirt set off her dark skin to perfection.

"You look great, Lo," I said, hugging her. "Who are you?"

"Van Helsing," she said. "Complete with a stake for subduing all these vampires." She pulled out her "sword," which turned out to be a pointed metal rod for staking up shrubs. "I decided I'd rather be a vampire killer than a victim." She gestured over the railing at three Mina-esque girls, all wearing long nightgowns ranging from diaphanous to modest, chatting with two vampires.

Typical Lo. If she'd been the "victim" type, she'd never have been able to help raise Axie after their parents' deaths, get a scholarship to A&M, and figure out how to make a living from the small farm she'd been raised on. "Thanks for getting the 'forest' moved over here," I said. "You must be exhausted."

"I'll sleep well tonight," she admitted with a smile.

I didn't bother telling Brooke she looked gorgeous, because she always looked gorgeous. She hadn't changed much since her reign as Miss Colorado.

"Troy's gone to get drinks," she said, referring to her husband.

"Is he Max?" I asked.

She pouted. "No, he didn't want to go to the bother. He's a vampire with nothing more than fake teeth and a cape. Party pooper."

I couldn't see droopy-shouldered, light-haired Troy as a vampire, but I didn't say so. But then, he wasn't my idea of Maxim de Winter, either. "At least he came."

"You are looking *très, très* hot in that catsuit, girlfriend," Brooke said.

"That's what I told her." Hart nodded.

I blushed. "Aw, shucks." Compliments always made me uncomfortable.

"Too bad catsuits aren't more practical," Brooke continued. "I mean, you practically have to strip to use the bathroom. Otherwise, I'd suggest you stock up. And who are you supposed to be?" she teased Hart.

"I'm Batman," he announced in a surprisingly good imitation of Michael Keaton's rendering of the campy line. He struck a pose with his hands on his hips.

"Foiled any villainous plots this evening? Taken down the Joker or the Riddler?"

"Not so far." He smiled. "But the evening's young."

"*Sh,*" I cautioned again. "You'll jinx it."

I hadn't even finished talking when raised voices drew our attention. They seemed to be coming from under the landing, and even though I leaned over the railing, I couldn't see who it was. "Now see what you did?" I said to Hart before hurrying down the stairs. He, Lola, and Brooke followed hard on my heels. I heard a clanking noise as we descended, but kept on going.

Partygoers had drawn back from the couple scowling at each other. Mary Stewart, beautiful and virginal in an embroidered white Victorian nightgown that reeked of "Jane Eyre," held a woman I didn't recognize by the arm. She was short, on the chunky side, and wore a glower that was incongruous with her nun outfit.

"Let me go. You have no right." She tried to jerk her arm away but failed. Mary must have been stronger than she looked, because the woman was no lightweight.

"Can I help?" I asked in a calm voice.

Mary's head turned toward me and she gave my attire a reluctantly admiring once-over before saying, "This is Eloise Hufnagle, the woman who has been stalking me."

"She stole my book," Eloise said loudly. "She shouldn't get away with it." Her already ruddy face flushed with anger.

"Let go of her arm, ma'am," Hart said with quiet authority, "and we can discuss this someplace private."

"The manager's office," I said, catching Wallace Pinnecoose's eye. He was headed our way; he had an eerie Spidey sense about trouble at his club.

"In other circumstances, I might find your assumption of authority appealing, Batman," Mary said, her gaze sliding along Hart's athletic figure in a way that made me stiffen, "but I'm not turning her loose. She's been creeping around after me all day. Maybe for weeks."

Silently, Hart flipped his badge over his utility belt.

Mary breathed in on a sharp *ooh*. "You're a cop. A real crime fighter. Great, she's all yours. Just keep her away from me. Last time I ran into her, she drenched me with blood. That's a crime, right? Assault, or at least vandalism? I should have had her arrested."

Eloise, who had been struggling to free herself, suddenly stilled, her eyes fixing on something behind us. "What are you doing here—?" she gasped.

Involuntarily, I turned to see whom she was talking to. Lucas, attracted by the fuss around Mary, was coming toward us, dressed, if I wasn't mistaken, as the portrait of Dorian Gray. I figured this out because he had a gilt-painted cardboard frame rising like a ruff behind his head. I gave him props for not doing the easy thing and coming as Rochester or a vampire. Allyson Aldringham, dressed in a Red Riding Hood cape, trailed behind him, looking both besotted and unhappy. Merle and Constance Aldringham stood a few feet away, both of them with a stiffness that said they'd been arguing. I was pleased to see I'd been right about the cowled monk being Merle. Constance wore a period dress I thought I recognized from the cover of one of her books. I couldn't recall the character's name, although I was darn sure she was a lot younger than

Constance. She shot Allyson and Lucas a look from narrowed eyes and beckoned for her daughter. Allyson's chin went up a notch, but then she drifted toward her parents. I was pretty sure Lucas didn't even notice her defection; he was intent on reaching his sister.

The stranger I thought might be a sailor was watching us while gulping down a mixed drink like he'd been at sea for six months without fluids of any kind. He hadn't bothered with a costume and seemed to be wearing the same jeans as earlier. He turned away when he noticed me staring at him, snapped his empty glass onto a nearby tray, and melted into the crowd. Weird. He practically knocked into Francesca Bugle, bustling toward us in garnet-colored Victorian garb, saying, "Mary, dear, is everything okay?" Cosmo Zeller came with her, dressed as a generic Victorian or Edwardian gentleman, complete with cane and pocket watch.

Eloise, taking advantage of our distraction, swung her purse with her free arm. It clonked Mary on the knee and Eloise tore herself free. Instead of running, she dug in her purse, pulled out a jar filled with red fluid, tore off the lid, and flung the contents at Mary. The red gook spattered everyone within a ten-foot radius, and Eloise took off as we all instinctively recoiled. Hiking up her nun's habit, she displayed neon-colored running shoes and surprising speed as she dashed toward the main doors. She dug out another jar and pitched its contents to her left and right, spattering partygoers with the fake blood.

There were gasps of outrage and disgust as people

backed away. I heard a muttered "Gross," and a wailed "My dress!"

"Catch that nun," someone shouted.

A couple of people half turned as Eloise brushed past them, and one man reached out his arm as if to grab her, but she eeled away and was out the door in a flash. Fog swirled behind her. No one gave chase. Mary was exclaiming over the ruin of her nightgown, Hart was calmly summoning uniformed officers, and I was digging in my utility belt pocket for the foil packets with the stain-removing wipes I always carried (along with bobby pins, safety pins, tape, needle and thread, pen, tissues, and various other emergency supplies that come in handy when a bridesmaid tears her dress, the birthday boy spills punch on his shirt, or a keynote speaker shoots buttons across the room because the last time he wore his tux shirt, he was seventy pounds lighter —true story). I handed most of the wipes to Mary, who took them with a muttered word of thanks and hurried toward a bathroom, followed by Lucas. I used a tissue to sponge at a streak of red infiltrating my cleavage. It smelled sweet. It wouldn't surprise me if the goo was Karo syrup mixed with red food coloring. I gave thanks that my costume was black and hoped it wouldn't stain. Noticing a sprinkling of red on Hart's forehead, I reached up to blot it.

"Thanks," he said. "I'll be back in a minute—I need to meet the officers outside. Can you hold down the fort in here?"

"Sure. The excitement's over."

I gently herded the guests who showed a tendency

to gawk back toward the ballroom, murmuring about food and drinks and a door prize drawing. Brooke swished along beside me, and Lola started to come, too, but then said, "Drat, I've lost my stake." She rattled the empty sheath.

"Don't worry about it," Brooke said. "It'll turn up."

Ignoring her, Lola pushed her glasses up, dislodging her eye patch, and said, "It must have fallen out on the stairs. I'll catch up with you."

The party got louder over the next half hour and had just begun to simmer down as a few people drifted out, when Wallace Pinnecoose appeared beside me. Half a foot taller than me, he was a solid man in his sixties, with bronze skin, iron gray hair slicked back from his brow, and a stiff posture that showed off his black suit and crisp white shirt. He could have walked into any British period piece and assumed the role of butler with no re-hearsal, or onto the set of a Western and acted the part of a warring chief. Those two roles should have been mutu-ally exclusive, but somehow they both fit Wallace. He waited while I finished a conversation, and then said in a low, measured voice, "Amy-Faye, we've got a problem."

I stiffened. I'd never heard Wallace use the word "prob-lem" before. He referred to "situations" (a thieving bar-tender) or "incidents" (a bridesmaid and a groom found naked on Wallace's desk during a reception) or "occur-rences" (a three-alarm fire in the kitchen) and dealt with them with sangfroid, never looking stressed or breaking a sweat. Right now, he definitely looked stressed, and sweat beaded his high brow. He dabbed it with a snowy handkerchief.

"What's up?" I asked, instinctively speaking in a whisper.

"Is Detective Hart still here?"

My unease ticked up a notch. Wallace never wanted to involve the police in any of the Club's incidents, preferring to keep things quiet so as not to harm the Club's reputation.

"I haven't seen him since the scuffle earlier."

Wallace tipped his head to the right and I followed him, weaving my way through the gradually thinning crowd. We left the party behind and turned down a dimly lit hallway that led to the Club's administrative offices. Golf and tennis trophies in glass cases were interspersed with framed photos from various tournaments and an oil painting or two of former chairmen of the Club's board of directors. Halfway down the hall, a door with a crash bar led to the parking lot, and just past that, on the left, were two restrooms. The faint scent of chemical-lavender cleaning products seeped from them. The crowd noise diminished as we neared the end of the hall.

We drew abreast of Wallace's office. The door was ajar and a bar of light fell through it to stripe the carpet. I gave him a questioning look and he nodded infinitesimally toward the door. "In there."

Reluctant to look, I took refuge in awkward humor. "There's no naked people in there this time, is there?"

When Wallace merely slid one heavy brow up a bare quarter of an inch, I steeled myself and approached the open door.

Chapter 7

I hovered on the threshold. There was no need to enter; indeed, I'd read enough police procedurals to know Hart would be pissed off if I mucked up his crime scene. I could tell from the doorway that it was a crime scene. All the signs pointed to it. A desk lamp was knocked over and glass from the bulb glittered on the carpet. Eight or ten books were tumbled on the floor. The one nearest me was a text on grass and soil cultivation for golf courses. The coppery smell of blood clogged my nostrils. The biggest clue, though, was the man slumped on the floor, facing the doorway, half-supported by Wallace's desk, a knife plunged through his heart. No, not a knife, I realized, my gaze fixed on the metallic length of it. A stake. *Uh-oh.*

With an effort, I turned away. My eyes met Wallace's for a moment, and then I called Hart's number.

He answered with, "I'm just coming back in. We've searched the property but can't find her. Chances are, she had a car."

I cleared my throat. "You need to come to the manager's office right away," I said.

There was a beat of silence and when Hart answered, the words were clipped. "On my way."

* * *

It wasn't until I got home at almost two in the morning that I realized I'd gotten my wish to see Hart work a crime scene dressed as Batman. It hadn't been nearly as funny as I'd imagined. He'd discarded his cape and mask, but couldn't do much about the rest of the costume, which drew no end of guffaws from the officers and forensics techs who showed up to work the scene. He'd inspected the body and the office, and then interviewed me and Wallace—separately—in someone else's office. After making sure I was okay, he'd been strictly professional and I'd followed suit, giving him a concise report on how Wallace had alerted me to the "problem" and assuring him I hadn't entered the office or touched anything.

"Do you know who he is?" I asked. The victim was the jeaned man with the short hair and the tattoos.

"No ID on him," Hart answered. "The coroner will run his fingerprints. Do you recognize him?"

I'd lived in Heaven all my life (even back when the town was Walter's Ford, before the town council renamed it to attract the destination wedding business), and Hart had been here only about six months, so it wasn't an unreasonable question.

I bit my lip. "I don't know him, but I saw him at the bookstore this morning and at the auction. I noticed him here earlier, too, when that Eloise person started flinging blood." Suddenly, I started to shake, the evening's events catching up to me. Through chattering teeth, I said, "Can I go home now?"

Hart relaxed his professionalism long enough to hug me and briskly run his hands up and down my upper arms to warm me. "Not quite yet. Hold it together, Amy-Faye. You're doing great."

I'd had to wait while the uniformed police took down the names and addresses of everyone still at the party, and then I'd had to try to remember who else had been there earlier. It was an impossible task because there hadn't been a guest list—anyone who bought a ticket was welcome to attend. And some people's costumes had hidden their identity. It was, I slowly realized, a setup to make a murderer's job much easier; at least, it would make it easier for him or her to escape unnoticed.

The stake, of course, belonged to Lola. She was so distraught by the idea that an item she had brought to the party had been used to kill a man that I drove her home when the police finally said we could leave. She sat in the van's passenger seat, eye patch pushed up into her hair, hands clenching and unclenching on her thighs. "I hope the police won't think I had anything to do with it," she said.

"Of course they won't, Lo! You didn't even know that man, did you?"

She shook her head. "Uh-uh. Never saw him before. I don't think he's from around here. That didn't keep Lindell from asking me twenty different ways if I recognized him, knew him, or had ever seen him anywhere."

"I saw him at Gemma's store during the author panel, and then again at the auction," I said. "I don't think the police know who he is yet. Hart said he didn't have any ID on him."

"Maybe it was a robbery, and he fought back," Lola said. "The self-defense books all say you should just hand over your wallet if you get mugged, not make a fuss, and run if you can."

I kept my attention on the road, ill lit this far out of town. I didn't point out that the robbery theory didn't account for Lola's stake being the murder weapon.

"I must have lost the stake when I went downstairs during all that fuss," she said, raking her fingers through her short hair. "But it wasn't on the stairs when I went back to look."

"No telling who picked it up. It might have been a staff member, getting it out of the way, or a Good Samaritan partygoer planning to turn it in to the Club's lost and found," I said.

"Or it might have been the murderer." Lola turned her head to stare out the window.

We drove under a streetlight as I made the turn into the Bloomin' Wonderful driveway, which also led to the small house Lola shared with Axie and her grandmother. In the dark, I couldn't make out any of the blooms in the fields, although my headlights glanced off the glass panels in the greenhouses. Stopping near her front door, I put a hand on her shoulder. "None of it is your fault, Lo. The killer went for a weapon of opportunity—if it hadn't been the stake, it would have been something else—a steak knife, a deer antler. I know it feels icky to think that you brought the murder weapon to the party, that you held something that later got stabbed through a man's guts, but—"

"You're not helping, Amy-Faye," Lola said.

I shut up. "Sorry." I leaned over and hugged her awkwardly. "Hart will figure it out."

She opened the door. "He'd better do it quick, because otherwise I'm going to." She closed the door firmly on the final word and marched toward the house, where the porch light and a dog's barks welcomed her home.

It was enough to make me want a dog, I thought, unlocking my own door and stepping into the quiet dark of my bungalow. My erratic hours wouldn't be fair on a dog, however, and I didn't think a gerbil or a goldfish would fill the same void, so I remained pet-less. I shucked off my Catwoman outfit in the dark, brushed my teeth, and flopped into bed, emotionally and physically exhausted. Thank goodness tomorrow was Sunday and I had nothing on my calendar except the Readaholics meeting. I'd meant to finish *Rebecca* tonight, but . . .

"Gothic heroines aren't much like today's female cops, PIs, or even amateur sleuths, are they?" Kerry said, buttering a biscuit. Even though she phrased it like a question, it sounded like a statement. Kerry never shied away from making statements. Maybe it came of being a politician, even a small-town one.

We were sitting in Lola's cramped kitchen, having voted previously to have brunch while discussing *Rebecca*, since we were meeting on a Sunday (to accommodate my schedule). Lola's grandmother had insisted on cooking for us, so we were feasting on scrambled eggs with sausage, homemade biscuits with strawberry preserves Mrs. Paget had put up in the summer, and pancakes topped with pecans and bananas. It was more food than I'd generally have for breakfast in an entire week, but I was enjoying every bite of it. I poured more melted butter onto my pancakes.

Axie was at a friend's house and Mrs. Paget had left for a Bible study after cooking our breakfast, so it was just me, Brooke, Kerry, Maud, and Lola in the small kitchen with its cheery wallpaper printed with chickens, gingham curtains, and butcher-block counters that Lola complained about every time she had to refinish them. It felt very 1950s to me. The red Formica-topped table had a metal rim and legs, as did the padded chairs. Somehow, it also felt homey, even though it was nothing like the kitchen in the house I'd grown up in and where my parents still lived. The smell of coffee pervaded the air as Maud poured herself another cup.

"That no-name protag was pretty helpless, I'll give you that," Maud said. "No gumption. No grit."

"I wouldn't say that," Lola said. She looked tired, with dark circles under her eyes. "She was a product of her times. Women weren't raised to stand up for themselves then, not physically, not financially."

"Why didn't she have a name?" Brooke asked. Even on a lazy Sunday morning she was perfectly made-up with her hair gleaming in the sunlight that streamed through the windows over the farmhouse sink.

"It makes her kind of an 'everywoman,' don't you

think?" I asked. I'd finished the book hastily this morning, skipping church, and hadn't had time to analyze it as much as I usually do.

"No," Maud said. "The average woman doesn't meet a handsome millionaire, marry him, live in a mansion, and duke it out with a dead former wife and demented housekeeper. I should have dressed as Mrs. Danvers last night. I can play sinister." She narrowed her eyes and tightened her mouth into a thin line.

"You creep me out," Kerry agreed.

"The heroines in gothic novels should make it a practice to fire all the servants the moment they walk through the door of the spooky old mansion," Brooke said. "And call the Ghostbusters. That would solve a lot of their problems up front."

When we stopped laughing and humming the *Ghostbusters* theme song, I said, "Okay, maybe not an 'everywoman,' but I think it's the same ploy you see in modern suspense fiction—a normal person living a normal life gets caught up in extraordinary circumstances and has to cope."

"If you can call what she did 'coping,'" Maud sniffed, still down on the protagonist.

"I think du Maurier not giving her a name is an identity thing," Brooke said. She flipped her hair over her shoulder to keep from trailing it in the syrup on her plate as she forked up the last morsel of sausage. "Names are powerful. Names give immediate impressions. I mean, you'd have a different idea of someone named Arabella than you would if she was called Mildred. Du Maurier is playing with that, making us decide who this woman is without giving us a clue via the name."

"That's deep, Brooke," I said, half admiringly, half mockingly.

She made a face at me.

"No, it is," Lola said. She rose and started to collect our plates. "I think du Maurier's playing with all the names. De Winter, for example. That conjures up a cold feeling to me, and I think the husband is a cold man. Or"—she cocked her head to consider—"maybe he's *become* cold as a result of his experiences with Rebecca."

"She was evil," Kerry said.

"And do you know what her name means, what 'Rebecca' means?" Lola asked, returning to her names theory. We looked at her and shook our heads. "'Tied' or 'bound.' I looked it up."

I crinkled my brow. "What are you saying she was bound by, Lo?"

"Not her marriage vows—that's for sure," Maud said, making us all crack up.

"Maybe her evil nature," Lola said slowly. "I think sometimes that when you choose to do the wrong thing time after time, when you choose to hurt others, eventually it's not a choice anymore—you can't break out of the habit."

"Wow, this is an unusually cheery discussion," Kerry said.

Lola slumped into her chair, cupping her hands around a coffee mug. "Sorry. I'm not feeling too cheery today."

"That wasn't an attack on you," Kerry said, looking

dismayed that Lola had taken her words that way. "It wasn't a cheery book."

"And last night didn't exactly end on a cheery note, either," I said. The murder was the elephant in the room we'd all been avoiding mentioning.

"Do the police know the victim's name yet, Amy-Faye?" Brooke asked.

"I haven't talked to Hart today, so I don't know."

"I wonder how he ended up in the manager's office," Kerry said, focused, as usual, on logistics.

"Someone lured him there," Brooke suggested.

"Or more than one someone," Maud said.

We groaned. "Not everything that happens is part of a conspiracy," Kerry said tartly.

"Most everything is." Maud was unrepentant. "Even in *Rebecca*, you can tell Mrs. Danvers and that smarmy Favell are working together to—"

"Maybe the manager had something to do with it," Brooke said.

I immediately shook my head, setting my ponytail swinging. "No way. I've worked with Wallace Pinnecoose for years. He's not the murdering type."

"That's what people said about Jeffrey Dahmer," Maud said.

"And Ted Bundy," Kerry added.

"And—"

I tossed my napkin at Brooke before she could add another serial killer to the list. "Right, I got it. Everyone liked Jack the Ripper, too. He was a swell guy to his friends and his dog. I'm just saying I don't think Wallace had anything to do with it."

"When the police find out who he was, maybe it'll be clear who killed him," Lola said quietly.

Kerry patted her arm, and I said, "I hope so, Lo."

"And, if not, we can figure it out," Maud said. She put her cup down with a decisive click, her tanned hand strong and bony against the delicate china. "Nothing about the murder is remotely your fault, Lola, but if it will give you peace of mind to know what happened, then we'll find out." Even though she liked Hart, her activist days at Berkeley in the late sixties had left her convinced that all police were corrupt, incompetent, or both.

"You know," I said, thinking out loud, "that guy—let's call him Doe for now—Doe was at all the author events. Maybe he's in town because he knew one of them."

"Or maybe he likes books," Kerry said. "Or he was passing through on his way to, oh, Salt Lake City, and saw the posters and decided to check out the Celebration of Gothic Novels for fun."

I gave her a doubtful look, but didn't argue.

Lola stood and said in a voice that meant she was ending the discussion, "Let's wait and see who he turns out to be. Then we'll decide what to do."

Chapter 8

"The victim's name was Trent Van Allen," Hart said Monday noonish, handing me an aromatic bag from the Munchery and a larger plastic bag that contained his Batman costume. Saturday night, before I left the Club, I'd offered to return his costume to the rental place in Grand Junction when I dropped mine off, knowing that with a murder investigation under way he wouldn't have time to do it himself. He'd been grateful for the offer and we'd arranged to have lunch together. I tucked the Batman duds under the table I use as a desk, and put the lunch bag on the blotter and opened it, burying my nose in the pastrami scent rising from it. Hart settled himself in one of the grass green velvet upholstered chairs that went so well with the pale lemon walls. "Van Allen—ring any bells?"

I shook my head. "Not even a tinkle. Who is he?"

"Hails from Idaho originally. Did a stint in the marines. Came back from the desert, got mixed up with drugs, moved on to armed robbery and grand theft auto, was recently released from the Illinois state pen."

"So maybe it was a robbery gone bad," I said.

"Anything's possible." Hart's tone said he wasn't buying it. "The question is, what was he doing in Heaven?"

"Tourist?" I ventured.

Hart cocked a skeptical eyebrow. Carefully maneuvering a cardboard bowl of soup from his lunch bag, he levered the top off it and ripped the plastic covering off a spoon with his teeth.

"Teeth are jewels, not tools," I murmured, repeating a phrase my mother had dinned into me, my three sisters, and my brother, Derek, from the moment we sprouted teeth. She had harbored a not-so-secret wish that one of us would become a dentist, but we all disappointed her. "You know," I said, remembering my conversation with the Readaholics the day before, "I saw that guy—Van Allen—at all three of the events yesterday. He might know one of the authors."

"Did you see him talking to any of them?" Hart asked, the plastic spoon looking small and ineffectual in his large hand as he scooped up the black bean soup. The garlicky smell fought with the scent of my pastrami.

I closed my eyes, trying to remember. "No-o. He asked a question at the panel discussion, but I don't think he directed it to a particular author. He didn't bid at the auction, as far as I know, although Cletis kept it moving so fast I might have missed it. At the costume party, he wasn't dressed up—well, you saw—and I only spotted him once, when Mary Stewart had it out with Eloise Hufnagle. He was standing near Constance and Merle Aldringham, but I don't know if they were conversing." I shrugged. "Sorry."

"We struck out with Hufnagle, too," Hart said morosely. "We tracked her to the Merton Inn, but she had already checked out."

The Merton Inn was a run-down place on the I-70 access road, a good ten miles out of town. Picturing it made me think about the Columbine for some reason. I started. "Oh, I did see him one other time. I had to run over to the Columbine, where all the authors are staying, and he was there. He came out from behind the B and B, I think, and walked west."

"Now, that's interesting," Hart said. He put the lid back on his empty soup bowl, stowed it in the bag, and tucked it into my trash can.

"How was he killed?"

"The ME hasn't done the autopsy yet, but I'm guessing that metal spike did the job. From the angle, and the relative lack of blood, it looks to me like it went up under his rib cage and into his heart. Either someone knew what they were doing, or they got lucky. I'd guess death was more or less instantaneous. It's possible the ME will find something else, though."

I felt a bit queasy and put down my sandwich. The greasy pastrami sat heavy in my stomach. "TMI."

He shrugged. "You asked. By the way, did you have a photographer at the ball? I'll need all of his or her photos from last night."

Having anticipated this request, I had Sam Ayers's card ready and I passed it to Hart. "I already gave her a heads-up that you'd be calling."

His expression was both amused and impressed. "Thanks. What have you got on your plate for the rest of the day?"

I gestured toward the large whiteboard behind my

desk with our upcoming events carefully lettered on it. We had some weddings booked as far out as two years from now, and a slew of events over the holidays. "This week is pretty slow," I said, "so I'm getting a head start on our holiday parties. I'm ordering supplies, buying decorations, researching new ideas for holiday-themed parties, and interviewing a new Santa Claus."

Hart quirked an eyebrow, and I elaborated. "Our last Santa decided to move to Tallahassee to be closer to his grandkids. It's a shame, because his beard was real and no one ever complained about his breath. You laugh," I said, mock-severely, "but Santa's breath is a big deal. When you're sitting on his lap, begging for a skateboard or a puppy, you don't need a blast of halitosis."

"Is that part of your interview—sitting on the candidate's lap to assess breath quality? If so, I might be tempted to apply." He patted his lap.

I pretended to consider, and then shook my head. "No, I'm afraid you're not a good candidate. Not fat enough, not old enough, not hairy enough."

He rubbed his smooth-shaven jaw. "Wow. I'm pretty sure I've just been the victim of sizeism, ageism, and hairyism, all in one blast."

I laughed and got up. "And now you're going to be the victim of go-away-ism so I can get over to Grand Junction to return these costumes, and look for bargains at my favorite holiday-decor supplier."

"Yeah, I need to get back to the office. I've got a murderer to catch."

"That makes my to-do list sound awfully shallow," I said, walking him out of my office to the reception area, made up of a love seat, a solitary wing chair, and a coffee table. Al's desk (currently empty, since he was at lunch) and an overgrown ficus took up the rest of the small room. Framed photographs of events we'd organized hung on one wall above the love seat, and French doors opened to the garden and walkway.

"Hey." Hart raised my chin with his index finger, hearing the undertone beneath my joking words. His brown gaze held mine. "Helping people have fun is important. You help commemorate the significant moments in people's lives. You distract them from the ugliness, put it in perspective. That's important stuff."

Grateful, I stood on tiptoe and planted a kiss beside his mouth. "Thank you."

With a smile, he left, and I returned to my office to collect the costumes, my shopping list, and my purse. Leaving a note for Al to remind him where I'd gone, I locked up and headed to the van. There was a nip in the air today, but it was clear, and once I got close to Grand Junction, I felt like I could see halfway across Utah. Grand Junction was only a hop, skip, and a jump away from the Utah border. There is no blue as clear or intense as a Colorado sky. Looking at it was like falling up into an endless swimming pool. The costume shop was two blocks away from Colorado Mesa University, where Al went to school, and students clad in shorts despite the chilly temps slouched to classes. One of them worked behind the counter at the costume rental place and accepted my returns with an efficiency that surprised me a little. Maybe I was a bit ageist, I thought. The clerk brushed aside my apology for any fake-blood stains that might be on the costume.

"We gotta get 'em all dry-cleaned anyway," he said. "Musta been quite a party. Yours isn't the first one turned in today with that stuff on it. People are nuts," he stated in the voice of one explaining that the earth is round. "And something about putting on a costume increases their nuttiness, like an electron multiplier. Physics major," he said in response to my look.

I thanked him, and exited to the parking lot. Before I could get into my van, a voice hailed me.

"Amy-Faye! I guess you're here for the same reason I am." Gemma Frant stood beside her aging Honda Civic and hefted a bag from the rental place. She was pale without makeup, and her frizzy hair was escaping from its loose bun. I hadn't seen her to talk to since before the body was discovered.

"Gemma, I'm so sorry about the—" I stopped, unsure how to phrase the rest of my apology. *I'm sorry about the murdered guy discovered in the middle of your party? I'm sorry I had to call the police to investigate a homicide during your gala? I'm sorry someone was inconsiderate enough to get himself killed in the middle of a party I organized?* None of it struck quite the right note. "I'm sorry," I said simply.

She waved away my apology by fluttering both hands, no mean trick since she clutched the bag in one of them. "Don't worry about it, Amy-Faye. It wasn't your fault. I wish—well, of course I wish it hadn't happened, and

I feel sorry for that poor, poor man, but . . ." She twitched her brows together. "Do the police have a suspect?"

"No, but they know who he was. Trent Van Allen."

She shivered, even though it wasn't that cold. "The police asked me and asked me about him—they said he was in the store during the panel discussion—but I didn't recognize him, not even when they showed me a photo. I don't know that name at all. Van Allen? I don't know any family from around here with that name. He must have been a tourist, just passing through town, although why he was at the ball . . ." She licked her thin lips nervously. "Surely it was a mugging, a random thing, and the poor man was just in the wrong place at the wrong time?" Her anxious gaze pleaded with me to agree. "I mean, it couldn't have anything to do with my Celebration of Gothic Novels. That would be too horrible."

"Of course not," I reassured her, seeing that she was close to tears. I didn't point out that people rarely got mugged in the manager's office at the most exclusive country club in the western half of the state.

It wasn't until I was at the party supply wholesaler, waist-deep in napkins, tablecloths, and centerpieces featuring hollies, reindeer, menorahs, polar bears, angels, and other holiday figures, that I took in what the clerk had said: Mine wasn't the first costume he'd seen today with red stains. Leaving the startled saleswoman behind, I dashed into the parking lot to call Hart. I got his voice mail and left a long message about how he needed to confiscate all the costumes and test them for real blood. "You probably already thought of that," I wound up, "but when the costume shop guy said he'd seen other costumes with red stains, well, I thought I should let you know. Call me." I hung up, returned to the shop, and placed an order that made the saleswoman's day.

On the way back to Heaven, I pulled into the long driveway that led to Bloomin' Wonderful, knowing Lola would want to know the murder victim's identity. Even though her nursery was only five minutes outside Heaven, it felt like I'd traveled back in time, to a more peaceful era, when I trundled down the gravel road leading to her farmhouse. On one side, a field of daylilies, mostly browning foliage at this time of year, but with some apricot and yellow blooms, stretched out in neat rows. Greenhouses lined the other side of the road, their panes steamed. I knew they held all sorts of flowering shrubs and potted trees, as well as other perennials. The farmhouse was small and painted lavender with white trim. A hound bayed when I parked the van, but no one came onto the porch. Misty, the longhaired gray kitten I'd rescued in May and given to Lola, came running to meet me. She was much leggier now, and carried her tail like a gray plume.

"Mer-eow," she said, rubbing against my shins.

I stooped to stroke her silky back and she butted against my hand. "Where's Lola?" I asked her.

As if in answer, or maybe because I stopped patting her, she took off at a slow trot, rounding the corner of the largest greenhouse. I followed her and found a dusty Lola pitchforking what looked like old mulch materials into the open hatch of a commercial-sized composter.

Spotting me, she swiped her wrist across her forehead, leaving a clear path in the dust. Misty took advantage of the opportunity to leap into the wheelbarrow and tackle a waving length of twine.

"Watching you do that makes me grateful that I get to argue with brides about whether the table linens are salmon-colored or coral for a living," I said.

Lola smiled. "I know it's hard work, and it's for darn sure messy, but it's very satisfying. I like the idea that everything gets recycled and turned into a fertilizer that will help everything grow again, without having to use chemicals." She thumped the side of the composter. "It's important to me to be organic. What brings you out here—a wedding order?"

I persuade a lot of my brides to get their flowers from Bloomin' Wonderful. "Not today. The police ID'd the guy from the costume party. His name was Trent Van Allen."

Shaking her head slowly from side to side, Lola said, "I don't know the name. He's not local, is he?"

"From Idaho originally, Hart said. He was an ex-con."

Lola frowned. "None of it makes sense. What was an ex-con doing at a book festival? Unless—did he steal collectible books or something like that? He could have been after the first-edition books at the auction."

"Not as far as I know. Hart mentioned armed robbery and auto theft—doesn't sound like a guy who would be dealing in first-edition Twains or Thackerays on the side."

"No, it sure doesn't. Shoo, you."

As the last words were apparently addressed to Misty, I didn't take offense. Misty, holding the twine between her teeth, jumped out of the wheelbarrow and Lola went back to shoveling its contents into the composter. The pitchfork tinged against the wheelbarrow with each scoop. She worked in silence for a long minute, and then said, "Someone here in Heaven knew him, knew Van Allen. His death wasn't random."

"I agree." I waited to see where Lola's scientific mind would take her.

"I think he was here specifically for the Celebration of Gothic Novels." She wrinkled her nose as a particularly sharp odor drifted from the composter, then shut the hatch with a thud. "You said he was at all of the events. That's what he came for."

"What's what he came for?"

"Something—or someone—involved with the festival." She gazed at me unblinking from behind her glasses, which were speckled with tiny mulch bits. "The timing is too coincidental otherwise. Think about it: Stranger comes to town, attends three events associated with the gothic festival, and then is killed by someone not tied into the festival? Uh-uh. I'll bet you next month's heating bill that it's all related to Gemma's shindig."

"You don't bet."

"True." She smiled, her teeth dazzling against her dark complexion. "I'm still right." Grabbing the wheelbarrow's handles, she trundled it back toward a shed. I

picked up the pitchfork and followed. Misty had disappeared. "We need to talk to the people in town for the
festival, the authors."

I thought about reminding her that the police were
on the case, but I knew she felt irrationally guilty because her spike had been the murder weapon, so I
merely said, "Who do you want to start with?"

Chapter 9

We decided to start with Maud Bell, since she had an in with Constance Aldringham and her family. Maud endorsed both Lola's analysis and her plan to talk to the visiting authors.

"You know Sandy sets out munchies and has a little happy hour at the Columbine every evening at six," Maud reminded me when I called. "It's really for guests, but Merle invited me and Joe for tonight. Joe left this morning for Costa Rica to photograph spider monkeys, so why don't you and Lola come along? As much business as you throw Sandy's way, I know she won't mind giving you a handful of peanuts and a glass of wine. We can casually work Van Allen into the conversation and see how people respond." Her voice rang with enthusiasm.

I felt a little uncomfortable crashing Sandy's happy hour, so I called her to make sure it was okay. She said she was happy to have us, but Lola insisted on bringing a bottle of wine anyway, even though she doesn't drink. I picked up a Chianti at the liquor store while Lola cleaned up, and then we met Maud outside the Columbine. Maud looked a tad chicer than usual in a silvery gray knit tunic that set off her silver, white, and gray hair to perfection. She wore it over slim black slacks and looked like a model for a senior living magazine. I wondered if the extra effort was for Merle.

We climbed the B and B's steps, three abreast, and I fought the urge to link elbows and compare us to Charlie's Angels. We really needed Brooke to be the Angels, though, since she looked so much like a young Jaclyn Smith. Actually, since there weren't any black Angels or senior citizen Angels over the course of the show's run, I needed to think of another trio of sleuths we could be. Unfortunately, the only trios that came to mind were the Three Stooges and the Kingston Trio. Since I didn't plan to break into song or poke anyone in the eyes, they didn't seem apropos. I puzzled over it for a minute, thinking that as many mysteries as I read, I should be able to come up with a crime-solving trio, but they were all duos (Nick and Nora, Rizzoli and Isles, Elvis Cole and Joe Pike) or hard-core loners.

I let go of that train of thought as Maud pushed the door open. A muted babble of conversation greeted us, coming from the parlor where I'd seen Constance and Allyson the other day.

"Let's do it," Maud whispered, taking the lead and striding into the room. Lola and I followed in her wake.

The small room felt crowded. Bottles of liquor and wine sat on the wheeled cart where the coffee urn had been the other day. The garnet-colored drapes were half-drawn, framing a rectangle of twilight, and sconces provided a warm glow. An Aubusson rug (or reproduction) cushioned the hardwood floors underfoot and made the room feel cozier. What looked like all of the inn's guests were assembled for free drinks, chatting in twosomes and threesomes: The Aldringham family had one corner staked out, Francesca Bugle and Mary Stewart chatted with the movie producer, and Lucas Stewart poured himself a hefty tot of bourbon before returning to a conversation with Sandy.

"Maudie!" Merle caught sight of her immediately (almost as if he'd been on the lookout) and came forward to kiss her cheek.

"Joe's off to Costa Rica," she said, "so I brought Amy-Faye and Lola along. I think they want to hear stories about our activities at Berkeley."

Merle looked uneasy, which made me want to hear about what had gone on at Berkeley.

Everyone murmured hellos and Sandy beckoned us toward the drinks trolley. "You didn't need to do that," she said, taking the wine bottle Lola proffered, "but thanks. It won't go to waste. Who knew authors drank so much?" she whispered to me as Lola helped herself to a ginger ale and joined Maud with the Aldringham clan. "Although I will say that reading Constance's latest book almost drove me to drink. What dreck! I didn't make it past the second chapter. Give me a good biography any day." She tidied up the bottles, and said, "Stick around as long as you'd like—I've got to check on Dave. He's got a nasty cold, and you know how men get. Two sneezes and a cough and they're acting like they've got bubonic plague." We laughed and she bustled away, holding an empty bottle by its neck.

Pouring myself a scant glass of white wine, I edged toward the group made up of Francesca Bugle, Mary

Stewart, and the movie producer, who was holding forth about his upcoming release. He was dressed all in black again, trendy glasses pushed up on his head. He held a tall glass with the remnants of a gunky green smoothie coating the sides. I tried to dredge up his name—it was something weird that started with a C. Casper? Cuba? Cosmo! Cosmo Zeller. Mary greeted me with a smile and Francesca edged over to make room for me.

"—ad placement on *The Walking Dead*, *Grimm*, *Gotham*—just fifteen-second spots to whet viewers' appetites. You'll start seeing them next week. Just tell me if they don't make you jump!"

When he paused to slurp down the last bit of his smoothie, Francesca said, "The casting is almost complete on *Barbary Close*."

"Unfortunately," Cosmo jumped in, "Jennifer Lawrence had a prior commitment, so we're still looking for our Avalon. That casting will be crucial to the movie's success. Avalon's got to be beautiful and innocent, but with a core of steel." He wrapped the fingers of his right hand around his clenched left fist, to demonstrate the core of steel. "Young girls identify with her. You"— he nodded graciously at Francesca—"have the soul of a twenty-two-year-old to be able to make Avalon so real."

"Well, I was twenty-two once," Francesca laughed. She wore another hat tonight; this one was royal blue with three little feathers sticking up from one side.

Mary's expression said, *Not recently*, although she didn't verbalize it.

"We're thinking about filming right here in your

quaint little town," Cosmo said, looking at me. "The gazebo by the lake, the downtown district, the mountains—all of it says 'Barbary Close' to me. We'll cast some of the locals as extras, put this town on the map."

He clearly expected me to applaud or at least gush, but all I said was, "Sounds like a good thing for the town." Taking a deep breath, I used his comment to bring up the topic I was here to pursue. "I'm glad the murder Saturday night didn't make you think Heaven wasn't a suitable location. We have an extremely low crime rate. The victim wasn't from Heaven and I doubt his killer was, either, so I'm sure there's no reason not to film the movie here."

There was dead silence for a full fifteen seconds in our little circle. Cosmo stared into the dregs of his smoothie, Francesca worked her lips in and out, and Mary fingered a strand of her red hair. She finally asked, "So the police have identified that poor man, the one who was murdered?"

Nodding, I said, "Trent Van Allen. Did you know him?"

She reared back. "Me? Of course not. Why would I know him?"

Without answering, I looked from Francesca to Cosmo. "How about you?"

"I don't even know why you'd ask that," Francesca said, pulling her chin back so she looked like a turtle and giving me a frosty look.

I blinked disingenuously. "Well, he was from out of town and he went to all the book events, so I thought he might be connected to one of you."

"You mean like a deranged fan stalking one of us?" Mary asked, casting a look over her shoulder as if expecting to see a dark figure advancing on her with a raised butcher knife.

"Possibly," I said.

"I've already got that batty Hufnagle woman following me around," Mary said. "I think that fills my quota of deranged stalkers. The murdered guy must have been following you." She smiled sweetly at Francesca. "Or maybe Constance."

"A deranged fan," Cosmo mused. "If we spin it right, that could drum up a lot of free publicity for the movie. Too bad he didn't break into your house, or attack you."

Francesca, Mary, and I shared a look, totally in accord for the moment. "'Too bad'?" Francesca asked tartly. "'Too *bad*'?"

"Oh, I wouldn't have wanted you to get hurt," Cosmo backpedaled quickly, holding up a defensive hand. "I only meant—"

"Come to think of it," Francesca said slowly, "someone did break into my room here."

"What?" Mary squeaked. "And you didn't say anything?"

Cosmo Zeller took advantage of the opportunity to edge away, holding his glass up as if he was going in search of a refill.

"When?" I asked.

Francesca shrugged. "I didn't notice anything missing, so it didn't seem worth making a fuss about. It was Saturday sometime. When I got back from the high school, I knew someone had been going through my things."

Saturday. That was when I'd seen Van Allen skulking around the inn.

"It was probably housekeeping," Mary said dismissively.

Francesca shook her head. "No, because the maid hadn't been in yet. My bed still wasn't made up and I didn't have fresh towels."

Sandy had a couple of college girls who helped her with the cleaning on weekends when the inn was full.

"I know I locked my door when I left to go to Book Bliss, but it was unlocked when I got back. And the things in my tote, where I keep my notebooks, research files, and laptop, had been disarranged."

"Jewelry?" Mary stroked the moonstone necklace circling her neck.

"Didn't bring any."

"You should tell Sandy, and maybe the police," I said.

Francesca gave me a world-weary look. "Hon, the police aren't going to get excited about a break-in where nothing was stolen. They've got better things to do—like catch whoever killed that Van Alston guy."

"Van Allen," I said. "Trent Van Allen."

"That was the dead guy's name?" Without my realizing it, Lucas Stewart had come up behind us. Now he looped an arm over his sister's shoulders and gave us all a smile. I wondered if he knew how devastatingly sexy it was the way his eyes crinkled the tiniest bit at the corners.

I nodded. "Did you know him?" I asked, knowing his answer in advance.

"Never saw him before Saturday," he said.

"You saw him?" Mary slipped out from under his arm and stared at him.

"Heck, yeah. He was all over the place. He asked a question about pen names at the panel thingie in the morning, and he was seated on the far right of the auditorium during the auction. He didn't bid on anything, though. Then, I noticed him at the costume ball. Well, I mean, he was damn noticeable, being the only one not in costume."

"You've very observant," I said.

"Have to be, in my line of work," he said.

"Which is?" I tried to guess what Lucas did for a living. I ruled out the obvious, like underwear model and soap opera actor, since I couldn't see that those would require any observational skills.

"I'm a bodyguard."

I blinked at him and Francesca said, "Well, I never!"

He grinned, pleased to have startled us. "Yep. I'm between jobs at the moment, and thought I'd tag along with Mary on this tour after what happened in Birmingham."

"Fat lot of good you've been," Mary said, clearly irritated. "Where were you when I got into it with Eloise Saturday night? Too busy flirting with anyone stupid enough to give you one iota of encouragement."

The glance she threw at Allyson Aldringham made it perfectly clear whom she was talking about. Mary was clearly one of those sisters who took a somewhat proprietary interest in her brother's romantic life. I grinned to myself at the idea of being jealous of any of my brother Derek's hapless girlfriends. Of course, he went through them quicker than an allergy sufferer went through Kleenex during ragweed season, so I didn't even meet most of them. Come to think of it, my youngest sister, Natalie, had gotten into it once with Derek when he took a girl she didn't like to a friend's wedding. Maybe the jealousy was a younger sister–older brother thing.

Lucas gave his sister a darkling look. "Mare, we talked about this—"

"Do you carry a gun?" Francesca interrupted.

"Sometimes," Lucas said. To forestall Francesca frisking him, he said, "I'm not carrying now. This assignment didn't seem to warrant it. Besides, these hands"—he held them up—"are lethal weapons."

He smiled and I couldn't tell if he was serious or making fun of himself. Before I could puzzle it out, something smashed through the window and glass went flying.

Chapter 10

There was a loud thud, followed by the tinkle of glass falling like sharp rain. I caught my breath and put a hand over my eyes to shield them.

"Get down," Lucas shouted. A couple of people dropped to a crouch. Merle Aldringham threw his arms around Maud to shield her, leaving his wife to fend for herself. Hmm. Allyson grabbed a pillow from the sofa and held it up. Someone let out a strangled yelp. Lucas raced for the door, and his footsteps pounded toward the main door, which creaked open suddenly and slammed shut.

After a moment of silence, when nothing exploded or went up in flames, I straightened and edged forward to inspect the missile. Everyone quickly gathered around.

"A brick," Constance said with disgust. "Hardly a threat to life and limb." She eyed her husband, who had sheepishly let go of Maud.

"Really, Merle, I can take care of myself." Maud laughed, shaking her top to scatter any glass slivers, and running her fingers through her hair. "Bricks aren't nearly as nasty as the tear gas canisters the police used to break up our Vietnam War demonstrations, or as lethal as the Kent State riot."

"I'm bleeding," Allyson announced, at the same time I spotted the note rubber banded to the brick. Lola used a napkin to stanch the trickle of blood on Allyson's hand, and I nudged the brick over with my foot. I read it aloud. "'You won't get away with it.'"

"Who is 'you' and what is 'it'?" Maud asked. "I hate sloppily used pronouns with unclear antecedent references."

"It's got to be Eloise," Mary said, looking a little pale.

Sandy arrived, drawn by the commotion probably, and took in the situation with one quick glance. "I'm calling the police."

Before she could dial, Lucas strode back in, breathing hard. "I couldn't catch him. I heard running footsteps, and I took off after him, but he got away in a car. I wasn't close enough to get the license, or even the make." He smacked a fist into his palm in frustration.

"Or her," Mary said. "Oh, Lucas, it had to be Eloise."

His eyes narrowing, he said, "If so, she's escalating. The fake blood was a nuisance, but this—that brick could have hurt someone."

It hardly seemed possible, but he was even sexier when he was worried and intense.

Mary wrapped her arms around herself. "Oh, do you think she's trying to kill me? Is my life in danger?" She shivered.

I couldn't help but think she was overdoing the melodrama a bit. Apparently, Maud agreed.

"If so," Maud observed drily, "she's the least competent assassin ever. She threw a brick through the window, for heaven's sake; she didn't spray the room with an AK-47."

"The police are on their way," Sandy announced. "Let's move into the breakfast room—I don't want anyone cutting themselves on all this glass."

I didn't know if she was more worried about people dripping blood on her expensive rugs or of getting sued.

She made herding motions and we all trooped across the hall into the pretty wainscoted breakfast room with the antique buffet, six square tables already set for tomorrow's breakfast, and long windows hung with gold velvet drapes. Lucas immediately crossed to the windows and drew the drapes across them. It looked like he was taking his bodyguard duties a little more seriously. Sandy, eyeing her variously nervous, irritated, and unsettled guests, ducked out of the dining room and returned minutes later with the drinks trolley. Constance, Merle, Lucas, Mary, and Francesca dove for it. I still had my original glass of wine, but I set it down and helped myself to a bottled water. Lola was refilling her ginger ale and asked in a low voice, "Do you think the note is about the murder?"

I shrugged. "I don't know. Could be. Or it could be about the manuscript-theft lawsuit, like Mary thinks."

"Or something else entirely," Lola said.

A young female HPD officer I'd never met arrived before we could hash it out any further. I wondered if she was new—she might be the replacement for Officer Ridgway, who had supplemented his department paycheck by selling information on HPD activities. She earnestly inspected the brick and wrote down what we had to say about the incident. Bagging the note, she suggested Sandy put plywood over the broken window for the night, told us to call if anything else happened, and left. Sandy disappeared in search of a whisk broom to clean up the glass, and I held the dustpan while she brushed stuff in. We discussed an upcoming sorority reunion she was hosting, and I agreed to come over on Saturday morning to help her plan the event. Lola, Maud, and I left as soon as the police officer drove away.

"Ice cream?" I suggested as we stood on the walkway. I hadn't even finished one drink; I figured I deserved a little indulgence. I was pretty sure I had nothing edible in my fridge, so the ice cream could be dinner.

"You're on," Maud said. "We can do a debrief."

"We're not in MI5," Lola said, chuckling. "But I'm up for a strawberry fro yo. Why don't we try that new yogurt place where Allenby's used to be?"

We rendezvoused at the yogurt place, a small storefront on the edge of the downtown district, squashed between a Western boutique called West of Eden and a Thai restaurant. On a Monday at dinnertime, we were the only customers in the brightly lit and tiled place. Our footsteps echoed. I filled my cup with a blend of coffee and chocolate yogurts and topped it with Heath pieces and chocolate sauce. If you're going to indulge, might as well go whole hog, right? Lola stuck with strawberry yogurt and fresh fruit, while Maud indulged in a key lime yogurt with gummies and crumbled animal crackers. When we had weighed the yogurt and paid up, we went back outside to one of the three metal tables arranged on the sidewalk. It was a clear, quiet evening, without much traffic. The aroma of coconut and curry drifted from Lanna Thai. There was a definite nip in the air now that it was dark, and I was glad for the drapey gray sweater I'd pulled on before going to the Columbine.

"I'll start," Maud announced.

No surprise there—Maud was never shy about offering an opinion, an observation, or a comment.

"The Aldringham household is one unhappy place," she said, licking a bit of green yogurt from her upper lip. "In a way, it's a study in how time exaggerates our dominant characteristics, I think." She sounded a little melancholy.

"How so?" Lola asked.

Maud gave it some thought, knitting her brow. "Well, Merle always was a persuadable guy, the kind of guy who went along to get along. Now it's almost as if he's so in the habit of doing whatever Constance wants that there's not much Merle left. I have a feeling that chatting with me is the first rebellious thing he's done in many years, and that's not much of a rebellion, heaven knows.

"He worked in an accounting firm the first ten years or so after they got married, but it sounds like when Constance hit the big time, he quit. He says he's daytrading now."

"That can be really hard on a marriage," Lola observed. "When one partner is totally dependent on the other."

"Especially when the 'other' is Constance Aldringham," Maud said tartly. "When we were in college, she was always looking out for herself, only interested in a cause if there was something in it for her. She always had to be in charge, had to be the center of attention. Now she's a black hole sucking in everything that comes within her gravitational pull."

I raised my brows. "That sounds a bit . . . harsh."

Maud gave a wry grin. "You're right. I'm just angry on Merle's behalf, and on Allyson's. Have you heard the way she talks to that girl? When they were at our place Saturday night, it was 'Allyson simply can't hold a job' and 'All of Allyson's friends have their own places now, but she's simply not ready,' with the girl sitting right there. She's so dismissive and hurtful, it makes me want to pop her." She paused and worked her jaw from side to side. "We used to be friends."

Lola put a hand on Maud's arm. "Friendships run their course."

"Looking at them makes me wonder which of my qualities has become more prominent as I've aged," Maud said.

"Your independent spirit," I put in before she could come up with something negative.

"Your passion for making a difference in the world," Lola said.

"Thanks," Maud said with a grateful smile. "I have done my part to keep our local government and business folks honest with my blog." She twitched, as if to shake off her unusually reflective mood, and said, "Now, that Allyson . . . Merle hinted that she's got issues."

"What kind?" I asked, crunching on a large chunk of Heath candy.

"He wasn't very clear on that. I got the feeling she'd maybe been in trouble with the law, but I could be wrong."

"Drugs?" I asked.

"Possibly. Or it might just have been that she never finished her degree and can't hold a job. She's been living at home and working as Constance's personal assistant for over a year now, Merle said. She was involved with some unsuitable guy, and when that went bust, she moved back in."

"Not so unusual these days," Lola said. "Lots of the middle-aged folks who come to Bloomin' Wonderful talk about having their kids move back home after college. It's hard for kids to find jobs these days, to get on their feet. That's why I'm so happy Axie is working for you, Amy-Faye. I think having some work experience under her belt will give her a head start. Not to mention that it helps her understand the value of a dollar."

"Not much these days," Maud groused. "You know the Washington pols and the bankers are like this"—she entwined two fingers—"and they're conspiring to set policies that disadvantage—"

A car with a bad muffler rumbled past, drowning her out. I jumped in before she could get into full spate. "Francesca said someone broke in to her room on Saturday afternoon. She said they didn't take anything, but she's sure someone went through her things."

"That's strange. Maybe it was the maids," Lola said.

"That's what Mary Stewart suggested."

We ruminated on it for a moment, but when none of us could make anything of it, I said, "Did anyone react to the name Trent Van Allen? Did you get the feeling anyone knew him?"

Maud shook her head. "I didn't pick up on it if they did. I tossed the name out while all the Aldringhams and Lucas were standing there, and they all acted as if they'd never heard it. It's too bad we didn't have a photo to show them. Constance seemed to think Wallace Pinnecoose killed him—that they were up to some kind of financial hanky-panky together." She blew a raspberry.

"And Merle seemed inclined to think it was a random murder," Lola said.

"A serial killer who just happened across the stranger who just happened to be hanging out in Wallace's office?" I didn't try to hide my disbelief.

"I didn't say it made sense." Lola smiled.

"There has to be a connection between Van Allen and someone involved with the gothic festival," I said, frustrated. "It doesn't track otherwise."

"Maybe the police have come up with something," Lola said.

"Fat chance."

Maud had little regard for "society's authorized forces of repression," as she referred to anyone in a uniform. Well, maybe not Girl Scouts or flight attendants.

Lola stood. Stacking our empty yogurt cups together, she put the spoons inside them and carried them to the trash can near the curb. "I've got to get going. I told Axie I'd pick her up from Thea's in ten minutes."

"And I'm freezing," I said, standing and rubbing my hands together. "I'll call Hart in the morning and see what he has to say about the brick."

With quick hugs all around, we headed for our cars and home.

Chapter 11

Al Frink beat me into the office on Tuesday morning. When I came through the door, he rose and handed me two message slips. One was from a woman wanting me to organize a baby shower. A new customer—yippee! The other said that Flavia Dunbarton had called. She was a reporter for the *Grand Junction Gabbler*, and I'd met her after my friend Ivy Donner died. I eyed the inoffensive pink slip dubiously.

"What did she want?" I asked Al. As if I didn't know.

"To talk about the murder," he said, confirming my suspicion. "She sounded hot. Is she hot?"

"Hot?" Al didn't usually react this way to our clients.

"Hot. Sexy, beautiful, a bombshell." He looked at me eagerly.

"A femme fatale."

"She is?" His eyes lit up.

"No, I was just playing our game." I gave it some thought. "She's attractive. Dark hair, nice smile. Late twenties." Which made her three or four years older than Al, I guessed.

"I guess I can judge for myself." He moved to pick up a file folder so he wasn't facing me. "I told her you were free at nine."

"Al!"

"Yes, boss?" He gave me an innocent look.

"Don't call me 'boss,'" I said querulously, stomping back to my office.

I barely had time to glance at the schedule board and make a couple of phone calls related to events later in the week before Al appeared in my doorway with Flavia Dunbarton peering over his shoulder.

"Your nine o'clock is here, bo—Amy-Faye," he said. The fatuous look he gave Flavia told me she fit his definition of "hot."

I didn't see it. She was a thin woman, with shoulder-length brown hair, thin lips, and a long face. Still, she did had an energetic quality to her, a feeling of being alert and alive, and maybe that's what attracted Al.

"Would you like coffee, Ms. Dunbarton?" he asked.

I noticed he didn't ask me.

"Flavia." She smiled at him. "No, thanks."

He lingered in the doorway until I said, "Thanks, Al." Reluctantly, he withdrew and closed the door.

Flavia plopped into a chair and pulled out a small recorder. "Right. Let's talk murder."

I couldn't help but laugh a little. "Hi, Flavia, how've you been? How's the newspaper business? Did you have a good summer?"

She looked a little taken aback by my gentle sarcasm, but then grinned, her cheeks squishing her eyes into engaging half-moons. "Sorry. I can be a bit too focused on business. My mom used to tell me to take a breath and look around sometimes when I was caught up in a project. How are you? Are you getting past what happened last May?"

I didn't know if I'd ever "get past" my friend's murder, and almost being killed by her murderer, but I didn't feel like going into it with Flavia. "Life goes on," I said.

"And here you are, involved in another murder." Flavia's eyes lit up.

"I'm not 'involved,'" I said. "I happened to be at the Club when the body was discovered—that's all."

"Tell me about it." She set the recorder on the edge of my desk.

Dodging the request, I said, "Why are you talking to me? There were hundreds of people at the party."

"Yes, but not too many of them saw Van Allen's body," Flavia said. "And the police are pretty much at a dead end—they can't even locate his car or where he was staying—so I'm reduced to beating the bushes to get something worth printing by deadline. Help me out, please? I heard you knew the guy."

She heard entirely too much, I thought, probably from one of the cops or ambulance people on the scene. "I didn't know him, but I'd seen him a couple of times that day." Giving in, and thinking I might drum up some business for Gemma, I talked at length about the Celebration of Gothic Novels and Gemma's bookstore, and only a little bit about Van Allen having been present at some of the events.

"Why do you think he was hanging around the gothic festival?" she asked.

I thought briefly about telling her my theory about his having a specific interest in one of the authors, but it was mere speculation, so I shrugged and said, "Maybe he grew up reading Daphne du Maurier and watching *Dark Shadows*. Maybe he wanted to buy a book for his mom or his wife. Did he have a wife?"

Flavia shook her head. "Not according to the police. At least, he didn't have one while he was in prison. He might have acquired one as soon as he got out, one of those prison groupies who get off on marrying inmates."

I was sure my expression of distaste mirrored Flavia's. "Ugh," we said together.

"Anything else you can tell me?" Flavia asked.

"Nope."

She turned off the recorder and gathered her things. "If you think of anything, let me know. This story will run tomorrow morning, but I'll need something for later in the week, too, since my editor wants follow-ups. It's not often we get a story with famous authors and murder in Heaven or Grand Junction."

She said it with a shade too much relish for my taste. "Thankfully," I said, rising. Mindful of Al's crush, I called, "Al, can you show Flavia out?"

He appeared with the speed of the Flash. The scent of aftershave preceded him and I suspected he'd slapped some on for Flavia's benefit. I bit back a grin as he said, "Certainly! Right this way, Ms. Dun—Flavia," he said, for all the world as if he were guiding her through the Minotaur's labyrinth instead of shepherding her twenty-five feet through the reception area to the clearly visible French doors. When he didn't come right back, I suspected he was walking her all the way to her car, and I laughed as I picked up the phone to call Hart.

When he answered, I said, "Hey."

"Hey, yourself."

I heard the smile in his voice and smiled in return. It flashed through my mind that I hadn't felt this goofy about a man since the early days of my relationship with Doug.

"You're calling about the brick, aren't you?"

"You heard, then?"

"Of course. It was the most exciting thing that happened last night. Well, unless you count old Mrs. Beasley locking herself out of her house in her nightie and calling for assistance, which I don't, since that happens at least once a week."

"Wow. Being a cop is a thrill a minute."

"If Mrs. Beasley were twenty-two instead of eighty-two, and her nightie was more Victoria's Secret than Queen Victoria, the troops might find it more thrilling to go to her rescue. As it is . . ."

I laughed. "Seriously, did you learn anything from the brick or the note?"

"No. Bricks aren't made for holding fingerprints, and we couldn't lift any from the paper, either. Not too surprising. Unless someone saw whoever threw the brick . . ."

I heard the shrug in his voice. "Mary Stewart and her brother think it was that Eloise Hufnagle. They're worried that she's escalating, getting more violent, that she might hurt Mary."

"Unlikely. It's a far cry from splashing stage blood on someone or tossing a brick through a window to assault and battery. If she's worried, Stewart should take simple precautions—not walk down dark alleys alone, stay with a group of people."

"Did you know her brother's a professional bodyguard?"

"Anyone can call themselves a bodyguard," Hart said, clearly unimpressed. "It's not like there's a licensing organization or required training. On the other hand, if he's halfway alert, that should be all it takes to keep Hufnagle away."

We made arrangements to have dinner on Wednesday night—the only night of the week I didn't have an event planned—and hung up. As I replaced the phone, I heard Al come back. He was whistling. I bit back a smile when he appeared in the doorway, a fatuous grin on his face.

"She asked me out," he said, the grin getting wider, if that were possible.

"She did?" There was too much surprise in my voice, so I added, "On a date?" Not much better. "Uh, what did she say? Where are you going?"

"We were standing by her car—she's got a sweet ride, a 1968 Corvette she says she and her pop restored, turquoise with white leather interior—and I told her it was cherry. We went back and forth about cars, and she asked me if I was going to the muscle car show in Grand Junction this weekend, and I said 'yeah,' and she said we should go together." He tweaked his bow tie straight.

"That's great, Al. Sounds like fun." Fun for Al, and apparently fun for Flavia. I'd rather watch asphalt cure than go to a car show. But Al was a car nut, and I knew he'd have a great time. He might not even get around to looking at the cars if Flavia was nearby. "You'll have to tell me about it on Monday."

"Sure thing," he said. His brow creased. "What should I wear?" He immediately winced, and said, "Delete that. That was such a girl question."

I laughed as the phone rang and he scooted back to his desk to answer it. I called the caterer working tonight's birthday party to let her know one guest had a strawberry allergy and another wanted a gluten-free meal, and then devoted some time to Thursday's corporate off-site and the party for five hundred on Saturday night. I had only last-minute details to attend to for both events, so when I rang off with my point of contact at Delaney Construction, I called Brooke and talked her into taking a walk with me around Lost Alice Lake. I knew she and Troy had the appointment this evening to talk to a mother-to-be who was planning to give up her baby, and I wanted to take her mind off it. Brooke has always been a worrier.

Swapping my low-heeled pumps for walking shoes, I checked my e-mail one last time and headed out. I had to tell Al twice that I was taking a long lunch and would be at Lost Alice Lake. He was caught up in a daydream—about Flavia, I was sure. "Yeah, okay, later, boss," he responded absently. I suspected I could have told him I was headed to Mars for a little look-see and he would have given the same response. He was probably still trying to sort out his wardrobe options for the date. The dark-wash jeans or the distressed ones?

Brooke was waiting when I pulled up beside her Mercedes ten minutes later. Her dark hair swung in a ponytail and she had an Athleta jacket over slim-fitting workout pants. She gave me a hug. "Thanks for getting me out of the house," she said. "I was just sitting there stewing."

"I know. You are the Queen of Stewing. Remember how you lost four pounds waiting for the acceptance letter from CSU? And the time you threw up because you were so worried about how your dad would react when you scratched the car door?"

"I'm better than that now," Brooke protested as we made our way down the slight incline to the path that circled the lake. A cold front had come through last night and I zipped my fleece against the bite of the wind made keener by the water. The lake gleamed blue, dappled by sunlight and riffled by the breeze. With the already snowcapped Rockies in the background, it looked like a postcard. Grasses waved from the bottom by the shore, and I glimpsed a foot-long trout before a flick of his tail hid him among the waving fronds. A handful of people were enjoying the beautiful fall day, conscious that soon the path would be covered with snow and the lake frozen over. Two high-school-age kids who should probably have been in school were tossing a Frisbee, and other people walked or jogged. Brooke set a brisk pace down the path; she was much more conscientious about working out than I was.

I filled her in on last night's cocktail gathering and the brick, and told her about Flavia Dunbarton coming by this morning.

"Lucas Stewart is a bodyguard?" she asked.

"Out of all that, the first thing you pick up on is that Mary's brother is a bodyguard?"

"C'mon, A-Faye. That's interesting. It's like having Kevin Costner or Jean-Claude Van Damme in our midst. Remember that movie Costner made with Whitney Houston? What was it called?"

"*The Bodyguard.*"

"That's it. I'll bet Lucas has all his own hair, which makes him way hotter than Costner."

"Oh, I don't know," I said, huffing a little and swinging my arms to keep up with her longer stride. "Costner's engaging. Likable."

Hronk, hronk. A V of geese flew low overhead, headed south, a bit late in the season, in my opinion. I watched them for a moment, and then said, "Do you think the brick's related to the murder, the lawsuit, or something else?"

Brooke cocked her head, considering. "I think we don't know enough about any of the players," she said. "Troy Sr."—her wheeler-dealer, powerful father-in-law—"says you never sit down at the negotiating table with someone until you know them better than their wife or dog does."

We weren't negotiating anything, but I got her point. "You think we should find out more about the authors."

"About everyone who came to Heaven for the gothic thingie," she said. "The authors, bodyguard Lucas, Constance Aldringham's hub and daughter, the movie guy, and that Hufnagle woman. I don't suppose Hart would fill you in?"

I shook my head, then palmed a strand of hair out of my eye. "No. He lets a kernel fall now and then, but he's not going to turn over dossiers on all those people. I don't even know how much he's looked at them."

"Well, we can Google with the best of them," Brooke said. "I'll find out about Mary Stewart—"

"You just want an excuse for cyber-stalking her brother. What would Troy say?"

She ignored me, which was justified, since I knew she was still madly in love with Troy and was only funning about Lucas.

"—and Maud can research the Aldringham clan, since she knows them from the olden days. Kerry can look into Francesca Bugle, and Lola can take Eloise Hufnagle."

"I'll find out what I can about Cosmo Zeller," I agreed, liking the plan as much because it would keep Brooke occupied for the afternoon, and help her not worry about the adoption interview this evening, as because we might learn something useful about the murder. "Can you phone the others and let them know?"

"Happy to."

We were about halfway around the lake's three-and-a-half-mile circumference, and I stopped to take a pebble out of my shoe. Once I had retied my sneaker, we walked another twenty-five minutes in companionable near silence, commenting on the beauty of the day and betting on when the first significant snowfall of the season would happen. We'd already had a couple of dustings, but nothing to call out the snowplows. Brooke and I always made snow angels together the first time we got enough snow. When we got back to the parking lot, I hugged Brooke again, holding her for an extra moment. "Good luck tonight," I said. "Call me and let me know how it goes."

"Will do," she said with a strained smile.

"And don't forget to call Lola and Kerry and Maud," I added, "and see what you can dig up on the Stewart sibs."

"I know what you're doing," she said, giving me a little shove.

"I'm not doing anything," I said, all innocence.

"Yes, you are, and I appreciate it. I'll try not to worry. Promise. If this mother doesn't choose Troy and me, the next one will." She got in the Merc, blew me a kiss, and drove off.

Chapter 12

Wednesday morning started early. I had been hired to put together a networking breakfast for professional women in a three-county area, and I'd set it up at an orchard that boasted a large room used for farmers' markets on summer and fall weekends, and other gatherings the rest of the time. When I arrived at six a.m., it smelled strongly of peaches; in fact, the aroma of peaches was heavy in the air before I turned into the long, curving driveway leading to the orchard. As I crested a hill, the orchard lay spread out below me with the Colorado River winding behind it, tinted peach (appropriately enough) by the rising sun. Puffy cumulus clouds glowed pink and coral and red, and I stopped to take a photo with my phone. It was too beautiful to ignore.

Two baker's vans and Al had beaten me to the orchard, and the owner's yawning daughter let all of us into the barnlike space to set up. I had worn jeans and brought work gloves in anticipation of shoving the rustic tables and benches into position, and I was sweating by the time Al and I flapped a vinyl tablecloth onto the last table. I could have hired someone to do it, but that would have cut into my profits, and it's not like I was doing anything else at this hour of the morning. Bushel baskets of peaches made lovely centerpieces, and the goodies unloaded by the baker and her assistants added a yeasty, sugary smell to the room that made my mouth water.

"Smells delicious," Al said, swiping the hem of his shirt across his damp forehead.

"Scrumptious."

"Delectable."

"I'm having one." I made for the trays of pastries and chose a still-warm cake donut. Al swiped a peach and soon had juice dribbling down his chin. After we enjoyed our snack, we unloaded a podium from the van, and tested the rudimentary microphone and sound system the orchard supplied. There wasn't going to be much in the way of speeches—just a welcome from Kerry Sanderson, whose brainchild the event was— before the women began schmoozing and eating.

About seventy-five women had signed up for the event and they began arriving in ones and twos. Helping themselves to pastries, juice, and coffee, they chatted in small clumps until Kerry strode in, very mayoral in a cream-colored suit with a colorful scarf, and made a few remarks. She was witty and welcoming and soon had the women chuckling and nodding their heads as she talked about the importance of making connections across communities. When she finished to genial applause, she headed toward me, where I stood catching up with a couple of women I knew from Grand Junction. As a small-business owner, I was as much a participant in this event as its organizer.

"Have you heard from Brooke this morning?" she asked when the other women drifted away. She patted a stray hair into place on her short do. "How'd it go for her and Troy last night?"

"I haven't heard from her yet. You know Brooke—she's no early bird. I'll call her on my way back to town."

Kerry nodded. "Let me know. When she called yesterday to say you thought it would be a good idea to find out more about our suspects, she mentioned the appointment. Good thinking, by the way. I spent an hour last night looking into the life and times of Francesca Bugle."

"And?"

"And it was an unrewarding task, because as far as I can tell, there was no Francesca Bugle before her first book came out eight years ago." Kerry gave me a meaningful look.

I wasn't sure there was anything very meaningful to that. "It's a pen name."

"Of course, but usually you can find out the author's true identity by checking copyrights, or reading through the bio to get hints, or via Web sites that make a practice of matching authors' real names with their pseudonyms. But not in this case. Her bio is carefully written to not even mention a state by name, and although it talks about her mother's early death, farming, and living a hand-to-mouth existence, the photos of a decrepit barn and cornfields are stock photos, straight off the Internet. I suspect the photo of the pigtailed girl with her overalled brother is, too. And her Facebook page is the same. All her posts are related to her books. The recent ones are focused on details of the movie deal, the production process, et cetera, et cetera. Nothing even as personal as 'My cat ralphed up a hair ball today,' or 'Happy birthday to my great-gran, Mildred Fluffernutter, who is a hundred and three today.'"

I chuckled. "She's creating a brand," I said, well aware of the necessity for that as an entrepreneur myself.

Kerry snorted. "I'm a politician, for heaven's sake—I understand about staying on message. But this goes beyond that, it seems to me."

"Maybe she's just a private person."

Kerry looked skeptical. "Could be, but—"

A trio of women interrupted us then to try to get Kerry's support on a measure they wanted to bring before the Heaven town council. I circulated, meeting new people and possibly drumming up business. A couple of women referred to Flavia's article in this morning's edition of the newspaper, and mentioned they'd seen my name. They all had theories about the murder. I got a chance to talk to Kerry only briefly as she was leaving.

"Let's meet tomorrow night to discuss what we've come up with," she suggested. "I'll let the others know. Your place. Seven. I'll bring some zucchini bread—my plants are still producing, if you can believe that."

She was gone before I could respond. I shook my head. Kerry's efficiency—some might say bossiness—was occasionally annoying, but I couldn't deny that she made things happen and got things done. I had an event tomorrow night, but it was small and Al could handle it. I went in search of him to let him know, and to get started on the cleanup process.

Back in the office before noon, after a stop at home to shower and change out of my jeans, I called Brooke. No answer. Hm, not good. If she'd had a positive response from the prospective mother, she'd be shouting it from the rooftops, wouldn't she? I left a message for her to call, and listened to the messages on the office answering machine. The first two were for Al, nothing urgent, and I wrote them down. He wouldn't be back today— he had classes at the university. Preoccupied with a pen that was running out of ink, I almost missed the last message.

"This is for the Amy-Faye Johnson mentioned in the *Gabbler*," a New Jersey–accented woman's voice said. "If you want to know more about Trent Van Allen, meet me at the high school stadium at twelve today. If you don't show up, I'm outta here. Come alone."

I looked at my watch. Eleven fifty-six. I pulled out my keys and raced to the door.

I slid into the stadium parking lot six minutes later, hoping the anonymous caller would allow a couple minutes' leeway. Although there was moderate traffic around the high school across the street as classes broke for lunch, the stadium appeared deserted. The lot, where my dad had brought me to teach me to drive, had weeds growing between cracks in the asphalt and needed painting; the lines had faded to near invisibility. I scanned the stadium as I trotted across the lot, and thought I spotted someone standing in the top row of the bleachers on the home team side. If so, she ducked out of sight when I shaded my eyes and looked up. The stadium made a lot of sense as a rendezvous, I realized, passing the closed ticket booths, since someone could stand up there and have a 360-degree view of the surrounding terrain. If I hadn't come alone, for instance, the watcher would know.

I wasn't nervous as I made my way down the sloping concrete ramp to the field area. Maybe I should have been, but it was broad daylight, and I could hear kids shouting to one another as they peeled out for Subway or Arby's. A quarter-mile track, in good shape, surrounded the field area, where the grass showed scruffy patches from last Friday night's game against a Grand Junction high school team. Leaning back against the metal rail that ringed the field, I scanned the upper rows of seating. Two sections to my left, a woman waved at me from the topmost row.

I began the climb, wishing I were wearing my tennies instead of my tan pumps. Two rows below the woman, I stopped to assess her and saw that she was doing the same to me. She was fortyish, give or take, with multilayered dark hair streaked with meant-to-be-obvious blond highlights. Deep-set eyes under arched and penciled brows had crow's-feet at the corners. I saw why as she squinched her eyes against the smoke rising from her cigarette when she drew on it. Poppy-colored lipstick outlined thin lips and stained the cigarette. Her nails were long, clearly acrylic, and painted a deep mulberry with sparkly stick-ons that competed with the rings she wore on seven of ten fingers. Tight jeans, black leather booties, and a gray hoodie completed her look.

"You that Amy-Faye?" she asked, stubbing out her cigarette on the metal bleacher and letting it fall in a cascade of sparks.

I nodded. "Who are you?"

She used her tongue to lift a piece of tobacco from her lip, then peeled it off with her fingers. "Sharla." It came out like "Shawla."

"Sharla Van Allen?" I took a stab in the dark.

"Nah. Me and Trent didn't bother. It's only a piece a paper, right? Never mind about my last name. Come sit. I'm getting a crick in my neck looking up at youse." She patted the bleacher seat beside her and the metal rang hollowly.

I climbed the rest of the way and sat. My feet thanked me. Close-up, she smelled like cigarettes and a sandalwood-heavy perfume. I imagined it was called Oriental Rendezvous or something similar and sold by the bucket at Walmart.

"The paper said you found my Trent. Was he— Did he say—?" Her voice was husky.

"He was already dead," I said hastily. "I'm sorry for your loss."

"It sucks," she said, shaking another cigarette out of a packet but not lighting it. "Sucks big-time. I've been waiting four years for Trent to get out of prison, and then we have only a month together before he—" She broke off and put a forefinger under each eye to keep moisture from smearing mascara down her cheeks. Tears under control, she gave me a steely look. "I want to catch the bastard who did this to him. Trent never hurt anybody. He didn't deserve this."

I tried to remember what Hart had told me about Trent's criminal record. I seemed to remember lots of robbery but no rape or murder. "You should go to the police," I said. "Detective Har—"

"I can't go to the cops." She gave me a look that said I was dumber than a box of rocks. Her eyes were an unusual amber color, with flecks of lighter gold and caramel. "I got warrants out. You think I'da bothered with you if I could stroll into the local cop shop and tell 'em what I know? And I know plenty."

"I guess not," I said. "Why did you call me?"

"I read about you in the paper this morning, and it said you'd solved a coupla other murder cases, and I thought you might be able to figure out who offed Trent."

The bleacher's metal ridges were biting into my thighs and I shifted. "What do you know?"

"I know who killed him, that's what," she said triumphantly.

"Who?"

"Well, I don't know his name, but he's the guy Trent came here to see. Or it might be a gal—Trent wasn't too clear on that. Didn't want me knowing enough to get myself in trouble if the deal went south, see?"

Not really, but I nodded.

A reflective look came over Sharla's face. "Trent, he was a good guy—the best—but not much of a planner.

So, when he wrote to me a few weeks before he got out of the joint and said he had something going that would make us rich—well, not rich, but set us up solid, let us buy a garage from a guy Trent knew of—Trent was real good with cars, very handy, you know?—well, I had my doubts. But then he told me about how all he needed to do was get in touch with this person that was gonna be at this Celebration of Gothic Novels—I could never get into those kinda books. Give me a good Western any day—there's nobody can write a Western like Louis L'Amour, God bless him." She crossed herself. "Well, I began to think that maybe he was onta something. I shoulda known better." Noticing the still-unlit cigarette in her hand, she crumbled it into tobacco shreds and let them drift down. "Trying to quit," she said, pulling a key ring with a heavy silver-colored "VW" on it from her purse and jangling it.

I figured it was a substitute for the cigarette.

"So he mails me this package before he gets out, a box, tells me to keep it somewheres safe, and not to say anything about it to no one. So, I put it in this place that I use, not a bank or nothin' like that, but a safe place that not even Mama knew about before she died. God bless her soul." She crossed herself again. "Who knows what she knows about now?"

Interesting question. "What was in it?"

She looked affronted. "I didn't look. He told me not to. Said it was better if I didn't know, because Frankie the Cockroach would get cheesed off if he knew what we were up to. Besides, it was all wrapped around with about eight layers of tape and no way could I get it off without Trent seeing that I'd opened it."

Clearly, the mechanics of it had defeated her, and not her respect for Trent's warning. "How big was it?"

Sharla held her manicured hands about a foot apart and then held one above the other to indicate the package was perhaps three inches deep. "It was heavy, too," she said. "Not like gold heavy, but weighty. Five pounds, maybe? Trent asked me for it when he got out, and I gave it to him. He took it with him that night."

"Saturday night? The night he was killed?"

Sharla nodded, her hair-sprayed do swinging stiffly. "Yeah."

"So where is it now?"

"Well, that's the sixty-four-thousand-dollar question, now, isn't it? Either the perp got it or Trent tucked it away somewheres, maybe in the car."

I perked up at that. "The car? You mean he drove to the Club, but his car is still missing?"

"That's what I just said, isn't it?" She looked wistful. "I wanted to go to that party—I love a good costume party. Trent and me once won a prize at a Halloween party, for best couple's costume. It was a party at the restaurant where my cousin Delania works. They got the best fried shrimp in Trenton, although Delania tells me they recycle the rolls off customers' plates—just pop 'em back into the warmer to serve again. Can youse imagine? Anyways, I got a big box, tall as I am, and cut out holes for my arms and head, and then I painted it red. I was a brick, and Trent went as a bricklayer. Get it?" She gave a throaty laugh, delighted by the memory.

"Saturday night?"

"I was just gettin' to that." She gave me a hurt look. "So, Trent tells me I can't come, even though I am the sexiest vampire that ever lived if you just give me some fishnet hose and a set of fangs." She bared her teeth. "He says that I have to stay at that fleabag motel or go to a movie while he meets the mark. That's what he called him—or her—'the mark.' He took the package with him, and said he should be back in two hours, three tops, with the money. Five hundred K." Her eyes widened at the thought. "He said if he wasn't back by midnight that I should skedaddle, ditch the hotel, and get out of town."

"But you didn't."

"Is it likely I'm gonna let someone get away with killing my Trent?" she said, the steely look back in her eyes. It was odd how such warm-colored eyes could look so cold.

"Of course not," I said.

"If we were back in Jersey, I know plenty a guys I could call on to help me out with this, but out here, all I got is the cops"—she dismissed them with a wave—"and you. So, you gonna help me, or what?"

"What kind of car?"

Taking the question as my willingness to help her, she nodded with satisfaction and said, "Tan Volkswagen station wagon, older than dirt, with two hundred and twelve thousand miles on it. Total POS, but it got us from Chicago to here, so I guess I shouldn't dis it."

I wrote the details in my notebook. "License plate?"

She looked sheepish. "I don't remember the whole thing. *H* twenty-three something. We only got the car a month ago, bought it from some dude whose son had gotten a DWI, so he was teaching him a lesson by offloading his junker. Paid three hundred bucks, cash. We keep a crate of oil in the back because the gas guzzler burns about a quart a day."

"How are you getting around?"

"Well, I've got my scooter, don't I? We shoved it in the back of the wagon and brought it with us." She gestured to the east side of the stadium, where I imagined it was parked out of sight.

I thought for a moment, and then said, "It seems to me that if we could find the car, and the package was still in it, that it might tell us who Trent was meeting, or at least give us a clue."

"You think I haven't thought a that? Whaddaya think I been doon the last three days? Nothin' but riding my scooter on all the roads around that ritzy country club, looking for the car. Nada. All I got to show for it is a sore butt, a coupla dozen golf balls I can sell, and a great photo of a moose." She thumbed through the screens on her phone to show me a close-up of a startled bull moose with impressive antlers standing in the middle of a gravel road.

"You're lucky he didn't charge," I said, handing the phone back. "Moose are unpredictable."

"Oh, he did," she said, with a tight smile of satisfaction, "but turns out my scooter is faster than Bullwinkle here."

"I've got friends who can help look for the car," I said. I was also planning to give Hart the info, but thought it wise not to mention that to Sharla. "In the meantime, is there anyone else Trent might have talked to about whatever—"

She was shaking her head before I finished. "Nah. He knew better." She stood and arched her back to stretch it, and then looked over the stadium wall into the parking lot. "What the—?" She whirled to give me an angry look. "The cops! You brought the cops." She was already descending the bleacher steps as I jumped to my feet and peered over the wall. A police car was pulled to the curb, half a block down from the high school. I was pretty sure the cop was there to hand out speeding tickets to the high schoolers returning from lunch, but Sharla wasn't waiting for my explanation. She was halfway to the field by the time I started after her.

"Sharla—wait! I didn't—I want to help. How do I get in touch with you?"

She didn't slow down, just held up her right hand with the middle finger pointing up.

My heel caught on the edge of a step and my ankle twisted. *Yeow!* The pain pulled me up short. By the time I limped the rest of the way down the stairs, holding one pump in my hand, Sharla had disappeared. Ticked off and hurting, I pulled out my cell phone, but then decided it would be better to tell this story to Hart in person. Gingerly wedging my shoe back onto my foot, I hobbled up the ramp to the parking lot and my van.

Chapter 13

On the short drive to the police department, I worked out what I was going to say to Hart. My goal was to flood him with all the details Sharla had supplied, hoping to distract him from the fact that I'd agreed to meet a total stranger alone, and that I was once again sticking my nose into police business.

It didn't work. By chance, he and Chief Uggams were chatting in the reception area when I arrived at the police department. Hart, tall and lean, made the chief look even squatter and heavier by comparison. Chief Uggams, a black man with grizzled hair, a barrel chest, and a slight gut made more impressive by his uniform belt loaded with gun, cuffs, baton, and other paraphernalia, played poker with my dad and had known me from birth. He greeted me with a pink-gummed smile. "Amy-Faye, what brings you here?" He hugged me, and I caught a whiff of cherry Jolly Ranchers. "Did Norm send you down to gloat about that four of a kind he tripped me up with Thursday night?"

I smiled. "No, he didn't say anything about it."

Chief Uggams shook his head. "He played me like a fly fisherman after a trout, and I went for it hook, line, and sinker. No one bluffs like your dad—you remember that."

"I will," I promised.

Hart, who had been studying me since I walked in, broke in to say, "Why don't you come back to my office, Amy-Faye?"

"No hanky-panky on the city's dime," Chief Uggams said, laughing and giving us a knowing look. He went down the hall toward his office, chuckling.

My face warmed. Did the whole town know that Hart and I were seeing each other? I thought—and not for the first time—that one of the drawbacks of small-town life was the way everyone knew everyone else's business and didn't hesitate to bring it up at embarrassing moments. When Doug Elvaston and I had broken up after dating since high school, I suffered for months from the comments well-meaning neighbors and mere acquaintances had heaped on me, everything from condolences to dating advice. Thank goodness Mabel Appleman, the department's secretary/receptionist/dispatcher, wasn't sitting at the counter. If she had been, the chief's remark would have been all over Heaven before Hart and I got down the hall to his office.

Hart's office was a small room with windows on two sides, one looking out on the lot behind the police station, where three of the department's vehicles currently sat, and the other on the alley running between the department and A World Apart, the travel agency. Paint, flooring, and furniture were all taxpayer-funded blah and utilitarian, but a full set of Sherlock Holmes novels and short stories was bookended by a plaster deerstalker cap and pipe, a set of golf clubs slouched in one corner, and a stuffed bulldog wearing a red jersey perched atop the printer. His name was Uga and he was the University of Georgia's mascot. A framed photo of Hart's sister and his nephews sat on the credenza, next to a photo of a high-school-aged Hart with his folks and his brother and sister. Their matching smiles made me want to smile.

"What's up?" Hart asked, hitching one buttock onto the front of his desk while I sat in the ladder-back chair facing him. "You look like the cat who just ate the canary."

I gave it some consideration. "I don't think I actually got the canary," I said, "but I saw it." I launched into an account of my meeting and conversation with Sharla, glossing over how and where I met her. "So all we— you—have to do is find the station wagon," I finished, "and we'll know who Trent went to meet, with any luck."

Hart tapped a pencil on his desk. "What did this Sharla look like?"

I described her as he took notes. "She said she had a scooter," I added.

He nodded. "That's helpful." I thought he might congratulate me on coming up with information that might help solve the case, but he merely asked, "Who was this 'Frankie Cockroach' that she mentioned would be upset by Van Allen's plan, whatever it was? Extortion, it sounds like."

"I didn't get a chance to ask her that before she took

off." Dang. I wasn't cut out to be a police interrogator. I reminded myself that I truly hadn't had time to call Hart before meeting Sharla.

"Did you get the impression he might have followed Van Allen and Sharla here, that he could have caught up with Van Allen?"

It hadn't crossed my mind. I twisted my lower lip and bit it. "She certainly didn't say anything about that. She just mentioned the guy in passing."

He straightened and I got up. "This is good info," he said. "We'll put a statewide alert out on Sharla and the Volkswagen. It's possible the killer found it and disposed of it somewhere, but maybe we'll get lucky."

Relieved that he wasn't chewing me out, I smiled and said, "You don't mind if the Readaholics keep an eye out for it, do you?"

He eyed me. "Not as long as you promise that you'll call me if you find it."

I crossed my heart, the motion making me think of Sharla. "Promise."

He took a step closer until no more than two inches separated us. I felt the heat of him and his scent made me flush in a good way. "Still on for tonight?" he murmured.

"Absolutely. Where are we going?"

"How about my place? I can grill, we can drink wine on the deck"—he lowered his voice—"and then maybe there can be some of that hanky-panky the chief doesn't want going on on police property."

My blood fizzed through my veins like I'd been infused with champagne. "Sounds great," I managed to say. "Can I bring anything?"

"A toothbrush?"

His voice was half-serious, half-questioning, and it jolted me. Was he suggesting what I thought he was suggesting? Yes, of course he was. I drew in a breath, not sure if I was ready to move our relationship into bed. My body, warm and tingly with his nearness, informed me that it was definitely ready, but my head wanted to take things slowly.

"A bottle of wine it is," I said, licking my lips.

He smiled ruefully. "See you at six thirty?"

"Perfect." I stepped toward the door.

"And don't think I didn't pick up on the fact that you went to meet a possible murder suspect alone," he said, his voice reverting to "cop" as I twisted the doorknob.

Thinking it wisest not to reply, I scooted through the door with a hasty, "See you later." His description of Sharla as a possible murder suspect got me thinking, though. Could she have killed Trent? She could have donned her sexy vampire getup and slipped into the party, found Lola's metal stake, and used it to impale her boyfriend, but why kill him there if she wanted him dead? And why come to me for help with finding his murderer? She was already in the clear, with no one having the least notion that she even existed. No, I decided, Sharla wasn't the murderer.

It was after one o'clock and I was starving, so I swung through the Munchery to grab a salad (the Catwoman costume had made me decide to lose five pounds) and an iced tea, and then headed toward Brooke's house. I got halfway there before remembering that she volunteered at the Heaven Animal Haven on Wednesday afternoons, so I reversed and drove to the animal rescue. HAH was located on five acres of land on the east side of Heaven. Bordered by a scraggly line of lodgepole pines and set three-quarters of a mile off the road, it wasn't the kind of place you'd run across by accident. A mobile home served as the office, while two buildings housing animal kennels and runs took up the rest of the clearing. HAH mostly cared for deserted cats and dogs, but people sometimes brought in wild animals, which volunteers rehabbed, if possible, and released to their habitat. The wild animals stayed on the far side of the compound, completely separate from the domestic pets and the people who came to adopt them.

Brooke's Mercedes was parked outside the office trailer and I parked alongside it. My ankle twinged when I got out, and I almost dropped my salad. Drat that Sharla. A gadget of some kind let out a loud "meow" when I opened the door, and Brooke looked up from the computer. She had her long dark hair back in a loose fishtail braid, and wore her usual subtle makeup. I didn't see any signs of tears, and she greeted me with a smile.

"I've come for lunch," I announced, looking around. Last time I was in here, there'd been a loose iguana and four people trying to corral it. Today, there was nothing more animated than a stack of kitty litter bags waiting to be hauled out to the cat kennels. Pulling a stool up to the counter where she sat, I plopped my salad container and iced tea onto the laminate surface. It looked clean enough. Animal intake was in the back building, although sometimes people—witness the iguana incident—brought strays in here by mistake.

"I see you didn't bring me any," she said.

"I figured you'd have eaten already," I said, "but if you haven't, I'm happy to share if you've got your own fork." I nudged the container toward her.

She shook her head. "Thanks, but I ate before I came out here."

"Sooo?" I said leadingly once I'd swallowed a bite.

Her eyes gleamed and an almost shy smile broke out on her face. "I think she's going to give us the baby, A-Faye."

I squealed. "Really? Congratulations! I am so, so, so, so happy for you."

Brooke held up a cautioning hand. "It's not for sure yet. She said she liked us best, that she thought we would be wonderful parents, but that she wanted to think about it overnight. She's supposed to call this afternoon." She checked her cell phone, which lay beside the computer. "That's why I didn't call you back—because we don't know for sure yet."

"I'm crossing all my fingers," I said, doing so and holding them up so she could see.

Her cell rang, playing "Call Me Maybe," and she snatched it up quickly, then sighed and took the call, mouthing "Troy." "No, she hasn't called yet," Brooke said. "Yeah. As soon as I hear." She set the phone down. "He's antsy, too," she explained.

I found that reassuring. I hadn't been sure Troy was committed to the idea of a baby at all, much less adopting one. And it didn't help that his parents were vociferously against adoption, not wanting a baby with "who knows what genetic predispositions and antecedents" (as Miss Clarice, his mother, put it) having the Widefield name. "Why would you adopt a mutt when you could have a purebred?" she had, in all seriousness, asked Troy and Brooke.

"The waiting is driving me bonkers. I've had to redo the inputs to this donor spreadsheet four times." She gestured to the computer screen. "Distract me," she pleaded.

"I met a woman this morning who said she knew who killed Trent Van Allen," I said around a mouthful of field greens.

Brooke's perfectly groomed brows soared. "What?"

"She didn't know the killer's name or gender, but other than that, she had him pinpointed." I grinned at Brooke's confusion, and went on to explain about Sharla's phone call, meeting her at the stadium, and my new quest for the tan station wagon. "Hart wasn't too happy about me meeting Sharla alone, but he says he's okay with us looking for the car, as long as we call him if we find it," I finished.

Puckering her forehead, Brooke asked, "What do you think was in the package?"

I shrugged. "Beats me. Sharla didn't really offer a theory. It could have been money—money's heavier than you'd expect, and you could get a bunch in a nine-by-twelve-by-three-inch package if you were using hundreds."

"That would suggest that Van Allen was buying something, rather than selling something," Brooke said.

"Who's to say he wasn't?" I licked the last glisten of Italian dressing off my fork. "If not, the possibilities are nearly endless. Collectible baseball cards? Incriminating photos—it'd be a bunch of them if the box weighed so much."

"Drugs," Brooke suggested.

"Definitely could be. Rare but valuable snakes," I guessed, having recently read an article about reptile smuggling.

"Were there airholes in the box?"

"Probably not. Sharla didn't mention any."

"Not livestock, then. Blood diamonds? Bearer bonds? Keys to a fleet of Maseratis!"

"A suitcase nuke—how big would that have to be? Sex tapes. A priceless artifact. A previously unpublished Agatha Christie novel!"

We were having so much fun with our increasingly outrageous guesses that it took a moment for the sound of Brooke's cell phone ringing to penetrate. When it did, we both shut up and looked at it where it vibrated on the counter. She almost dropped the phone as she grabbed it. Her lower lip trembled when she ID'd the caller, and I knew it was the expectant mother. My stomach felt hollow and I couldn't imagine Brooke's tension.

"Answer it," I hissed as she hesitated.

"What if she doesn't—"

"Answer it!"

With the air of a French aristocrat approaching the guillotine, she accepted the call and whispered, "This is Brooke."

Despite a desperate urge to eavesdrop, I figured she needed privacy, so I hopped off the stool and left the trailer, sitting on the steps to watch a couple of Steller's jays screeching at each other. When ten minutes had gone by, I became aware that I was jiggling my foot nervously. I got up and began to pace, scaring away the jays and a chipmunk that had emerged from under the trailer. I kicked at fallen leaves, satisfied by the crunchy-slithery sound they made sliding out of my way. Did the long conversation mean the woman had said yes, and she and Brooke were talking about the details? Or did it mean that she'd said no, and Brooke was trying to compose herself before facing me? Just as I was on the verge of barging back into the trailer, the door swung open.

I stopped on the lowest step and stared up at Brooke. Tears glistened in her eyes.

Chapter 14

I leaped up the stairs to put my arms around her, the lump in my throat making it hard to speak. "Oh, Brooke—"

She hugged me convulsively, but then gently disengaged herself. The look of startled wonder on her face told me I'd been wrong about the cause of her tears. They were tears of joy, not despair.

"I'm going to be a mother," she said. A smile curved her lips, gradually growing until she was grinning. "I'm going to be a mom! In seven months, I'm going to be a mother." She threw her arms up over her head and shouted, "Hear that, world? I'm going to be a moooom!"

She grabbed my hands, dragged me down the steps, and danced me around in a circle Ring Around the Rosy–style. Her giddiness infected me and we whirled quicker and quicker until dizziness made us stagger apart. I put a hand on a tree trunk to steady myself. Brooke hunched over, hands on her knees, braid dangling, trying to catch her breath.

"You're going to be a mommy," I said, so happy for her. "Do you know if it's a boy or a girl?"

"Not yet," she said. "I don't care. I'm happy either way. Troy kind of wants a girl to be a daddy's little princess." She suddenly straightened, the braid whipping over her head. "Troy! I've got to call Troy. He's going to be a father. Oh, my God." She raced back into the office, where she'd left her phone.

She emerged less than a minute later, still smiling. I figured the smile might be permanently imprinted on her face, at least until sleepless nights of getting up for four a.m. feedings wore her down.

"Troy's ecstatic," she reported. "Over the moon. He really liked Kay. That's the birth mother. He's going to tell Miss Clarice and Troy Sr., and meet me at home in an hour. We can have sex without worrying about getting pregnant for the first time in ages. Oops." She covered her mouth with overlapping hands. "TMI." She let her hands drop. "I'm just so happy I don't know what I'm saying."

She positively glowed in the way all the books say expectant mothers glow. Huh. I'd always assumed that was a hormonal thing, but apparently not.

"This calls for a celebration," I said. "Let's go get a bottle of champagne. The best part about adopting is that you can drink like a sailor throughout the pregnancy."

She looked uncertainly back at the office. "What about—? I'm supposed to—?"

"Lock it up and leave it," I said. "People can bring strays in tomorrow. This afternoon, we celebrate my bestie's impending motherhood."

As a result of our celebrating, I had a slight headache as I got ready to go to Hart's place for dinner. Even one glass of champagne does that to me. I took a couple of aspirin before showering and pulling on my jeans. As I shrugged into my clingy yellow top, my gaze fell on my pink toothbrush in its cup and I remembered Hart's suggestion. He had been to my house for dinner, but I had never been to his place and I was curious. A guy's place said a lot about him. I'd dumped one guy on the spot, an accountant who seemed nice and was kind of cute, when he invited me over to admire his plushy collection. He'd tried to introduce me to nearly a thousand stuffed animals, all of which he'd named, but I'd bolted after the third one, a chipmunk he called Absalom. A guy I'd dated briefly in college, during one of Doug's and my "off" phases, had had a place so obsessively neat that I knew we were doomed. I'm no slob, but I don't use a ruler to align the books on my bookshelves, or have labels on my fridge shelves to show where each condiment goes. I was mentally crossing my fingers that Hart wouldn't have a display of Farrah Fawcett posters, or piles of dirty laundry on every surface (as two other guys I'd dated had).

Hart had mentioned that his condo was a rental, and I'd been past the place numerous times, so I knew right where to go. He lived in a small complex, four buildings done up with timbers and stone to look like hunting lodges. They were built around a central courtyard with one unit per floor for a total of twelve units. Hart had the top-floor condo in the south-facing building. Looking up at it as I turned into the parking lot, I figured he'd have a great mountain view. The parking lot had recently been resurfaced with slots marked for visitors. I pulled into one and turned off the van.

Gathering my purse and the bottle of Varaison Merlot I'd brought, I climbed the stairs and knocked.

"It's open," Hart called.

I walked in to find myself facing a wall of windows and sliding glass doors that did, indeed, frame a spectacular view of the snowcapped mountains. Not a Farrah Fawcett poster in sight—a definite plus. I noted a sofa covered in sand-colored chenille and a matching chair arranged to face the sliding glass doors and a flat-screen television mounted over a gas fireplace. There were bookshelves filled with books—another plus—skis leaning against the wall by what I assumed was a coat closet, and a chess set on a table. The walls and the carpet were a neutral taupe, but a thick area rug that reached from the hearth's edge to the sofa added color with a geometric print in navy, reds, and tan. My gaze returned to the view. Smoke rose from a grill on the deck. I walked toward it, past the small dining room table, already set, and looked down at the barbered grass below, which merged with a meadow where four deer were feeding. The evening's chill seeped through the glass.

"I don't know what you're paying for this place," I said, "but it's worth every penny." Reluctantly turning away from the view, I angled to the right where Hart was working over the kitchen sink. He was vigorously massaging a delicious-smelling rub into two steaks that rested in a pan at the bottom of the stainless steel sink.

As I set the wine on the counter, he held up his crusty hands as an explanation. "Sorry I couldn't get the door." He leaned over to kiss me. He wore jeans with a hole at the knee and frayed hems, and a Rascal Flatts concert T-shirt, and smelled of soap and damp hair from a shower. His lips lingered on mine, and I began to feel light-headed. He broke away when a clump of oily spices fell from his spread hands to the floor. "Almost done here," he said, lifting the pan out of the sink and washing his hands.

I ripped off a paper towel and wiped up the marinade splotch. "Anything I can do?"

"Why don't you open the wine while I slap these on the grill?" He headed out to the deck and I searched three drawers before finding a corkscrew. Pulling the cork, I found wineglasses in a glass-fronted cabinet and poured just as Hart came through the sliding doors again, letting in a mouthwatering whiff of seared meat.

"If I get you a jacket, can we take these out on the deck?" he asked, indicating the wineglasses. "I don't want to overcook the steak. If it weren't so chilly, we could eat out there. That's what I've been doing all summer, but I'm afraid that's done for the year."

"Sure." I let him drape a red fleece jacket around my shoulders and followed him onto the deck. The air was bracing, but it felt good. My headache slipped away and I wrapped the fleece's sleeves around me, liking the faint scent of Hart that rose from the jacket. Leaning over the deck rail, I watched the mule deer with their outsized ears amble across the field and into the tree line that bounded it. I tasted the wine and let its rich berry and leather flavors fill my mouth. My shoulders relaxed. I hadn't realized how stressed I was until that moment.

"Peaceful, isn't it?" Hart said, watching me. "When I think about buying a house, I come out here and decide that until I can find a place with the same kind of quiet and view, I'll just stay here."

I turned to face him. "Have you been house-hunting?" That would mean he planned to stay. Happiness bloomed inside me at the thought.

Picking up the long-handled fork to turn the meat, he said, "Not formally. Not with a Realtor. I've been looking at listings online and driving around, scoping out the areas I like."

"I'm sure Kerry would be happy to work with you when—if—you decide to really do it." And she'd tell me the moment he contacted her, too, I thought. "She helped me find my house and get a really good deal on it."

"How do you like your steak?"

We moved inside when the steaks were done to medium-rare perfection, and settled at the small table. Night fell outside, turning the windows to black, as our conversation ranged from real estate values in the area to discussions of our favorite TV shows. Mine—*Scandal*; his—*The Walking Dead*.

"I'd have thought you'd like a detective show, with all the mysteries you read," he said. "*Law & Order, Blue Bloods, Elementary*."

"Funny, I'd have guessed the same for you."

"Too much like real work, or so ridiculous they make me cringe," he said, refilling our glasses.

"What's the worst?"

"*Castle*," he said without hesitation, spearing a round of grilled zucchini like he was stabbing the show's creators.

"Aw, I love Nathan Fillion," I protested. "He's so likable, and he and Stana Katic have such great chemistry, even though they're married now—I mean, their characters are married."

He looked at me over the rim of his wineglass. "You think marriage kills romance?"

"Only on TV," I said. I thought about his question a bit more and added, "I do think relationships change over time, though. The romance, the heat, waxes and wanes. Friendship is as important as chemistry."

"Don't you think friends have to have chemistry, too?"

I'd never thought about it. "I guess so," I said. I tucked a lock of hair behind my ear. "I guess there's a friend version of love at first sight, where you just know someone is going to be a good friend from the moment you meet them. Brooke and I were like that. Oh, did I tell you she and Troy are going to adopt a baby?"

We talked and laughed until the wine was nothing but dregs and the steak fat had congealed on our plates. Then, I cleared while he loaded dishes into the washer. When he wouldn't let me help with that, I wandered into the living room and inspected the titles on his bookshelves. There was a lot of history and biography, which didn't surprise me, and an entire shelf of poetry, which did. I angled my head to read the spines: Wordsworth, Frost, Oliver, Soto, Cisneros, Angelou, Kinnell. Some I knew; some I'd never heard of.

The scent of lemon danced around me and I heard his footstep behind me. I turned to see him holding two plates with what looked like iced lemon bread and forks. As I took one from him, our fingertips brushed and a spark arced between us. Drawing in a calming breath, I nodded toward the books. "Are you like Adam Dalgliesh?"

He wrinkled his brow. "Who?"

"P. D. James's Scotland Yard inspector—a cop who writes poetry."

He laughed. "I read poetry, but I don't write it. My poetic efforts run to 'Roses are red, violets are blue. Your breath is real stinky and your armpits are, too.' I think I wrote that in second grade. My mom still drags it out, along with all the family photos, whenever I come home for a visit."

"Wow, and you gave up such a promising poetic career to become a cop." I shook my head in mock amazement. "The world's loss." I forked up a bit of the silky lemon cake and almost moaned as the bright citrus exploded on my tongue. "Now, this"—I pointed with my fork—"is divine. If you made this, I demand you hand in your badge immediately and open a bakery."

He led me over to the sofa, grinning. We sat. "I made it, but it's my nana's recipe. I'm not the creative type, but I can follow a recipe with the best of them."

"Yes, you can," I agreed fervently, pressing my fork into the crumbs and licking them off.

"Seconds?" he asked, amused.

I held out my plate. "Please."

While he was gone, I swung my feet onto the couch, digging them under a throw pillow, and leaned back against the arm. My ghostly reflection swam on the dark glass doors. When Hart handed me my plate, he set two glasses of water on the coffee table, then sat and lifted my legs to lay them across his lap. The naturalness and intimacy of it made me catch my breath. I choked on a cake crumb. Grabbing for the water, I gulped.

"Okay?" Hart quirked a quizzical eyebrow.

"Fine," I managed. To distract both of us from my flustered state, I asked, "Any luck finding that station wagon?"

"No," Hart admitted. He picked up one of my feet and began to massage it through my nubby sock. "But I just put the alert out this afternoon, so that's not too surprising. Any more contact from Sharla?"

I shook my head, the feel of his thumb digging into the ball of my foot leaving me dumb. My sock was off now and both his hands were massaging my foot, kneading and stroking, thumbs digging hard into the arch and then stroking toward the ball. I spread my toes with pleasure. It was the single most sensuous thing I'd ever experienced. We talked about our favorite authors, but I couldn't concentrate; I was too distracted by what he was doing to my foot. He massaged each toe individually between thumb and forefinger, before sliding his fingers between the toes and then pressing them up. The stretch felt divine. He did the same thing with my whole foot, arching it down and then flexing it up. I swallowed hard. Heat rose from my core and flushed through my veins. I was totally incapable of speaking and wondered if he knew what kind of effect he was having on me. Then, his eyes, heavy-lidded and smoldering, met mine, and I knew that he did.

His fingers entwined with mine and he pulled me toward him. I went willingly, until I was sitting across his lap, his arm around my shoulders, his lips inches from mine. I moistened my lips with the tip of my tongue.

"I happen to have a never-used toothbrush or two," he offered conversationally, watching for my response.

I locked eyes with him and reached a hand up to draw his head down so I could kiss him. His hair was crisp under my fingers, not quite long enough for me to wrap my fingers around. When we broke the kiss, I smiled into his eyes. "That's okay. I brought mine."

Chapter 15

I hummed and sang my way through Thursday's corporate off-site, eliciting first Al's puzzlement, and then, by late afternoon, when the off-site broke up, a knowing grin.

"Don't go there," I warned him when it looked like he was going to comment. I had just responded to a text from Hart saying how much he was looking forward to seeing me this weekend. Al and I were working together in my office to figure out a seating chart for a wedding reception in two weeks. It was greatly complicated by the fact that both bride's and groom's parents had divorced and remarried. That in itself wasn't so bad—I dealt with that all the time—but the bride's father had married the groom's sister, a woman thirty years his junior, and the mother's family, Sicilians from the old country, had all sworn they'd get revenge on him. The groom's parents weren't too happy with him, or their daughter, either. I was seriously thinking about suggesting that the young couple elope.

"Go where, boss?" Al asked innocently. "I'll tell you the one place I'm definitely not going is to this wedding." He stabbed a finger at one of the crumpled seating charts we'd discarded. "I think we ought to have a metal detector at the church door."

"Know where we can get one?" I asked, only half-joking.

When we had done the best we could with the seating chart, Al left to set up for this evening's event, and I turned my attention toward my research assignment for tonight. As busy as I'd been yesterday—and last night, I thought, grinning to myself—I hadn't had time to look into Cosmo Zeller. I started with a basic search and netted more than twenty thousand hits. Whoa. I skipped through several pages of entries and realized that every time one of his movies was reviewed, his name got mentioned. Great. Slogging through all of this to find the kernels would take days. Weeks.

I waded in. Two hours later, my eyes were blurred and I had only a couple of paragraphs of information about Cosmo, starting with the fact that his birth name wasn't Cosmo; it was Phineas. He'd been born in a small town in Illinois and skipped town immediately after high school in search of fame and fortune as a Hollywood actor. There was a gap of several years in his bio, where I suspected he'd spent more time waiting tables or parking cars than in front of the cameras. He reemerged as Cosmo Zeller, with a nose job and capped teeth, in his late twenties, with an assistant producer credit on a forgettable romantic comedy. Two years later, he produced a blockbuster thriller and his fortune was finally made. He acquired a wife, divorced, and remarried, all before hitting thirty-five. He had three children with wife number two, and she had taken him to the cleaners in a recent divorce, if the tabloid reports were accurate. I whistled when I saw how much the courts seemed to think she and the kids needed on a monthly basis. I could pay off my mortgage for less than one month's alimony and child support.

Cosmo had produced a string of hits in the nineties and the early part of the next decade, earning comparisons with Bruckheimer and that ilk. Lately, though, it seemed to me, he had lost the magic touch. His last three films had been flops, one of them of such epic (and expensive) proportions as to earn it a place on the list of Top Ten Hollywood Box Office Bombs of all time, snuggled up between *Heaven's Gate* and the Johnny Depp *Lone Ranger*. His multimillion-dollar Hollywood Hills home, with its tennis court, indoor and outdoor pools, movie-viewing room, humidor room, and ocean view, was on the market. I wasted half an hour doing the video tour of the house and wondering about how someone cleaned the crystals on the chandelier hung twenty feet above the foyer floor, and how long it had taken to paint the elaborate trompe l'oeil murals of Roman ruins in the pool house.

Bringing my mind back to the task, I jotted a summary of Phineas "Cosmo" Zeller on a three-by-five card.

- self-made millionaire; one of Hollywood's top producers; two Oscars
- divorced, father of three, huge child support/ alimony payments—financial difficulties?
- industry sources say he needs a big hit; *Barbary Close* his ticket back to big time?

As six o'clock approached, I tucked the card into my purse and headed for home. In the back of my mind, I knew we were running out of time. Once the week was up, the three authors and their families and Cosmo Zeller would scatter, leaving Heaven for their normal lives. Once that happened, I didn't think we had a prayer of figuring out who had killed Trent Van Allen.

Just before seven o'clock, I surveyed my sunroom with satisfaction. It was a small rectangular space furnished with wicker chairs upholstered in bright floral cotton. Celadon-colored ceramic tile covered the floor. Floor-to-ceiling windows looked out to the front, side, and rear yards. I had the wooden blinds closed now that it was night, which made the room feel a bit smaller, but also cozier. Plants, hand-selected by Lola as her house-warming gift to me, dangled from baskets and sprouted from ceramic pots. It was my favorite room in the bungalow that was 99.9 percent the bank's and 0.1 percent mine. Feeling a little chilly, I dashed to the den to grab the afghan off the chair in there and bring it into the sunroom.

The doorbell rang, and I let in Brooke, still glowing with the joy of impending motherhood. Her glossy hair bobbed from a high ponytail and she seemed to dance as she walked. We went into the galley kitchen, where she helped herself to some Pinot Grigio from the box I'd bought on my way home. She was babbling about a conversation with Kay, her baby's birth mother, when she stopped midsentence and eyed me narrowly.

"Something's different about you," she said.

I opened the fridge door and hid behind it, pretending to search for a lemon in case someone wanted iced tea. "I don't have any. Lemons," I said, closing the refrigerator.

"Lemons, shlemons," she said, waving them away.

"Lola might want—"

Her eyes widened. "You and Hart didn't—"

I turned away and grabbed a sponge to wipe down the clean counter, but not before she caught sight of my telltale blush. Sometimes pale skin was a curse.

"You did," she breathed. "When? You didn't tell me! I want to know everything."

Even though Brooke and I had historically shared many details of our love lives, I felt shy about discussing what had happened between me and Hart. It was too new. Too . . . special. I was saved by the bell as the doorbell rang. I sprinted to open it and let in Lola, Kerry, and Maud. Misty trotted in with Lola, and I stooped to pat her. When I'd rescued her off the street, I'd thought about keeping her, but my schedule didn't mesh with a pet's needs. I'd given her to Lola, but it made me smile to see her back in my house. There was a flurry of greetings and drinks-getting, and Kerry busied herself, slicing the zucchini bread and handing it out on napkins. Brooke caught my eye as we all trooped into the sunroom, though, and her look promised that we would resume our conversation later.

Lola sat beside me on the love seat with Kerry in the chair to Lola's left and Brooke on my right. Maud sat on an ottoman across from me, and Misty leaped onto the low, deep windowsill and batted the blinds cord. We had barely seated ourselves when Kerry announced, "I'll go first."

"Wait," I said. "Something happened yesterday. I got a call from Trent Van Allen's girlfriend. She filled me in on a few things." I recounted as much of my conversation with Sharla as I could remember. "She ran off before I could ask her any questions, really," I finished, "but we should all keep a lookout for a tan station wagon. If we find it, and the package is still there, well, it will probably point to the killer."

Maud rubbed her hands together. "A modern-day treasure hunt," she said. "I'm in."

"I'll keep an eye out while I'm making deliveries tomorrow," Lola said.

"If anyone finds it, though," I cautioned, "you've got to call the police. I promised Hart."

Kerry gave a brisk nod, and said, "Can I report on Francesca Bugle now?" She slid her cheaters from the top of her head to the bridge of her nose and peered at a printed page. "I researched Francesca Bugle, and I'm here to tell you there's no such person." She gave us all a meaningful look over the top of her glasses.

"Pen name," Maud said dismissively, just as I had earlier. "There's no such person as Carolyn Keene, either. Actually, she was several people, at least one of them a man. Fact." She leaned forward with her forearms on her knees. "When you think about it, the whole writer-for-hire thing is a conspiracy of sorts, with publishers and agents and writers conspiring to convince the reading public that—"

Kerry interrupted her ruthlessly. "I don't think there's

any conspiracy related to Francesca Bugle. I do think she's got something to hide." She sat back and flipped her notebook closed.

"Maybe she just likes her privacy," Lola said. "I can understand that."

"Let me tell you what I learned about Cosmo Zeller," I said, sensing that the Bugle conversation wasn't going to go anyplace useful. "He is definitely not the shy and retiring type. There are more articles about him online than there are about global warming." I saw Maud's eyes light up and hurried on before she could launch into her spiel about the global warming conspiracy. I told the group what I'd learned about Cosmo, finishing with, "So, he may be having financial problems. Or not. Just because he's selling his house doesn't mean he's on the verge of bankruptcy."

"He could be off-loading it because of the divorce," Brooke suggested. She sipped her wine. "It could contain too many memories, or he might not want such a big place now that it's just him."

"I looked at a video of it online," I confessed. "He's probably dumping it to avoid the maintenance bills. It must cost a fortune in cleaning teams, pool boys, heating and cooling—you name it. Anyway, all the pundits seem to think this movie, *Barbary Close*, will be a huge hit and put him back on top."

We tossed around ideas about where Cosmo and Trent Van Allen might have crossed paths, but other than the fact that they had both lived in Illinois once upon a time, nothing popped. We realized we didn't know enough about Van Allen to determine where his path might have intersected with that of any of the suspects, and I made a note to ask Hart if he could share some details from Van Allen's file. "Hart mentioned Van Allen was a marine," I said. "Did any of our suspects spend any time in the military?"

Everyone shook their heads no. "Of course," I pointed out, "the murderer doesn't have to have known Van Allen personally. Van Allen could have come across something the murderer wanted, or evidence of wrongdoing the murderer wouldn't want revealed, and approached the killer with it. I mean, all of these people are public figures, to some extent. It wouldn't be hard to track any of them down."

The others let that sink in for a moment, and then Lola pushed her glasses up her nose and pulled up a document on her notebook computer. "I've got a report on Eloise Hufnagle. She's really a very interesting woman. As you know already, she's from the Atlanta area. She grew up in a middle-class neighborhood. Her mom was a teacher—she died of breast cancer eight years ago. Her dad works for the post office."

"Bad genes there," Maud quipped.

"Eloise won a full scholarship to Emory University, where she got a PhD in biochemistry with an emphasis on pathogen transmission. She wrote her dissertation on environmental factors in aerosolized transmission of pathogens in commercial airplanes. I managed to find a couple of her papers online. They were quite interesting. She works for the CDC now, the Centers for Disease Control."

Of course Lola, with her master's in chemistry, would find the scientific angle appealing.

"I couldn't find as much about her fiction writing, but from newspaper reports about the court case, I gathered that she's been working on publishing a novel for some time. Years. Apparently, the manuscript she was working on has a story line and characters a lot like those in Mary Stewart's novel *Blood Will Out*. Eloise called hers 'Marked by Blood.' She was part of a writers' critique group and suspects that one of her feedback partners knows Mary Stewart and gave her a copy of the manuscript." Lola stopped, a look of concern on her face. I could tell she sympathized with Eloise Hufnagle.

"Which Mary Stewart categorically denies," Brooke put in, waving a sheaf of papers she had pulled from her purse. "Stewart says that any similarities are coincidence, a case of spontaneous ideas arising simultaneously. At least, that's what her lawyer says. Stewart doesn't talk about the case. Anyway"—she twiddled the ends of her ponytail—"Mary Stewart has been a writer from the get-go. She grew up in Boise—"

"Wait a minute." I straightened. "That's where Van Allen was from. I think." I screwed my eyes shut, trying to remember what Hart had said. "Yes, I'm sure Hart said he was from Idaho originally, although he didn't mention Boise specifically."

"Worth looking into," Lola said.

"Lots of people are from Idaho," Kerry said.

"Anyway," Brooke continued, "Mary was into writing from middle school on, winning all sorts of contests and awards. She left Idaho to go to college at the University of Virginia, where she was active in Pi Beta Phi. She's one of my sorority sisters." Brooke smiled. She'd been social chairperson of her sorority chapter at Colorado State University. "She was briefly engaged to a fellow student, Jonathan Logan, but broke it off a week before the wedding. Cold feet, I guess."

"She doesn't strike me as the type that would return either the ring or the wedding presents," Kerry said.

I looked a question at her and she shrugged. "Gut feeling. There's something cold about that woman. Calculating. I had a Realtor like her in my office once— could sell the proverbial fridge to an Eskimo—but I caught her colluding with a listing agent to jack up the price one of our clients would have to pay for a house, so I canned her. She moved to Montrose and I hear she's been agent of the year in the Re/Max office there three years running." She flared her nostrils.

Brooke continued. "Mary had a few short stories accepted for online publications and then sold a couple to print magazines. You know," she said, looking around at all of us, "I read a few of the stories. They were pretty good; at least, I enjoyed them. But not one of them featured a vampire or anything vaguely fantasyish or paranormal."

Lola leaned in. "You're saying you think she stole Eloise's book?"

"I wouldn't go that far," Brooke hedged. "I just thought it was a little odd that all her short fiction was slice-of-life type stuff, and then her first novel is all about a vampire. It doesn't prove anything. Like I said, I just thought it was odd."

"I'll bet Hufnagle's lawyer has hired someone to compare the linguistic style of Stewart's short stories with the novel," Maud said. "You can't prove anything by subject matter, but writing style—that's a different matter."

"What about her family?" I asked. "And where does she live now?"

"I didn't look into her family much," Brooke said. "A couple of articles mentioned that her folks were divorced when she was ten and she lived with her mom and three brothers. I wonder if the other two look anything like Lucas. If so, they missed out on millions by not forming a boy band. Wouldn't matter the least bit whether they could sing or not."

We all laughed, which eased the gradually building tension and frustration. I thought we were all a little edgy, feeling like we weren't making much progress, that we were missing something.

"The police had me come down to the station yesterday," Lola said into the silence that followed the laughter. "They wanted my fingerprints." She rubbed her thumbs against her fingertips like she was trying to remove ink. "They're still trying to link me to the murder, as if my bringing that metal stake to the party wasn't link enough." Unusual bitterness sounded in her voice.

I put an arm around her shoulders. "The prints are just for elimination purposes, I'm sure. They already had mine on file," I said. "From when Ivy . . ."

We paused a moment, remembering our sixth Reada-holic, who had been poisoned in May.

"There's no way around the fact that I'm partially responsible," Lola said quietly. "If I hadn't brought that weapon—"

"The killer would have used something else." Kerry leaned forward to pat Lola's knee. "Don't beat yourself up, Lola. You're not responsible. The only one respon-sible is whoever stabbed Van Allen with it."

Lola gave Kerry a grateful smile but looked uncon-vinced. As if knowing her mistress needed comforting, Misty jumped into her lap and began to knead her thighs, making little *prrrp* sounds. Lola patted her and I could see the tension leaking out of her with each stroke. To get us past the moment, I turned to Maud. "What about the Aldringhams, Maud?"

Maud sucked on her thin upper lip, unusually slow to respond. "I shouldn't have volunteered to investigate them," she finally said. "Merle was . . . he and Constance were my friends, once upon a time. It felt wrong to go prying into their lives. However, I did it." Like Lola, she had a notebook computer and referred to it now.

"I'll skip over their growing-up years and our col-lege adventures, and get right to the stuff that might be germane."

Darn. I wanted to hear about the college adven-tures. Maybe I could get Maud to talk over a margarita one day.

"When Constance hit it big with her books, Merle quit his job as an actuary. When Allyson came along, I guess you could call him a stay-at-home dad, somewhat at the forefront of that movement, although they also had a nanny."

"It's hard on a man, giving up his work identity," Kerry observed.

Maud merely nodded and kept going. "More recently, the last eight or ten years, it looks like he's become a day trader, very active on the stock market."

"That's a risky route to riches," Brooke said. "My Troy played at day-trading for a while, but Troy Sr. put his foot down."

"It hasn't paid off for Merle, that's for damn sure," Maud said. "Over the past three years alone—the only years I could get the data for—he's lost over three and a half million dollars."

Lola gasped. I refrained from asking how Maud had gotten hold of the Aldringhams' financial records. I knew she did some hacking, usually in the service of outing conspiracies.

"What an idiot," Kerry said. "Surely they can't afford that kind of loss, no matter how well Constance's books are doing."

"No, they can't," Maud admitted. "They're inches away from being foreclosed on. They really need for *Autumn of the Lynx* to be a blockbuster. A movie deal would help, as well. I suspect that's the real reason they're still hanging around Heaven. Constance wants to work on Cosmo Zeller to option her novel.

"As if that weren't enough—" She paused to build suspense. "There's Allyson."

"What about her?" Kerry asked in a "get on with it" voice.

"I'm not quite sure. She was expelled from three private high schools, but I can't find out why. Accessing private school files is harder than breaking into DoD computers," she complained. "They're all so paranoid about being sued. I actually called one of her former headmistresses, said that Allyson had applied for a job with me and I was checking her references—"

"Smart," Brooke said.

"—but I got the runaround. She hemmed and hawed and said that she didn't feel she could be of use, since Allyson had left their school so long ago. She made a point of saying that Allyson had not graduated from her august academy, almost as if she didn't want Allyson's name associated with the school."

"Did Allyson ever graduate?" Lola asked. She shifted to look at Maud, and Misty jumped down, affronted that her napping place was unsteady. She came toward me and poked her nose into my glass, which I had set on the floor. I nudged her away.

"She got a GED," Maud said, "and then she scored a thirty on her ACT. She's bright enough, so I don't think her school troubles were related to grades."

"Lots of bright people blow off classes," Brooke said.

"Derek," I said. "He's at least as smart as I am, but he couldn't have cared less about his grades, so he was a C student all the way through high school. Drove my folks batty."

"Does she have a criminal record?" Kerry asked.

Maud pointed an approving finger at her. "I wondered the same thing. If she does, it's as a juvenile and it's sealed. I couldn't find anything on her as an adult, and I know my way around the courthouse databases. I can't help but think it might be drug related. Her folks had plenty of money; she was an only child with a mother who was more involved in her work than in mothering, and a father who, well . . ."

Maud petered out, clearly not wanting to say anything too negative about Merle. She swiped to the next screen on her notebook. "I called a couple of other people in California—it doesn't matter who. I made it sound like I was writing an unauthorized biography of Constance." She looked up. "It never ceases to amaze me how many people are willing to dish the dirt, given the slightest opportunity. Anyway, I picked up rumors that Constance had an affair some years ago with a writer." She named a thriller writer whose books routinely debuted in the top ten on the *New York Times* bestseller list. "His wife apparently found out and confronted Constance. What I wouldn't have given to be a fly on the wall during that encounter." She grinned.

"I never did like his books," Kerry said.

"My source said that Merle knew—the wife made sure of it—but that he and Constance worked it out. When they came for drinks the other night, they acted like a normal married couple, maybe a little bored with each other after more than thirty years, but not at each other's throats, not even in that passive-aggressive Updikean way. Sure, Merle still thinks about me in a 'What might have been?' sort of way, but he's absolutely not interested in pursuing it. And he wasn't even before he met Joe and saw how we are together. Except that Constance is a bestselling author, they could be any late middle-aged couple from any suburb in America."

She sucked on her upper lip again. "It's . . . deflating," she said after searching for the word. "We were such firebrands in our youth, sure that we were going to save the world, bring clean water to Africa, reveal government conspiracies, get equal opportunities for blacks and women. And here we are, forty years down the road, with nothing to show for it. Well, a few more wrinkles, a hip replacement or two, and a medicine cabinet full of laxatives and statins. Millions of people in Africa die from easily preventable diseases each year, we've got the most corrupt and least transparent government in my lifetime, education costs are out of control, and—"

"Since when are you such a Whiny Wendy?" Kerry broke in. "Just in the past couple years you've uncovered the last mayor's kickback schemes and gotten me elected—"

"Yeah, so happy about that," Maud said, tongue in cheek.

"—and caught on to that scam the school board was running, and wrote about how the Colorado Department of Transportation was wasting money with inefficient road-gritting operations, and dozens of other things, some of which were annoying, and some of which made a real difference in this town or the state. Pat yourself on the back, for heaven's sake, rather than moaning about how you haven't come up with a cure for malaria. You can only do what you can do. You make a greater difference in more people's lives than any six people I know." She sat back and *pfft*ed her bangs out of her eyes, her gaze challenging Maud to disagree with her.

"You're right, Kerry," Maud said, looking surprised.

"Never thought I'd hear those words come out of your mouth," Kerry said.

We all laughed.

"No more moaning. I guess I'm feeling unwontedly introspective, what with having Merle show up out of the blue and all. But I'm done with that now." She clicked off her notebook. "Let's go around and see who we each think did it. My money's on Sharla, the vic's girlfriend. Face facts: It's usually ones nearest and dearest who most want to do away with you. I can't explain why she would come to Amy-Faye after the fact, when it looks like she's gotten away with it, but maybe she needs help finding that car and the package in it."

I raised my brows; I hadn't thought of that. "I think it was Cosmo," I said. "He seems to be on a financial precipice. If Van Allen had something on him that would upset the applecart, well . . ." I looked at Kerry.

"I vote for Mary Stewart," she said. "I flat don't like the woman." She sat back with her arms crossed and looked at Lola.

"I don't think we can make an informed decision without knowing more about Trent Van Allen," she said, pursing her lips. "It would be like trying to record an experiment's results before adding one of the chemical agents to the mix."

She made a good point. "Van Allen's like that creep Jack Favell in *Rebecca*," I said slowly. "He's vaguely unsettling and out of place until you understand his relationship to Rebecca. Then, you see what his true role is."

"You might have something there." Maud nodded.

"Lola abstains," Kerry said, keeping us on task as always. "Brooke?"

My best friend looked around the room before saying, "I guess I'd go with Francesca Bugle. What Kerry said about her not having a background—I think that's a little odd. And she's so energetic and decisive and looks strong. I can see her confronting someone like Van Allen and, depending on how he reacted, things getting out of hand. Her books always have such twisty plots, too—she's totally capable of covering her tracks."

I whooshed out a breath, disappointed that we hadn't accomplished more. Lola, sensing my mood, leaned in and said gently, "It's all good, Amy-Faye. Pooling our information like this—it will help in the end."

I gave her a grateful smile and began to collect glasses and crumpled napkins. The women stood to leave. "So what's our next step?" I asked as we gaggled toward the tiny foyer.

"Find the station wagon," Maud said, at the same time Lola said, "Learn more about Trent Van Allen."

"I'll talk to Hart tonight—" I started.

"I'll bet you will," Brooke said sotto voce, with a sly smile.

"—and see if he can tell me more about Van Allen. Maybe we could team up tomorrow and look for the station wagon. Lola, I can help you make deliveries in the morning and we can look."

"Great. Eight thirty? Here, puss-puss," she called

Misty. The gray cat loped over and deigned to let Lola pick her up.

Brooke and Maud teamed up and Kerry said she had a house-hunting client to squire around in the morning, but would get her son, Roman, to go out with her in the afternoon. "He can drive," she said. "He's seventeen and still doesn't have his driver's license. The practice will do him good."

I locked the door after them and hurried to my phone to see if Hart had texted. He had. Twice. One of them warmed my cheeks and I started to text a reply, but then dialed his number. I walked into my bedroom and sat on the bed to take off my shoes, almost hanging up before he answered. It had been a darn long time since I'd slept with a man, and I'd forgotten how awkward the first conversation the day after could be. I hadn't spent the night. He'd walked me down to my van sometime after one o'clock and we'd kissed and made plans to see each other this weekend. Now the sound of his voice made me hesitate. "Hi," I said. I tossed my socks toward the hamper. Two points.

"Hi, yourself." He sounded amused. Maybe it hadn't been so long since he'd had a day-after-the-night-before conversation. "Last night was special. I went around with a smile on my face all day long."

His admission relaxed me. "I hummed show tunes all day. Al thought I was losing my mind."

"'There's a bright golden haze on the meadow,'" he sang in a light baritone.

I joined in and we finished out the chorus with silly flourishes.

166 / Laura DiSilverio

"Exactly." I laughed and it was okay. After a little more banter, I brought up Trent Van Allen. "Any chance you could give me a few more details about him?" I asked, wriggling out of my jeans. I sniffed them and draped them across my footboard, a graceful arc of white-painted iron, decorated with porcelain knobs. It, like most of my bedroom furniture, had come from my folks' attic. The mattress and the box spring were new, but the off-white matelassé bedspread had been in the attic, as had the blond maple dresser, which listed oh-so-slightly. One bedside lamp, pottery with raised daffodils on the swelling base, had come from a garage sale, along with the old steamer trunk I used as a nightstand. Once I'd cleaned it good and spray-painted it white, it made a dandy nightstand that I could store my out-of-season clothes in. The ceramic lamp on the other table had been made by my college roommate, who had wisely decided to give up ceramics in favor of becoming an accountant.

"I can do better than that—I'll make you a copy of his file. I might have to redact a few bits, but most of it's public record. I'll consider this a FOIA request. We've put out an APB on Sharla Winegard—she was listed as a known associate of Van Allen's on his rap sheet. There's a New Jersey warrant on her for shoplifting and grand theft auto."

I wasn't surprised to hear that, not after the way Sharla had reacted to the idea of going to the police. "Were either of them mixed up with drugs, that you know of?" Shrugging one arm out of my shirt, I switched the phone to my other ear so I could take it off over my head.

"Not that I recall. Why?"

I explained about how we were trying to find a point of intersection between the victim and the possible suspects. Hart was interested to hear that Allyson might have a record in California. "I'll make a call to the Sacramento police tomorrow," he said. "Even if her record's sealed, someone might remember what she was arrested for."

We talked for a few more minutes and then said good-bye. I hung up smiling, and padded naked into the bathroom for a shower.

Chapter 16

Lola drove and I ran vases of flowers or pots of flowering shrubs up to the doorsteps or offices where she was delivering Friday morning. The chilly temps forced me to wear a light jacket, but it was a fun job, since everyone greeted my appearance with a gasp of appreciation or a big smile. I kept my eyes peeled for a tan station wagon as we traversed the town and its outskirts. I spotted a tannish station wagon in the City Market parking lot and got all excited, but it was a Ford Taurus, not a Volkswagen. The young mother approaching it with a basket of groceries, a baby in a sling, and a toddler eyed us warily when she spotted us parked behind her ride. We drove off quickly, giving her a friendly wave. Our last delivery was to a funeral parlor and it took a good fifteen minutes with both Lola and me working to off-load all the arrangements.

"I'd forgotten how much faster it is with two people," Lola said, getting back into the commercial van painted yellow with "Bloomin' Wonderful" in pink script. "Axie goes with me in the summer, but when she's in school . . . well, it takes a lot longer when I have to find a parking space and make the delivery myself."

"Glad I could help. I've got an event tonight that will

probably have me out until past midnight, so I don't feel too guilty about playing hooky this morning. Al's on top of things." I'd already spoken to him twice.

As I slammed my door shut, Lola pulled out her notebook computer. "Look. I did some calculations last night. This"—she pointed to a square on the screen—"is the Club. I drew a circle around it out to two miles, because I figure Van Allen was most likely to park within that area. A two-mile walk would probably take him half an hour, maybe a bit longer in the dark. I don't think he's likely to have parked farther away than that, even if he was paranoid about not having the car spotted near the Club." She lifted her brows, asking if I agreed.

"That sounds reasonable to me," I said.

"Okay. Now, this"—she swept a finger across the area west of the Club—"is the golf course. There's nowhere there to park a car—at least, nowhere that wouldn't have been discovered and reported by now. This area farther west, though, is possible. He could park in this housing development or one of the shops along here, cut across the golf course, and be at the Club in twenty minutes or so." She zoomed in to show me the area she was looking at. I knew it. Jubilee Mansions was an upscale gated community. I thought a decrepit station wagon would stand out among the gleaming Jags, Audis, and Mercedes-Benzes. When I mentioned that to Lola, she agreed, but said, "There's the employee lot, though, where the yardmen and housecleaning staff park. I suspect the Volkswagen might blend in fine there."

She was right; I'd forgotten about that. "Let's check it out."

With a flash of white teeth, she swung the van into traffic and headed toward Jubilee Mansions. "I think we're going to get lucky," she said. "I feel it in my bones. My grandma said my horoscope said I was going to discover a pearl of great price today."

"Your grandma believes in horoscopes?" I asked, surprised that the devout woman, who always seemed to be in church or at a Bible study or serving dinner to the poor at a soup kitchen, believed in astrology.

"Not really," Lola said, making a turn, "but she reads them every morning."

We were laughing when I spotted a woman who looked familiar getting into a car. "Stop!" I told Lola, craning my head for a better look.

"What—?"

"Eloise Hufnagle. I'm almost sure of it. Back there— she was getting into a red car in that little lot behind the printing shop."

Lola flipped a U-ey at the next intersection, earning an indignant honk from an offended driver. She hunched forward over the steering wheel, eyes scanning the road ahead. I peered down each side street. "There!" I pointed to the left. "She's getting on Paradise Boulevard."

"You should call Hart," Lola said.

I shook my head. "Not until I'm sure it's her. Just follow her until she stops. Don't get too close."

"I don't want to lose her." Lola kept her attention on

the road while I kept my eyes pinned on the red car. Our higher vantage point in the van made it easier for me to keep her in sight, even when there were three or four cars between us. Once, it looked like she'd lose us at a red light, but Lola floored it and squeaked through the intersection on the yellow. Well, mostly the yellow. Law-abiding Lola looked stressed, her shoulders rigid and her jaw clenched, by the time Eloise turned into the parking lot of the Rocky Mountain Motel, one of a cluster of small hotels just off the I-70 exit.

The Rocky Mountain Motel was older than its neighbors, the Hampton Inn, the Holiday Inn Express, and La Quinta. It was a U-shaped two-story building built around a central parking lot, with rooms opening to the outdoors. An Indian couple owned it and had spiffed it up with a new coat of turquoise paint, a resurfaced parking lot, and window air-conditioning units. They had also recently opened a coffee shop adjacent to the motel, which sold, somewhat incongruously, the best Greek food near Heaven, including baklava to die—or diet—for.

"Park at the coffee shop," I suggested to Lola as the red car pulled into a slot on the left-hand side of the U, directly in front of a room. A maid's cart waited under the window, and the room's door was slightly open. A woman got out of the car, hefted a box, and slipped through the open door.

"I couldn't tell if that was Eloise," Lola said, a worry line between her brows. She idled the van in a spot in front of the busy coffee shop.

"Me neither," I admitted. "She seems about the right height and build, but the only time I ever saw her, she was wearing a nun's outfit."

"I saw enough photos of her online—I think I'll recognize her if I can just get a good look." Lola opened the door and leaned through the open window, trying to get a better view. Her glasses slipped and she pushed them up impatiently. As she did, the woman emerged from the hotel room across the way. She paused and seemed to be staring right at us, eyes squinting. I had to admit that the Bloomin' Wonderful van was not the most inconspicuous of vehicles.

"It's her," Lola said, her voice pitched a notch higher than usual. She had the presence of mind to drop down and pretend to look for something on the asphalt. "Call Hart."

I was already dialing, trying to keep track of Eloise from the corner of my eye. Before Hart answered, she threw herself into the red car, revved the engine, and peeled out. Lola scrambled back into the driver's seat, and threw the van into reverse. A horn honked a warning before she had backed up more than half a van length. We both looked over our shoulders to see a semitruck blocking us in as it tried to maneuver out of the small lot. The trucker was working one-handed, eating a gooey fistful of baklava as he drove. He gave us a cheery wave with a sticky hand as he pulled out of the lot. It was too late. Eloise's red car was out of sight.

I became aware of noises coming from my phone and lifted it to my ear to tell Hart we'd found and lost

Eloise Hufnagle. "She's driving a red Nissan Sentra," I told him, "but I never got the plate. She's got a room at the Rocky Mountain Motel off I-70."

"I know where it is. I'll be there in ten." He hung up.

Lola and I looked at each other and then at Eloise's room, its door still cracked open as the maid fetched small-sized toiletries from her cart and disappeared back into the room. "Are you thinking what I'm thinking?" I asked.

"No. Yes," she admitted sheepishly. "Probably. I'd love a peek at her room. What did Hart say?"

"Just that he was on his way over and would be here in ten minutes."

"We'd better hurry, then," Lola said, her mouth thinning into a determined line. We hopped out of the van, crossed the thin verge between the coffee shop and the motel, and hustled across the lot until we reached the slot where Eloise's car had been parked. Lola hesitated, but I gave her a gentle shove and she almost collided with the maid, a nineteen- or twenty-year-old girl who might have been the owners' daughter. She already looked worn-out, even though it wasn't yet noon.

"Oh," she said.

"My, uh, sister, Eloise, forgot her, uh, gum," I stuttered. Improvisation had never been my strong suit. "I told her I'd come back for it."

The maid shrugged a shoulder and stepped out of my way, checking a cell phone she pulled from her pocket. She sent a text or two and then wheeled the cart down another couple of doors.

"Don't touch anything," I reminded Lola. "Hands in your pockets like they do in all the police procedurals." I tucked my hands in the pockets of my khakis and nudged the door a bit wider with my elbow.

Lola peered over my shoulder. "It looks like the command center for D-day," she breathed.

I nodded, taking it all in. The room's furnishings could have been ordered from a catalog entitled "Bare-Bones Motel Rooms," but the place was spotlessly clean—kudos to the teen we'd met outside—and the colors were cheerful shades of rust and tan and pale green. The scent of a pine cleaner hung in the room. There were no clothes or shoes or books strewn about the room to indicate that anyone was in residence. However, Eloise Hufnagle had a series of corkboards propped against the walls, all of them covered with maps and charts and lists. We edged cautiously into the room. The largest bulletin board was held upright at eye level by the television; I guessed Eloise didn't feel the need to keep up with *The Voice* or *Rizzoli & Isles*. The pages tacked to the board had a series of connected circles with photographs pinned inside of them. In the center was a photo of Eloise herself, looking markedly less rabid than at the costume ball, wearing a white lab coat and black-rimmed glasses. Trim, professional, serious—not a bottle of faux blood in sight. At the far edge of the board was a photo of Mary Stewart, mouth ajar and chin tucked at an awkward angle. I wondered how long it had taken Eloise to find such an unflattering photo. Between the two main circles were smaller circles connected with lines that had handwritten notes inked above them. I didn't recognize any of the people, mostly women, in those circles. None of the lines went all the way from Eloise to Mary.

"She's doing a vector search," Lola said admiringly. "As if she were working with a disease and trying to track Patient Zero. See how she's working out from herself, and trying to find a connection that could have conveyed the disease—the manuscript, in this case— from her to Mary. So interesting!"

I left Lola to study the scientific precision of Eloise's work and wandered over to look at the corkboard propped against the wall by the bed. This one was full of dozens of photos of Mary Stewart—getting into her car, walking out of the grocery store, glad-handing fans at a book event, eating dinner at a restaurant with two other women. They were candid snaps taken by a mediocre photographer, many of them blurred, and some obviously taken with a long zoom lens. This evidence of Eloise's obsession with Stewart was a bit creepy. "Uh, Lola," I said. "Look at this."

She came over to study the new board. "Hm. I'm no lawyer, but I think this is going to constitute evidence of stalking when the police get a look at it. Looks like Mary Stewart was smart to get the restraining order."

A car door slammed and we jumped. Looking guiltily at each other, we scurried toward the door, moving awkwardly with our hands still dug into our pockets. I was afraid it was Hart, but when we looked outside, we saw a heavyset Indian man unloading boxes of toilet paper from a pickup truck near the small office. As we watched, he hefted two of the boxes and disappeared through the office door, presumably headed for a storage area. Ten seconds of watching him made me decide that running a mom-and-pop motel operation was not the way I wanted to make a living. I did my share of hauling stuff around as an event organizer, but I'd never had to stockpile toilet paper. Lola and I stepped onto the sidewalk in front of Eloise's room not four seconds before Hart's Chevy Tahoe came around the corner. I waved, as if we'd been standing there merely to help him find the right room.

He gave us a speculative look as he got out of the SUV. "I'm not even going to ask you if you've been inside. I see you were at least smart enough not to touch anything."

Lola and I jerked our hands out of our pockets. I felt mildly foolish.

"Wait here."

Even though the room's door was open, he approached the Indian man and had a short conversation with him. The man paused in his toilet-paper unloading, nodding several times, and Hart returned to us. I enjoyed watching his long stride, the way the sun sparked chestnut highlights off his brown hair, and the way his brown eyes crinkled at the corners against the glare. "Tell me how you found Hufnagle."

I explained about spotting her at the copy shop and following her back to the motel. I emphasized the fact that we hadn't approached her, that she'd spotted the Bloomin' Wonderful van parked at the coffee shop, and bolted. "We called you as soon as we were able to confirm it was her," I said virtuously.

"I'll nominate you for Citizen of the Year," he said

drily, and ducked into Eloise's room. Lola and I hovered in the doorway while he checked out the place, trying to gauge his reaction to the corkboard displays. He came out after five minutes, poker-faced, and made a call from the radio in his Tahoe. When he was done, he returned to us.

"Good work," Hart finally said. He smiled and I let go the breath I'd been holding with a loud whoosh. I hadn't wanted him to be pissed off at us. "We'll keep an eye on the place as manpower allows. The owner says he'll call me when Hufnagle returns. I can't see her abandoning all of her research and photos, so she'll probably sneak back at some point. When she does, we'll ask her a few questions."

"Do you think she's the killer?" I asked.

"If the victim were Mary Stewart, I'd look at her really hard," he said, rubbing his chin. "As it is, there's no photo of Van Allen in there, and no reference to him. That doesn't mean they didn't know each other, but there's no evidence of it."

I hadn't thought to look for photos of Van Allen and I let my shoulders slump with chagrin. Kinsey Millhone would have keyed in on that immediately, as would all my favorite sleuths. Well, maybe not Stephanie Plum. Her car would probably have blown up before she could take a close look at the photos. Or she'd have ended up in a tussle with Joe or Ranger on the motel bed. I felt marginally better.

"If Van Allen knew about Eloise's obsession with Mary Stewart, he could have capitalized on it in some way," Lola said thoughtfully.

Hart eyed her with interest and lifted a brow that invited her to continue.

"He might have offered to spy on Stewart for her. It must have gotten more difficult for her to keep track of Stewart after the restraining order. Or he might have offered to injure her in some way." Lola's brow puckered at the ugly thought. "I hate to think that about Eloise, but she could have wanted to punish Stewart for stealing her manuscript, and not been willing to harm her herself. I have a feeling that flinging paint is about the outer limit of Eloise's violent tendencies."

"You could be right," Hart said noncommittally.

I thought it was interesting that Lola was so sympathetic to Eloise Hufnagle, whom she called by her first name, and clearly less tolerant of Mary Stewart, whom she referred to by last name. Hart's radio squawking interrupted my thoughts. He bent to graze my lips with his, and said, "Duty calls. Talk to you later?"

The look in his eyes, and his openness about our relationship, warmed me. I nodded, and he climbed into the Tahoe. Lola and I started back across the parking lot to her van. She gave me a gently inquiring look. "Things are going well with Lindell?"

I couldn't suppress a smile. "You could say that."

Where Brooke would have said, "How well?" and pressed for details, Lola merely nodded and said, "I'm happy for you. It's about time you found a good man to get involved with. I was afraid when Doug got jilted in May that you and he—"

I shook my head. Not that the thought hadn't crossed

my mind; I mean, you can't be hung up on a guy for half your life and not think about getting back together with him when his fiancée leaves him at the altar, but no. I was done with Doug Elvaston for good, at least romantically.

"What about you, Lo?" I asked, climbing into the van. It smelled richly of loam and the sharp bitterness of marigolds. "Any interesting men on your horizon? Lucas Stewart is gorgeous," I hinted, thinking about the way she'd seemed interested in him last weekend.

"He gets less handsome the more you talk to him," she said. "That Dorian Gray costume was perfect." She thought for a moment. "It's hard to find time for men," she hedged. She started the van and we pulled out of the lot, headed back toward downtown Heaven. "Bloomin' Wonderful takes up twelve or more hours a day— well, you know how it is, running your own business. And then there's Axie and my grandma. It's too bad teens don't come with implanted GPS trackers. Then I wouldn't have to worry so much."

"You don't have to worry about Axie," I said. "She's a good kid."

"I know she's a good kid, but I love her so much. . . ." Lola trailed off. Her thin brown fingers flexed around the steering wheel.

"Think how good you'll be at parenting when you have your own kids," I said. "And you can leave them with their aunt Axie whenever you need a break."

Lola chuckled. "I might at that."

Back at the nursery, Lola's grandma came on to the

porch when we drove up. She waved at us. "I just made a pound cake," she called. "Come in and have a piece with warm peach topping."

I couldn't say no to Mrs. Paget's pound cake, so I accepted the invitation and spent a pleasant half hour catching up with Mrs. Paget and enjoying the rich cake. I tried to tell myself that the peaches made it practically health food, but I was sure my scale would reveal the truth when I got on it in the morning.

Chapter 17

My event Friday night was a bake sale with a twist—the goodies were being auctioned off to the highest bidder. The event was sponsored by the First Baptist Church of Heaven and the proceeds were going to pay for their new sanctuary. I'd orchestrated a major publicity push and I was pleased to see the parish hall was full to overflowing by the time I'd checked the sound system and coordinated the arrangement of the various baked goods (some of which were truly scrumptious looking), beautifully displayed on tables lining three sides of the room. Most of the room's space was filled with folding chairs laid out in neat lines, with an aisle down the middle. The high-ceilinged room, frequently used for wedding receptions, had a fully equipped commercial kitchen at the back, and a small dais at the front.

The bakers, several of them professionals from Heaven and its surrounding towns, had brought samples, and knots of people clustered around each table, scarfing down bite-sized morsels of cakes, breads, cookies, and pastries. The women of the church were selling beverages (nonalcoholic, of course) to wash down the sweetness and were making a mint if the lines in front of the coffee urn and the lemonade cooler were anything to go by. The pièce de résistance of the auction was a wedding cake—flavor and design to be determined by the winning bidder—supplied by Nona, hands down the best baker in town, who was notoriously hard to book because she was so busy and apt to go off to visit her grandkids in Dallas whenever she felt like it. She had brought a sample cake, four glistening tiers of lemon-colored frosting and bright fondant flowers. It looked divine. I noticed at least twelve engaged couples in the gathering audience. Perhaps I could get more business out of this, too. I'd left a business card on each padded folding chair, so maybe I'd get some calls.

With three hundred people crowded into it, the room was uncomfortably warm and I found a church staffer with a long-handled gadget to open the high windows. I was at the back of the room, propping doors open with hymnals, since I couldn't find rubber stoppers, when Cletis Perry, my go-to auctioneer, hobbled in, swinging awkwardly on crutches. A bulky cast encased his left foot and leg almost to the knee.

"Cletis," I said, hurrying over to hold the door wider. "What happened to you?"

He gave me his trademark grin. "I had a disagreement with a car and the car won. Broke my leg in three places, so the docs had to put a rod in. I'll be keeping the TSA folks busy from here on out, setting off the metal detector every time I pass through it." He looked a little pale under his tan, and the way he suddenly tensed made me think he must be in pain. Before I could ask, he beckoned to an assistant I hadn't noticed, and the young man (who had Cletis's slightly hooked nose and looked like he might be related) handed him a sheet of paper and then went forward to check out the setup and put Cletis's gavel on the podium.

"Dang crutches are a pain in the patootie," he said, trying to balance himself, hold on to the page, and extract a pair of reading glasses from the pocket of his pearl snap shirt.

"Let me." I drew the glasses out of his pocket and positioned them carefully on his face.

"Thanks, Amy-Faye. So we're selling cakes tonight, eh? Should be easier than my gig next week—I'm auctioning off the contents of storage containers whose owners haven't paid their fees. People store a lot of crap in those places." He made a dismissive face. "Why buy something if you're only going to hide it away in a storage place? Stupid. People today got too much stuff. But it makes me a tidy living, so who am I to get all judgmental on them?" He used a crutch to gesture toward the nave of the church, a dimly lit space opposite the brightly lit and noisy parish hall. "Maybe it's this place bringing out my holier-than-thou side." He chuckled.

"I hope your car wasn't totaled," I said, walking him past the wares toward the front of the room.

He crinkled his sunspotted brow. "My car? Oh, I get you. No, I wasn't in my car. Some fool tried to run me down in a crosswalk. He musta been texting or something, because he blasted through like he didn't even see me. Didn't even slow down. Luckily I'm spryer than I look and I heard him coming in time to jump forward, so he only clipped my leg. Otherwise, you'd be looking for a new auctioneer for your shindigs."

"Don't even joke about that," I said severely. "I hope he paid your doctor bills."

"Didn't stop." Cletis bit the words off. "It was a hit-and-run. A lady standing on the sidewalk who saw the whole thing and called nine-one-one, bless her, said it looked like he was gunning for me. That's ridiculous, though. I'm an easygoing guy, not much of one for making enemies, excepting my father-in-law, Howie God-fredson, who never did think I was good enough for his daughter, my Lisa. But he's been in his grave for coming up on eighteen years now, so I doubt it was him. And no one much benefits from my early demise, except young Clay up there"—he jerked his head toward the man who'd come in with him—"and he loves his old grand-dad too much to run him down." He watched his grand-son fondly. The young man apparently felt his gaze and looked over at us, beaming a smile at Cletis and circling two fingers in an "okay" sign. Cletis returned the smile and turned back to me. "It was probably a kid, too pan-icked by what he'd done to pull over. Afraid he'd lose his cell phone or car privileges. No one teaches their kids to be accountable anymore."

A sudden chill made me shiver. Maybe we shouldn't have opened all the windows. "I'm just glad you're okay," I told Cletis. "You're sure you're up to this?"

"This is nothing," he scoffed, tapping the cast lightly with the tip of one crutch. "I once conducted an auction with a fever of a hundred and four. Turns out I had meningitis. Never had such a bad headache in my life, but netted twenty percent more than the pre-auction estimates, and didn't pass out until I brought my gavel down on the last item." He mimed the gesture. "Sold!"

Refusing my offer of help, he made his way to the dais, exchanging greetings with six or eight people as he crutched his way forward. He went into his patter, and I watched from the back of the room, not really paying attention to the numbers or who won what. My mind was worrying the phrase "gunning for me," batting it around like a kitten with a catnip mouse. Cletis seemed to think the witness was mistaken, that the accident was simply an accident—a criminal one, since the driver didn't stop to help. What with Van Allen's murder, and the strange mix-up of items at last Saturday's auction, I wasn't so sure. Still, Cletis hadn't been at the costume party. He couldn't have seen anything that would threaten the killer. No, I was letting my imagination run away with me. Cletis was right: His broken leg was an accident, pure and simple.

Despite my late night, I arrived at the Columbine early Saturday morning to discuss the upcoming sorority reunion with Sandy. Hers was one of three Heaven B and Bs hosting the women involved, and she wanted my help coordinating van service between the B and Bs and the various event locations, setting up a spa day for the women, and putting on a dinner dance that would mimic the Greek events of their 1960s college days. She'd told me to come early because it was the one time she could guarantee we wouldn't be interrupted by guests. "Find me in the kitchen," she'd said.

Accordingly, I parked on the street at seven a.m. and hurried up the walkway to the door, chased by the chilly temps. It had dipped into the twenties overnight and the sun wasn't yet high enough to warm the air. I noticed Sandy had taken in the mums that had flanked the porch steps the last time I was there, probably to keep them from freezing. September in Heaven was the time of year when potted plants came inside for the winter. I let myself in through the front door. I closed it quietly, not wanting to disturb any of the guests. The potted mums on the entryway table drooped slightly and I hoped Sandy planned to water them soon. I was following the enticing aroma of baking scones toward the kitchen, when a small sound from the dining room caught my attention. Thinking I might find Sandy in there, placing fresh blooms in the bud vases on the breakfast tables, I detoured toward it.

"I'm sick and tired of this," a man's voice said as I neared the door. It sounded like Lucas Stewart. "You said we'd only have to pretend for a couple of months."

"The case has dragged on longer than anyone could have expected," Mary said, her voice soothing, "but the payoff will be worth it. You know that. We've been so careful. We can't afford to blow it when the money's practically in our grasp. The judge should hand down a final decision in a week or two. Then we can—"

"I don't want to wait for 'then.' I want now." Lucas's voice was a growl. Mary's faint, "Not here—" answered him, and then there was silence. I leaned my upper body forward so I could peer through the six-inch gap between the door and the jamb.

What I saw almost made me gasp aloud. Mary Stewart and her brother stood in profile to me, their arms wrapped around each other, kissing passionately. It was definitely not a kiss anyone could term sisterly or brotherly. No, it was a full-on, "let's hop into bed and make whoopee" sort of kiss; a potboiler-romance-cover kiss, complete with silk robe sagging off Mary's shoulder to show a swoosh of collarbone and a valley of cleavage; a nighttime-soap-opera-caliber kiss. It wouldn't have surprised me greatly if they had swept the chafing dishes off the buffet and gone at it right there in the dining room. A wisp of steam rose into the air and I wasn't sure if it was from a chafing dish or the hot-blooded couple.

I backed away silently, glad I was wearing athletic shoes. I felt uncomfortably warm, embarrassed by what I'd witnessed, appalled and puzzled by it. Mary and her brother . . . eew. Actually, incest was beyond "eew," and I blinked my eyes hard to try to rid myself of the images seemingly seared onto my eyeballs. Before I could open them, a hand clamped onto my upper arm, fingers digging in like iron vises. My eyes flew open and I saw Lucas Stewart standing in front of me, expression grim.

Chapter 18

Before I could do more than squeak, he dragged me into the dining room and shut the door, turning the lock. It rasped and slid home with a muted *thunk*.

"I told you I heard someone," he said over his shoulder to Mary, who was holding the robe closed at her neck, like a virginal heroine from a gothic novel, but her swollen lips and the flush on her pale skin betrayed her assumption of innocence. "She was practically peering through the keyhole."

"Amy-Faye! What's she doing here?"

"Spying on us." Lucas's full lips thinned into a straight line, and his square jaw jutted forward.

Recovering from my surprise, I waved the hand that wasn't controlled by Lucas. "Hey, I'm right here."

Mary's slit-eyed gaze landed on me. "Why were you spying on us? Who put you up to it? Eloise Hufnagle? You'd better see if she's got a camera," she told her brother.

"I wasn't spying—not on purpose—and I don't have a camera. You lay one finger on me," I said to Lucas when it looked like he was going to pat me down, "and I'll scream this place down." I opened my mouth to demonstrate my willingness to carry through with my threat.

"Sh," Mary hissed, and Lucas backed away, saying, "Okay, okay. Calm down."

I rubbed my arm, knowing it would bruise. I slid a foot backward, easing toward the locked door. "Look, what you two get up to is your own business. You're consenting adults. I don't care—"

"We're not really—" Mary Stewart began, at the same time Lucas said, "She's not my sister." He crossed to Mary and took her hand in his.

With a deep breath, Mary said, "We're married."

My jaw dropped. "What?"

"Eight months and three days ago," she said with a besotted look at her groom.

"Then why—"

"Can we trust you?" Mary asked, widening her eyes at me.

"We shouldn't tell—" Lucas started, but Mary talked over him.

"It's all because of Eloise," Mary said. "Eloise Hufnagle."

I was thoroughly confused. "Huh? What does she have to do with you being married or not?"

"It's a long story," Mary sighed. She let go of Lucas's hand and dropped into a chair. "I'll try to make it short. Lucas used to work with Eloise Hufnagle."

I edged another step closer to the door. "I thought he was a bodyguard." This story didn't jibe with what I knew about Eloise working at the CDC.

"He's a bodyguard now," Mary said, "or at least he will be when he finds someone to hire him. But *before*, he was a security guard at the CDC. That's where he met Eloise."

"She was a nice woman," he said, also sitting. "We used to chat when she swiped in or left for the day. Who would have guessed that she'd go all *Fatal Attraction* on me?"

"What does this all have to do with you pretending to be brother and sister?" I asked. Sandy would be waiting; I needed to get going.

They exchanged a glance, and then Mary took up the story. "He's too much the gentleman to say it. Eloise had a crush on Lucas. He tried to be kind without encouraging her, but some women can't take a hint. She talked all the time about this book she had written, going on and on about it. We were dating then, and he told me a little about it. From what he said, I could tell it had some similarities to the book I was writing, so I asked him not to talk about it anymore, to keep away from Eloise." Her fingers played with a couple of white rose petals that had fallen from the flower in the bud vase and she didn't meet my eyes.

"When *Blood Will Out* debuted, she went bonkers, railing that someone had stolen her book. I mean, she totally went off the deep end." She looked at Lucas for corroboration and he nodded. "When she started talking about a lawsuit, it made me nervous. We decided on the spur of the moment to get married, but decided to keep it quiet for fear Eloise would read something totally not true into the total coincidence of her know-ing Lucas and him knowing me."

Mary held my gaze with great earnestness, but she *totally* failed to convince me that there was anything coincidental about the situation. "So, what you're say-ing is that Lucas romanced Eloise to steal her book and you wrote it up as if it was your own? It probably started out like you said, with Eloise attracted to Lucas, but I'll bet when he mentioned the book to you, Mary, you told him to find out more, maybe even get a copy of the manuscript. Maybe he even took her on a few dates. Am I warm?"

The startled and hostile expressions on both their faces convinced me I was. Maybe he'd even slept with her, possibly with Mary's approval. Beyond sleazy. I felt sorry for Eloise. I thought of the vector charts in her motel room. "And now you're keeping your mar-riage secret and Lucas is ducking the limelight, so that Eloise won't make the connection between you." She'd probably already put it together. I remembered her saying something like "What are you doing here?" at the costume ball before flinging her red goo. I hadn't known what she meant at the time, but now it seemed clear that she'd spotted Lucas and been shocked to see him. "Because if she does, you lose the lawsuit and it's bye-bye, fat royalty checks. In fact, it's probably sayo-nara, writing career."

"I told you we shouldn't tell her," Lucas said. He was looking less handsome by the minute with a scowl on his brow and his upper lip drawn up in an ugly sneer.

"What do we do now?" Mary asked.

I'd been carried away with my deductions, but now a feeling of uneasiness crept over me. I was locked in a room—admittedly a room in a B and B with several other people around—with a couple who might well have murdered a man to keep their secret. If so, they'd managed that with hundreds of other people right down the hall. "Sandy's expecting me," I said, walking to the door with an unhurried and confident gait. If I acted like I was just going to walk out of there, maybe they'd let me.

"Not so fast." Lucas's hand fastened on my shoulder.

I wrenched away and spun to face him, wishing I knew tae kwon do or krav maga or any useful self-defense technique. My gaze darted around the room, searching for a weapon. My choices seemed to be fork, butter knife, or bud vase, none of which would have much impact in my hands. Kinsey Millhone probably knew eight different ways to kill or disable someone with a bud vase, but I would likely only cut my hand. "Is this what happened with Trent Van Allen?" I asked, hoping to distract them.

"What?" Mary was so surprised she let go of her robe and it gaped, showing a very sexy white teddy beneath it.

"He found out your secret and tried to blackmail you, didn't he? You met him at the party and one of you"—my gaze went from Mary to Lucas—"stabbed him to death."

"We're not murderers," Lucas said, taken aback. "Why would you think that? We didn't know Van Allen and he didn't have anything on us. The idea is ludicrous."

"You locked me in here. You keep grabbing me."

"I locked the door to keep other people from coming in. What—you thought we would hurt you?"

He seemed genuinely offended, to the point that I almost apologized.

He blustered on. "How would some ex-con know about me knowing Eloise Hufnagle? You're full of it." He crossed back to Mary and put his arm around her shoulders, pulling her close.

She bowed her head, red hair draping her face. "It makes me want to cry," she said, forcing out a couple of tears, "to think that you would think such vicious lies were true. I never stole Eloise's story, and I certainly never killed that man. I could never kill anyone—well, only in a book, but not in real life! I don't even squish spiders, and they give me the willies." She looked at me from under her lashes, perhaps to see how her story was going over.

She reminded me of the women in some Southern gothic classics: a core of steel veiled by fluttery lashes and a veneer of wide-eyed innocence. They usually managed to flirt and tease their way into getting a man to do their dirty work for them. Kathleen Turner in *Body Heat*. I decided some strategic dissembling was in order. "I can see that now, Mary. I was just thinking aloud, a stream-of-consciousness thing. It's a bad habit." I fumbled with the lock and it finally turned. It was like the turning lock opened my lungs and I could breathe deeply again. I sucked in a rib-cage-stretching breath and let it out slowly. Safety lay on the other side of the door.

Before I could pull the door open, Lucas said, "Wait." He held his hands up at shoulder height to show he wasn't going to harm me. "We want your word that you won't say anything."

"To Eloise," Mary clarified.

"Or her lawyers," Lucas said. "About us being married."

"I don't even know Eloise Hufnagle," I said, conveniently not mentioning that I'd followed her to her motel yesterday. "I've got better things to do with my time than hunt her down." True, but not the promise they were looking for.

A light footstep sounded in the hall and the door swung inward, almost clipping my face. I jumped back and Sandy stepped in, bringing the faint aroma of yeast with her. "There you are," she said. "I wondered where you'd gotten to." She noticed the Stewarts. "Good morning. Breakfast will be up in about ten minutes. Pecan waffles this morning. I'll bring some juice while you wait, if you want."

"Cranberry, please," Mary said with a smile. Her gaze swiveled to me and I couldn't quite read it. Plea? Warning?

I exited into the hall while Sandy promised Mary her juice and Lucas a mug of coffee. Throughout my meeting with Sandy, conducted in the cozy environs of the B and B's kitchen, part of my mind mulled over what I'd learned from the Stewarts. *Hm, what was Lucas's real name? Maybe he had taken Mary's last name when they married? Beside the point.* Lucas had seemed surprised and offended when I accused them of murdering Van Allen. I hadn't been able to read Mary as well. It seemed to me that she was the driving force in that partnership. I'd have bet my last nickel that she egged Lucas on to steal Eloise Hufnagle's novel, and she was clearly the one dictating that they not reveal their true relationship.

When I had wrapped things up with Sandy and reviewed all my notes, I went to the police station. They operated with a skeleton crew on nights and weekends, but Hart had told me he was working today. In addition to telling him about the Stewarts, I wanted to pick up the copy of Trent Van Allen's file he said he'd give me. The female officer who had come to the Columbine when the brick got thrown through the window was sitting at the desk. She had short black hair tucked behind her ears, and a smattering of freckles across a pug nose. Her name tag said HARDAWAY. She perked up when I walked in, and I figured she was bored with the Saturday morning shift. I'm sure Saturday nights had a bit more action in Heaven.

"Can I help you, ma'am?" she asked.

When I told her I wanted to see Detective Hart, she said he was out. I was disappointed, but thought to ask her if he'd left a file for me. "I'm Amy-Faye Johnson."

Interest sparked in her eyes and I knew she'd heard rumors. Oh, the joys of small-town life. She dug through a pile of envelopes and folders in a tray, and extracted one. "Here you go, ma'am. Should I tell Detective Hart that you came in?"

I was shy about saying I'd just call his cell phone, so I said, "Have him call me, please."

With nothing much on my agenda for the rest of the morning, I decided to continue the hunt for Van Allen's station wagon, which had been interrupted by tailing Eloise Hufnagle yesterday. Lola's plan was still a good one, and I called her to see if she wanted to join me. She was busy, as was Kerry. Brooke didn't answer her phone, but Maud did and said she'd love to go treasure hunting with me. I told her I'd swing by her house in five, and rang off.

Maud was waiting outside, dressed in her usual multipocketed pants and henley shirt, topped with a Windbreaker. Her gray, white, and silver hair was loose today, and she brushed it off her face impatiently as she got in the van. She folded her lanky frame into the seat, and asked, "What's the plan?" I filled her in on Lola's idea, and she said, "Good thinking. Brooke and I struck out yesterday."

I headed down Paradise Boulevard toward Jubilee Mansions, barely concentrating on my driving as I filled Maud in on my encounter with the Stewarts. When I got to the part about seeing them in a clinch, she observed, "Very Faulknerian."

I choked on a laugh. "Yeah, but it turns out they're not sibs. They're married."

Maud's eyebrows shot toward her hairline. "Married? Really?"

"So they say. But wait—there's more." I finished telling her about their shenanigans with Eloise Hufnagle's manuscript.

"So Lucas slept with Hufnagle and stole her book," Maud mused.

"That's how I read it," I admitted, "although they didn't cop to it."

"It sounds like they have a doozy of a motive for murdering Trent Van Allen, assuming he knew their secret."

"That's the kicker." I glided through the gates of Jubilee Mansions with a wave to the gate guard. That's one of the (few) benefits of driving a van with "Eventful!" swirled on the side: People like gate guards assume you're on your way to set up an event and don't hassle you. I'd done an event up here a bare two weeks ago, and the guard remembered me and my van. "Keep your eyes peeled," I said.

Maud scanned the streets. There were few cars parked at the curb, either because the HOA covenants forbade it or because people liked to keep their Escalades and Infinitis safely tucked away in garages. "How much do you suppose Stewart's book is worth?"

"I don't know. It's been on the *New York Times* bestseller list ever since it came out, hasn't it? And there's undoubtedly a movie deal in the works. And it's not just *Blood Will Out*, either. I mean, this is her whole writing career at stake. If it comes out that she stole a manuscript, no one will ever buy another of her books, I wouldn't think. So, potentially high six figures, or even a few million?" I didn't know enough about what authors made to feel sure of those numbers, but it felt like enough to commit murder for.

"Many a murder's been done for less," Maud concurred. "Look—isn't that the turnoff for the staff lot?"

I swung the van to the right, taking the unmarked

side road that led toward the small lot. A scrim of trees veiled it from the main road, probably so the rich homeowners could maintain the illusion that house elves and yard fairies kept their homes and acreages clean and mowed. We came around a bend, and the lot lay in front of us, shielded by another thin belt of trees from the golf course. It contained a black scooter chained to a pine tree, a grimy pickup truck with plastic sheeting duct-taped over the broken passenger window, an ancient sedan plastered with bumper stickers promoting everything from Save the Manatee to the right to life, and a station wagon. A tan station wagon with Illinois plates. Satisfaction and anticipation rose in me. We'd found it.

Chapter 19

"There it is," Maud said. She unbuckled and started to get out of the van before I'd come to a complete stop.

"Wait," I said. "We have to call Hart. I promised him."

She made a face, but stayed put. I dialed Hart's cell phone number and when he answered, I told him we'd found the station wagon.

"Great work," he said. "I'll be there in fifteen. Don't touch the car. Where did you say this lot is?"

I gave him directions and hung up to see Maud giving me a sly grin. "You slept with him."

My face warmed. How could she tell that from the thirty-second conversation I'd had with him?

"There's something in your voice," she answered my unspoken question. "Good for you. He seems like a stand-up guy, for a cop."

"I like him a lot," I said, not able to keep a big smile off my face. Not wanting to get into a discussion about Hart and our relationship—talking about it might jinx it—I leaned over to pick up Trent Van Allen's file from the floor. "Here." I handed it to Maud. "Something to entertain us until Hart gets here. It's the dossier on

Trent Van Allen. Read it out loud—I haven't had a chance to look through it yet."

Her long, tanned fingers flipped quickly through the three pages the file contained. She returned to the beginning and began reading. "Trent Van Allen. Born Pocatello, Idaho, April 12, 1973. That makes him forty-three. His Social's been blacked out—too bad because I could have discovered everything there is to know about him with that." She rubbed her long nose with her forefinger and resumed reading. "Enlisted in the Marine Corps in 1990. It says here he was infantry. Saw action in Kuwait during Desert Storm. Purple Heart, Commendation Medal. Two lines blacked out here, too. Transferred to Camp Pendleton. Honorable discharge in 1996." She looked up from the folder. "I wonder why he left the marines. It seems like he was good at it."

I shrugged. "Tired of getting shot at? Tired of taking orders?"

"He got a job at Jose's Repair and Body Shop in Barstow. Desolate place, Barstow. Hot, dry, windy, where I-40 and I-15 hook up. Two years after he shed his uniform, he got busted for drugs—cocaine. Possession with intent to distribute. A few more drug busts after that, a two-year stint in a California prison, and then he relocated to the East Coast, looks like Virginia for a while and then New Jersey."

"That's probably where he met Sharla," I said. The greenhouse effect was warming the car, so I opened my door to let a breeze in. A slightly noxious smell came with it and I wrinkled my nose.

"Looks like he got mixed up with stealing cars for

chop shops, maybe mob-related, if the names of his known associates are anything to go by: Louie 'Big Lou' DiLuzio, Andreas 'the Carp' Fezatte, Gina 'Mama G' Umstine." She looked at me. "What would my mob nickname be, if I were a 'made' woman?"

I laughed at the idea. "Fast Fingers Maud?" I mimed typing on a keyboard. "We could shorten it to an acronym: F2M, or F-Squared M."

"You could be the Organizer. Amy-Faye 'the Organizer' Johnson. It sounds sinister in that context." She resumed reading. "He did three years in a New Jersey prison for grand theft auto. He got a light sentence because he ratted out his partner, the aforementioned Big Lou. When he got out, he apparently drifted to Illinois, where he resumed his old activities and added some armed robbery—a couple of banks. Back to prison he went. Did four years. Got paroled five weeks ago. It says here he never met with his parole officer. Must have skipped town immediately, a violation of his parole." She shook her head.

"So where did a guy who's been in prison or hanging with lowlifes and stealing cars most of his adult life get something that he thought he could sell to someone associated with the Celebration of Gothic Novels?"

Before Maud could speculate, Hart's Tahoe came around the corner in a cloud of dust. He parked beside the van, on Maud's side, and got out, wearing a sport coat and olive green slacks. The wind riffled his brown hair. He greeted us. The smile in his eyes as they met mine made me tingle and I almost forgot why we were there. I remembered when he pulled a crowbar out of the back of the SUV, and disposable gloves from his pocket. He didn't object when Maud and I followed him to the car. As we got closer, the stench I'd noticed earlier got stronger. *Uh-oh.*

"Reeks," Maud observed.

I nodded, concentrating on breathing shallowly through my mouth. Hart's expression was grim. I'd read enough police procedurals to know what the odor likely meant. There was a body hidden in the car. I couldn't imagine whose it could be. Had Van Allen had a partner Sharla hadn't mentioned? She might not have known. As far as I knew, no one from Heaven had gone missing. The station wagon's windows were tinted, and it had one of those pull-across screens that hid the contents of the back section from view. A sun visor lay across the dash. Hart tried all the doors, but they were locked. The Volkswagen was so ancient that he had no trouble popping the two front doors with a slim jim he took from his coat pocket. He left them ajar, letting the air circulate.

"You might want to stand back," he said, inserting the tip of the crowbar under the lip of the station wagon's access hatch.

I shuffled backward a few feet, but Maud inched in closer. Positioning the crowbar near the lock, Hart leaned into it. Metal creaked. Pumping on the tool, Hart put his whole weight into it. The lock popped with a screeching bang that made me jump. The hatch flew up, barely missing Hart's chin. A wave of fetid, rotting air rolled out, almost viscous in its intensity. I gagged. Maud pulled a pot of Carmex from her pocket and calmly rubbed some beneath her nose. She offered the pot to me, but I declined. Hart found the release button that freed the screen drawn across the back of the station wagon and it sprang back, rolling up in its case.

At first I couldn't process what I was seeing. The body was bloated and swollen. Its head was canted at an awkward angle and its fur matted with blood. It was a deer, a small doe, probably from this spring's crop of fawns. I flopped over from the waist, giddy with relief that it wasn't a human body. Hart circled the car again, bending over to inspect the grille, and then came over to put a hand on my back.

"Are you okay?"

I nodded. "I thought it was going to be a body."

"There's front-end damage," he said. "Van Allen must have hit the deer on his way to the Club. I guess he loaded it up, thinking to get some venison steaks out of it. Then, of course, he never came back and it's been baking in the back of that wagon for a week. Damned if I know who to call about this. I need to search the car, but until that carcass is out of there, I'm not going near it."

"I know a couple of guys," Maud said, punching a number on her cell phone. "They're dead-animal removers. Usually they deal with livestock, but I'm sure they can handle the deer."

Maud's guys said they'd come. I used the intervening half hour before they showed up to tell Hart about my encounter with the Stewarts, husband and wife, not brother and sister. He winced when I described them kissing, but looked interested when I told him they were legally married. "At least," I added, "that's what they say now. I suppose they could be lying about that, but I don't know why they would. I'm ninety-nine percent convinced that they stole Eloise Hufnagle's book, like she claims, and they've been doing this charade so she won't connect them."

"They'd have been smarter to stay away from each other completely," Maud pointed out, "but I guess the newlyweds didn't want to give up their, ahem, marital intimacies for what might be a year or more. So, they may well end up losing out on millions because they couldn't keep their hands off each other for a few months. I'll bet the disappointment and blaming takes more of a toll on their marriage than being separated would have."

"You talk like it's a foregone conclusion that Mary Stewart will lose the court case," I said.

Maud gave me a pointed look. "I suspect word will get back to Eloise Hufnagle somehow, don't you?"

Now that she put it that way, I did indeed think Eloise was likely to find out about the secret marriage. The words "secret marriage" made me think of gothic romances and I thought it ironic that Mary Stewart should be living out so many of the clichés of her genre.

When the knackers arrived, Maud and I strolled through the narrow greenbelt to the edge of the golf course. Clouds scudded the sky now, and I zipped my fleece jacket against the chill. I did not need to watch the doe being pulled out of the station wagon. Hart stayed, saying he had a responsibility to oversee the operation and safeguard any evidence. Once through the strand of scraggly oaks and small pines, Maud and I found ourselves midway down the fairway for the fourteenth hole with a clear view of the Club across another fairway and the eighteenth green.

"Wouldn't have taken him more than seven, eight minutes to walk from here to the Club," Maud said, narrowing her eyes to measure the distance. "Maybe ten in the dark."

I tried to put myself in Van Allen's place, imagining the walk across the manicured grass, dodging sand traps. He could enter the Club through the pro shop—I tried to remember what time it closed on a Saturday night—or walk around to the front. He had either bought a ticket for the gala earlier in the day, possibly from Gemma, or paid at the door. Once inside he had . . . what? Gotten a drink, helped himself to a plate of hors d'oeuvres, and gone searching for the person he had come to find. Had he set up a meeting, or had he just known the person would be there?

"It was prearranged," Maud said when I asked her opinion. Her pale blue eyes looked almost gray in proximity to her gray Windbreaker. She still had it open, apparently unfazed by the cold and stiffening breeze. "He was going to trade whatever he had—information, photos, valuable object—for money and hightail it out of Colorado. Why take the risk of meeting the target twice?"

That made sense. "So he met up with his mark and they went to the office, or they had prearranged to meet in Wallace's office, which would suggest a pretty good knowledge of the Club's layout."

Cocking her head, Maud gave it some thought. "I think the office was spur-of-the-moment, a deserted and quiet place to have a conversation and do the trade."

"They couldn't have done the trade there," I pointed out. "Not if Van Allen left whatever it was in the station wagon. And I can't see the blackmailee traipsing around the costume party lugging a briefcase or gym bag full of money. I can't imagine Van Allen was prepared to take a check or a credit card." I tried to remember if I'd seen anyone Saturday night with a duffel or a box, but no one came to mind.

"Okay," Maud said. "So they were going to do the swap at the car. One of their cars. No one with half a brain would be willing to hike across the golf course to this lot with an ex-con, so my guess is that Van Allen was going to come back here, get the 'package'"—she put air quotes around it—"and rendezvous with the mark at his or her car, where he'd get the money."

"He wasn't in costume, not masked," I mused, "which seems to mean he didn't mind the victim knowing who he was."

"Interesting point," Maud agreed, nodding.

Before we could dissect the events of Saturday night further, Hart called us back. We found him standing beside the station wagon, empty of everything except fluids and stench. We carefully positioned ourselves upwind, and I was suddenly grateful for the colder air and the gusty breeze. He had stripped off his sport coat and donned a white coverall that zipped up the front, paper booties, and a puffy cap like surgeons wear. I knew he wasn't so much protecting his clothes from deer blood as protecting what might be a crime scene from the introduction of outside elements, namely, his hair and fibers from his clothes. I'd read enough Patricia Cornwell and Tess Gerritsen to know how easily evidence is mucked up by improper crime scene protocols.

"I thought you might want to be here when I searched the car," Hart said. "Your reward for finding it." He flashed a smile.

"You're not so bad, Hart," Maud said. "I may have to reevaluate my opinion of your species."

He looked a bit taken aback. "Men?"

"Cops."

Hart laughed, and then eased the passenger-side door wider with his elbow. Trying to touch as little as possible, he went through the glove box first. "Nothing in here but the registration, a bunch of napkins, and this." He straightened, displaying a gun, which dangled from his forefinger by the trigger guard. He sniffed at the barrel but didn't comment before tucking it into a plastic evidence bag.

Maud and I went around to the driver's door and peered in, able to see nothing more exciting than stains and pebbles on the worn mats, a tin of chewing tobacco, what looked like receipts tucked under the sun visor, and a half-full bag of cheese puffs. Hart worked his way methodically from the front seat to the back, finding nothing more. Finally, the three of us gathered around the open hatch at the back. Hart eyed the blood-soaked carpet with distaste.

"Only place left to look is under there." He nodded

to the stiff piece of flooring that covered the spare tire's hidey-hole. Hooking his fingers under the cover, he lifted it.

Maud and I crowded closer, looking over his shoulder. All I saw was the spare tire and the jack and lug wrench tucked into a niche. Hart lifted the tire out and ran his fingers inside the rim, but then shook his head. "Nada."

Disappointment flowed through me. I'd been so sure we were on the verge of figuring out why Van Allen had been killed, and probably by whom.

"Is it possible that the gun is what Van Allen was selling?" Maud asked. She stood with her hands on her hips, a line between her brows. "Perhaps it was used in the commission of a crime and has the murderer's fingerprints on it."

I was impressed. "Ooh, that's a great idea."

Hart's response was more muted. "It's possible. Unlikely, but possible. We'll certainly test it for prints and run the serial number. It may well have been used in a robbery or other crime, but given Van Allen's record, I suspect he's the one who used it." Stripping off his gloves, he tucked them into a coverall pocket. "I've got to arrange for a tow to Grand Junction so the forensic guys and gals can take it apart." He lowered his voice and leaned in closer to me. "See you tonight?"

"After my event," I said, unable to keep a goofy smile off my face. "It might be late, after ten, undoubtedly."

"Doesn't matter," he said. "I'll be up."

His smile made me wish life had a fast-forward

button so we could skip straight to tonight. Resisting the urge to pull his head down so I could kiss him, I squeezed his hand and joined Maud at the van. I settled into the driver's seat, feeling instantly warmer out of the wind.

Maud didn't say anything about the interchange between me and Hart, which made me glad it was she and not Kerry or Brooke with me. Either of those two would have been grilling me for details, and probably giving me advice on what lingerie to wear. Maud was more task-focused. As soon as I reversed the van and headed out of the lot, she said, "So where did Van Allen stash his package?"

"Maybe someone stole it."

She shook her head. "Don't think so. No one broke in to that car. I think his girlfriend was wrong. He didn't leave the package in the car—he took it with him. Which, when you think about it, makes more sense anyway. He wouldn't have to come all the way back here to get it once the deal's made with whoever he was meeting."

"Sounds like he made the trade-off. Whoever he met killed him and got away with the package and the money." I gripped and released the steering wheel a couple of times, frustrated by this turn of events. I really wanted to know what was in that package. It felt like it was the key to the whole case.

"Shoot." Maud slumped in the passenger seat. "It does look that way, doesn't it?"

I gave a dispirited nod. It didn't seem like we were getting anywhere with this case. I thought about Lola, and how guilty she felt about having brought the murder weapon to the party. I wanted her to at least know that the killer was going to be punished for his or her crime.

A hundred feet from the intersection with Jubilee Parkway, a car was pulled over on the shoulder, and I slowed. As we passed it, I noted the flat tire. A man hauled off and kicked it as we drove past.

"Wasn't that that movie guy?" Maud asked, craning her neck to get a better look.

I was already slowing and pulling over. He looked like he needed help. When we got out, the man was coming toward us. It was indeed Cosmo Zeller, looking less polished and urbane than he had at the cocktail party. His black blazer was rumpled, his tan silk shirt had a splotch of oil shaped like Florida on it, and his face and lips were wind-reddened.

"Thank God you stopped," he said. "Hey, I know you." He snapped his fingers twice. "Amy-Kay, right? The event planner. And you're Maud." He gave Maud an appreciative once-over. Despite her being over sixty and making zero effort to attract the opposite sex, there was something about her that appealed to men of every age.

"Amy-Faye," I said, "but close enough. Anything we can do to help? Looks like you've got a flat."

"Damn rental. Not only do I have a flat, but the spare's missing and my phone's out of juice. You'd better believe the rental company is going to hear from my lawyer. If you could let me borrow your phone to call them, that'd be great." Maud handed over her phone and he made the call, gesticulating with his free hand as he talked. "They're bringing another car to the B and B," he said, giving the phone back. "I'm supposed to leave the keys with this one and they'll fetch it later. Any chance I could get a ride back into town with you?" He smiled a plea, showing lots of white teeth. "These shoes aren't made for hiking." He held out one foot, elegantly shod in an expensive-looking leather loafer. No socks, despite the cold.

"Happy to give you a lift," I said, "but I don't have a seat in the back of the van. As long as you don't mind roughing it . . . I'll try not to crash, since you won't have a seat belt."

"No prob," he said. "Your van is a luxury vehicle compared to the heap I rode around in last month in Burundi. Rusted metal, seat upholstery thinner than a slice of prosciutto, and no shocks to speak of. No doors, so I was looking death in the eye every time we turned right. The driver drove like we were being chased by the zombies from *World War Z*. I didn't know if I was going to die of lockjaw or be jolted to death. When a lioness charged us, I almost welcomed a quick death. And the driver had the nerve to charge us five hundred dollars a day." He scrambled limberly into the back when I slid the van's door open. "What is this? Moving day?" he asked, looking at the boxes of tableware and linens, the fake potted plants, and the life-sized stand-up figure of tonight's birthday boy, who was turning fifty.

"Tools of the trade," I said.

He seated himself gingerly on a sturdy plastic tub and Maud and I returned to the front. I started the van and pulled onto the road gently, trying to take it easy so Zeller wouldn't rattle around in the back like a loose marble.

"What were you doing in Burundi?" Maud asked. "Joe was there two years ago and loved it."

"Scouting locations," Zeller said. "Like I was doing here." He flipped a hand to indicate Jubilee Mansions as a whole. "Someone told me there was a great house up here, with an observatory at the top, and a couple of turrets. Sounded perfect for one of the scenes in *Barbary Close*. You know the one. I took a wrong turn, and the car crapped out before I could visit it, though."

"We can drive you past, if you want," I said, with absolutely no idea what scene he was referring to, since I hadn't read the book. I turned right on the main drag through the housing area, rather than left to exit past the gatehouse. "It's just up here." I slowed as we drew near the Gaebler mansion, not the largest but definitely one of the most distinctive homes in the area. It was made of gray stone with crenellated turrets at either end. The house was mostly two stories, but a segment in the middle rose to three stories and was crowned with a glass dome. Against the now steely sky, and surrounded by wind-whipped trees, bare of leaves, and a nine-foot-high iron fence topped with pointy arrow-shaped finials, it looked properly gothic, someplace Dr. Frankenstein might perform his experiments. I'd done an event for the Gaeblers once, though, and I knew it was much warmer and homier on the inside than it looked from here.

Zeller hung over my seat to get a better look through the windshield. He smelled of spicy cologne. "Blimey. What an eyesore. It's perfect. Think the owners would be willing to let us use it?"

"No idea," I said, pulling into the driveway so I could turn around. "They're an older couple, and they spend the winters in Florida. I don't know if they've left for Clearwater Beach yet or not."

"I'm sure we can come to terms." He tried to input something on his smartphone, remembered that the battery was dead, cursed, pulled a business card out of his wallet, and jotted a note.

"Where else are you planning to film around here?" Maud asked.

"I'm in talks with the management of the Rocky Peaks Golf and Country Club, and I think my company can make it worth their while to let us film on the back nine for a week. My buddy Seb McManus is going to let us use his ski lodge, too."

Sebastian McManus was the billionaire who owned the closest ski resort to Heaven.

"You know," he said, "when we start filming, I can make sure you both get parts as extras. Maybe even a line or two of dialogue." He announced it like he was conferring a knighthood on us, or at least telling us we'd won the Lotto.

"I've got a SAG card," Maud said, surprising me but apparently not Zeller.

"I thought you looked familiar," he said. Snapping

his fingers twice, he ended with a forefinger pointed at Maud. "*The Lost Ones*, am I right? You played the skinny prostitute."

Maud nodded. "The pinnacle of my acting career."

"You should've kept at it," he said. "You had a future."

I drew up at the curb in front of the Columbine. "End of the line," I said.

Zeller jumped out of the van. "I appreciate the ride," he said. "Keep an eye on the local rag. We'll advertise when we start looking for extras. You two are *in*." He thumped his hand against the van and walked up the sidewalk toward the inn.

"So, you're ready to relaunch your screen career?" I teased Maud. I knew she'd done some acting, but I hadn't realized she was serious enough about it to have a Screen Actors Guild membership.

She stretched her legs out and flexed her feet in their socks and Tevas. "It was a short-lived phase, but it was fun while it lasted. I didn't have the patience for it. There's a lot of standing around and waiting in the movie biz. If I'd kept acting, I'd have done more stage work."

I cranked the ignition. "How many movies were you in?"

"Five," she said, "but one never got released. This was back in the days before flicks that didn't live up to their producers' expectations got released straight to video."

"Did you ever work with anyone famous?"

"Jack Nicholson," she said with a reminiscent smile. "They used to talk about Warren Beatty being a playboy, but he had nothing on Jack."

I snuck a glance at her profile, and saw the smile widen, deepening the lines bracketing her mouth. Somehow, I had no trouble believing she'd attracted Jack Nicholson's attention.

I started to angle into the road, when I glanced in the side mirror and saw a police car pull up across the street. Officer Hardaway got out and marched into the Columbine with a purposeful stride. I stomped on the brakes, bringing us to a lurching halt, at the same time Maud said, "Stop. That's an HPD vehicle. What's it doing here?"

I was already halfway out of the van. "I don't know, but I think we should find out, don't you?"

Chapter 20

Jogging back to the inn, Maud and I burst through the door to find a chaotic scene in progress. It seemed like every guest at the inn was gathered in the foyer. Francesca Bugle was on the stairs, dressed to go out with a rust-colored boiled-wool jacket and a black felt hat with an embroidered design. Cosmo Zeller looked over her shoulder, nostrils flaring like he smelled a bad odor. The Aldringhams were clustered near the dining room door, Allyson sandwiched between her parents. Her face was ghost white. Mary and Lucas Stewart were squeezed into the small hallway that led to the kitchen, and also looked nervous. Surely they didn't think their charade was arrest-worthy? Or was there more to the story of the stolen manuscript than I suspected? Sandy Milliken stood in front of Officer Hardaway, a bucket with a mop standing in it at her feet. Everyone was talking and asking questions. Officer Hardaway seemed overwhelmed by the hubbub and was having trouble making herself heard.

Maud put two fingers in her mouth and shrilled a whistle. Everyone shut up.

"Thank you, ma'am," Officer Hardaway said. "Now,

as I was saying, I need to escort Allyson Aldringham to the police station. Which of you is Allyson?"

Allyson took a hesitant step forward. "I'm Allyson," she said. She wore a short baby-doll-style dress of pale blue that made her look younger than her years.

Constance shoved past her daughter. "What is this in reference to?" she asked haughtily. "I simply must know why you want to see my daughter. I'm sure there's been a mistake."

Her contemptuous attitude straightened Officer Hardaway's spine. "I'm not at liberty to give you details," she said, sounding happy to be able to frustrate Constance's quest for information. "We are hoping she can help us with our inquiries. Ms. Aldringham can fill you in when she gets back. If you please, ma'am?" She gestured for Allyson to precede her out the door.

"I'm going to call a lawyer," Merle said.

Constance looked at her husband with rare approval. "Don't say a word until the lawyer gets there, Allyson. Not a word."

As if taking her mother's advice immediately to heart, Allyson nodded mutely and let Officer Hardaway escort her from the inn. At least she wasn't in handcuffs. I couldn't imagine what new evidence had appeared in between our leaving Hart and arriving here. I wasn't too sure he would tell me.

"I need to find a lawyer," Merle said. "Someone local."

He was talking to Sandy, but I answered. "Doug Elvaston. He's the best in town." I reeled off his cell phone number from memory. We'd dated off and on since we were high school juniors; that number was engraved on my brain forever. Merle thanked me and went outside to call Doug.

Francesca Bugle descended the stairs, with sharp *pock*ing sounds from her low-heeled pumps at every step. "Well, I would never have guessed that sweet girl was involved in a murder," she said, shaking her head.

"It's like in a TV show," Mary Stewart put in.

Everyone turned to look at her, puzzled. She made quite a picture wearing skinny jeans and a white top printed with gray flowers. Her hair was a flame cascading over her shoulders. She widened her eyes and blinked once. "The culprit on TV detective shows is always the least likely seeming person, who doesn't really have a reason for being in the show at all, and who doesn't have an immediately obvious motive. I wonder what her motive was."

Lucas, looking concerned, nudged her before she could speculate further about Allyson's possible motives.

Constance drew herself up and spoke in tones that would freeze lava. "Allyson wasn't involved in that murder in any way whatsoever. She simply isn't capable of killing someone. She doesn't have it in her." She sounded confident, but her hand trembled as she adjusted the pashmina draped over her shoulders, pulling it closer.

Merle came back inside. His hair was mussed and his beard had furrows, as if he'd raked his fingers through it. Worry tightened his sun-mottled brow. "The lawyer says he'll meet us at the police department," he said. "Come on, Connie."

Maud put a hand on his arm. "Is there anything we can do, Merle?"

Giving her a grateful look, he said, "Not right now, but thanks. I'll call you later." Taking Constance's elbow, he hustled her down the narrow hall leading to a back door and the inn's small parking area. Even in the midst of the drama, it tickled me to see him take charge. I'd thought he was a total milquetoast, under his wife's thumb, but clearly there was more to him.

"That's the old Merle," Maud said in a low voice, a smile hovering around her lips.

Now that the show was over, Francesca hooked a purse over her arm and went out the front door, saying something about wanting to do some souvenir shopping. Cosmo Zeller and the Stewarts disappeared upstairs.

When it was only Sandy, Maud, and I left in the foyer, Sandy said, "This has been the longest week. I don't know why, but I thought authors would be a nice, quiet bunch of guests, easy to get along with, tucked up in their rooms writing most of the time. Instead of which, I find them all over the house at the strangest hours—they argue, drink like sailors on liberty, and are finicky about their food. As if that weren't enough, one of them pisses someone off bad enough that I get a brick through my window—thank God for insurance—there's a murder, and now an arrest."

"She wasn't arrested," I said.

"As good as." Sandy shook her head. "On top of all that, my dishwasher broke and flooded the kitchen—we'll have to replace it, so there goes our weekend in

Denver next month—Dave's cold has turned into walking pneumonia, and I can't find the snow globe paperweight my parents brought back from their honeymoon in Japan." She patted the registration counter. "You remember it—it always sat right here."

Maud spoke up. "Who was arguing, and what were they arguing about?"

Good question.

Sandy rolled her eyes. "Who wasn't? The diva—"

I took that to mean Constance.

"—harangues her husband nonstop. She was tearing a strip off him about losing money on the stock market when I walked in on them in the sunroom. And she cuts that daughter of hers no slack, either. Pearl, one of my maids, heard her through the bedroom door, telling Allyson that she was done, that she wasn't bailing her out ever again, and that she was tired of being embarrassed in front of her friends. Whatever that means. Treats me like a scullery wench, too, when I made more money on Wall Street in one year than she makes in five years." Dropping her voice and glancing up the stairs, she continued. "That Stewart gal's brother has a temper on him, too, although I must say she gives as good as she gets. You can tell they're brother and sister by the way they bicker. My brother, Mike, and I were just like that."

I kept a straight face at that and avoided looking at Maud.

"That movie guy doesn't fight with anyone, but he's an odd duck. Hasn't unpacked a single thing. Keeps all his duds in his suitcases and keeps them locked." She sniffed. "My gals are all bonded—we've never had trouble with theft at the Columbine." She let out a long breath. "I will be glad to see the back of them come Monday morning. I'm sorry. I shouldn't be talking to you like this. I needed to let off some steam, and with Dave under the weather, well—I'm sorry I unloaded on you."

"No problem," I said. "I get that way myself. I know you're busy, so we'll get out of your hair." Impulsively, I hugged her. She disengaged almost immediately, but gave me a crooked smile.

"I'm not usually much of one for hug therapy, but that helped. Now, shoo, you two, so I can get the floors mopped and pop some cinnamon scones in the oven."

Maud and I shooed.

After dropping Maud off at her house, and extracting her promise to call me the minute she heard from Merle, I drove home and pondered my options. It was just noon, and I didn't have to be at the Club to set up until five o'clock. I drifted into my bedroom and dumped the contents of my laundry hamper onto the floor. I sat cross-legged on the floor, and began to sort the clothes, placing a yoga top in the cold pile and a pair of jeans in the warm pile. My hand sorted automatically while I thought. I could stay home and do some cleaning and laundry, but that had little appeal. I wanted to make progress on this case, find out who killed Van Allen and why, set Lola's mind at ease, and make sure a murderer didn't leave Heaven on Monday morning. I knew there was no point to calling Hart and asking why Officer Hardaway had picked up Allyson for questioning, and even less point in calling Doug, who would never breach client confidentiality. I chewed on my lower lip. Socks in warm, bra in cold, yellow blouse in cold.

A thought came to me. What if . . . what if Maud was right about Van Allen taking the mysterious package with him to the Club, but wrong about the killer stealing it? Van Allen was a career criminal, nobody's stooge. Would he walk into a meeting with a blackmail victim without taking some precautions? I didn't think so. At least, I amended, I hoped not. Maybe he was stabbed because he refused to give up the package, or maybe Van Allen tried to steal the money from his mark without giving up his package, planning to continue to bleed him or her for years to come. He miscalculated by not realizing the mark had a weapon and was prepared to use it in such a public place. I wished I had a way to get in touch with Sharla and ask her more about Van Allen. Wait a minute. . . . I did have a way to get in touch, albeit a roundabout one. I pulled out my cell phone, located Flavia Dunbarton's number, and punched it in.

When she answered with, "*Grand Junction Gabbler*, Dunbarton speaking," I said, "It's Amy-Faye Johnson. If you're interested in some breaking news on the Van Allen murder, you might want to check with the HPD."

She tried to get me to give more details, but I figured I was skating close enough to the line by giving her a heads-up; I wasn't going to risk Hart's wrath by telling her about the car or about Allyson "helping the police with their inquiries." I promised her a quote if my name happened to come up during her conversation with the police.

She thanked me for the tip and hung up. I returned my cell phone to my pocket, hoping that she would get a story out of Hart or Chief Uggams, and hoping that Sharla would get back in touch when she read it. Throwing the load of whites into the washing machine, I climbed back into the van and headed for the Club. If Van Allen had hidden the package, it would be at the Club somewhere. Anticipation tingled through me. The treasure hunt was back on.

I decided to start my search in the pro shop. It was open until seven o'clock on Saturday nights at this time of year and it made sense that Van Allen would have come in this way. I had stopped for a sub sandwich on my way over, so it was coming up on one o'clock when I parked on the golf-course side of the building. Even with a wind stiff enough to knock balls well off course, the fairways and greens were crowded with golfers trying to get in an extra round or two before a big snowfall ended their season. I thought I saw Troy Widefield Jr., Brooke's husband, piloting a cart, and waved, but he didn't see me. I pushed through the glass door to the pro shop. Betty Bullock, the Club's pro, was ringing up a Windbreaker for a customer, but looked up when the bell over the door pealed. A short, no-nonsense woman in her sixties who had competed on the LPGA tour for six or seven years, she had skin the texture of an old leather golf bag, baked by too many rounds in the sun, and white crow's-feet where the skin hadn't tanned because she was smiling or squinting. She wore a polo shirt with "Rocky Peaks Golf and Country Club" embroidered over her left breast, and a matching skort. Her straw-blond hair, liberally laced with gray, was shorter than I remembered, and waxed into soft spikes.

She grinned at me when the customer left. "You're not here for a lesson, I hope?"

I smiled in return. Ever since I'd taken a few lessons from her, discovering that I had no aptitude whatsoever for hitting a little white ball with a long metal stick, she had teased me that if I ever came back for more, it was going to be her cue to retire. "No, you don't get to ride off into the sunset today," I told her. "Actually, I'm hoping you'll let me search the place."

"Did you lose something?"

When I explained what I was after, she looked intrigued. "I wasn't working Saturday night—Louis was on—so I didn't see the guy you're talking about. Heard about it all the next day, of course. There hasn't been so much gossip floating around this place since that busboy started a fire in the kitchen because he was mad at the pastry chef for cheating on him." She came around the counter. "I'll help you look. I know every inch of this store, and every item in inventory, so I can't imagine that I wouldn't have tripped over this mysterious 'package' before now, but let's have a go at it."

We searched for half an hour with Betty occasionally attending to customers. I unstacked the golf ball twelve-packs, looked inside the spinning garment racks, pulled golf clubs out of bins to look down inside them, and rearranged all the shoe boxes. Betty even checked the stockroom, although she said it was unlikely that a customer would have gained access to it. At the end of the half hour, we had nothing to show for our labors. "It's not here," Betty announced.

"No, I guess not," I said. Damn. I had so hoped Van Allen's package would be in the pro shop. Searching the entire club was a much larger task, and I wasn't sure Wallace Pinnecoose would be thrilled about my poking around. For Wallace, the Club's reputation took precedence over any other consideration. I was sure he'd be happy to let a murderer escape justice if that would keep the Club from being dragged through the mud. I was disappointed, but nowhere near giving up. The package was here somewhere. It had to be.

Before I could decide whether to tackle Wallace for permission to search now, or to search surreptitiously tonight when I was back here for the fiftieth birthday party, my phone rang. It was Maud.

"Merle called," she said. "He needs a sounding board and I'm elected. I'm meeting him at Elysium, if you want to join us."

Boy, did I ever want to join them. I said a hasty thanks and good-bye to Betty and hit the road.

Chapter 21

The Elysium Maud spoke of was Elysium Brewing, the first brewpub in Heaven, on the easternmost outskirts of the town. It happened to belong to my younger brother, Derek. I had invested in it, though, as had my folks, so I was happy to see quite a few cars in the lot at the tail end of the lunch hour. The building, a former factory, was three narrow stories. Inside, sunlight streamed through the small windows and lit up the booths with their orange leatherette upholstery. When I'd heard the pub's decorator was going with orange, I'd been skeptical, but against the dark wood and the bar's brass fittings, it looked really good, especially in the evening under the soft glow from the antiquey-looking pendant lights. A wide staircase on my left led to an open area with eight pool tables and an auxiliary bar on the second-floor, offices on the third floor, and a rooftop space that would eventually be a venue for private functions. Derek hadn't moved ahead with gussying up the roof yet because only a month ago his partner had been murdered there. A humongous stainless steel vat with tubing spiraling around it took up a large chunk of space. It sat in a glass enclosure so Colorado's craft-beer enthusiasts could watch the brewing process in action. Derek was inside the enclosure, so intent on checking gauges that he didn't notice me.

I spotted Maud and Merle in a booth and went to join them, waving to my mom behind the bar as I did. She was busy with two men eating at the bar, but she waved back. When Derek's business partner died, she and Dad took on some responsibilities at the pub. She'd been enjoying her retirement from the library, and I thought she'd get tired of helping to manage the bar and its employees, but she seemed to thrive on it. Maud scooted over to make room for me on the bench seat, and I sat. Merle, across from us, wore a lugubrious expression as he buried his face in a foamy mug of beer. He lowered the glass to show bits of foam speckling his mustache and beard. The foam flecks weren't much paler than his face.

"We ordered lunch," Maud said, "but we were waiting for you to discuss Allyson's situation. Okay now, Merle, tell us what happened."

He started to answer but was interrupted by the arrival of a server I didn't know. When she had left with my order for water, Merle cleared his throat and said, "The police found Allyson's fingerprints in the manager's office at the country club."

Ooh, not good. Off the top of my head, I couldn't think of a single legitimate reason for Allyson to have been in Wallace's office.

"Where?" Maud asked.

Merle licked droplets of beer off his mustache. "On a display case and on a golf trophy."

"Lucky the victim wasn't clubbed to death with that," Maud said.

Small comfort. "What does Allyson say?" I asked. "Did she say why she was in there?"

Rocking his heavy-bottomed mug back and forth so the beer sloshed, and watching the suds rise up one side of the glass and then the other, he said, "She said she got turned around on her way to the restroom. When she realized she was in the wrong place, she looked around out of curiosity. I understand the manager has some nice artwork in there. I'm sure no one can blame her for taking a look." He sounded defensive. Not surprising.

Maud and I carefully didn't look at each other and there was an awkward moment of silence. I didn't think either of us was buying Allyson's story; I certainly wasn't.

The server appeared with my water, and slid bowls in front of Maud and Merle. Maud's was tomato basil soup, and Merle had shepherd's pie. I could tell by the lovely aroma of lamb rising in the steam. They each sampled their lunches, and then Maud directed a piercing look at her old friend.

"Merle, you and I have known each other a long time, long enough for me to say, 'Hogwash.' That story won't fly. If you don't want your daughter locked up for killing Trent Van Allen, I think you'd better come clean with us. You clearly know more than you're saying—it's written all over your face. You never could tell a lie, my friend. Remember that rally for student rights at Berkeley, and what you said to the dean when he questioned you? Even a two-year-old would have seen through it."

"Dean Pugh certainly did," Merle said with the ghost of a smile. He seemed to be recovering some of his color as he ate the shepherd's pie. "I thought he was going to expel me. It was a near-run thing. That wasn't as bad as the time when—"

It seemed as if he was going to seize the opportunity to wander down Remember-When Lane, but Maud brought him ruthlessly back to the point at hand. "Allyson," she said.

His shoulders slumped and he drained the rest of the beer in his mug. "Allyson," he finally said, his Adam's apple working, "was probably in the manager's office to steal something."

Maud and I goggled at him. He acknowledged our reaction with a small, rueful smile, and added, "My daughter is a kleptomaniac."

"That explains it," Maud said, more to herself than to Merle.

"Explains what?" he asked.

"Her expulsions from school, her inability to hold a job. She steals and gets caught, then gets kicked out or fired, right?"

An ugly maroon flush flooded his face. "How do you know that? Have you been digging into our lives, snooping on us?"

Maud shifted as if the seat had suddenly grown too hard. "We did a little research, yes. We Googled everyone we thought might have a connection to Van Allen."

I knew her research had gone way beyond Googling, but I kept my mouth shut.

"My God, Maud, how could you invade our privacy like that?" He set his hands against the table's edge and pushed back as far as he could go, denting the upholstery of the booth's back. He glared at his old flame. "What else did you find out? I used to admire your 'research' skills when we were in college, when you were using them to discredit the people and organizations responsible for strip-mining and DDT use and unlawful disposal of toxic waste, but I never thought you'd turn against me."

"I haven't 'turned against' you, Merle," she said crisply. "Far from it. I want to help Allyson, and unless you—or she—comes clean, that won't be possible. What did your lawyer say about her case?"

He took a couple of deep breaths, breathing out heavily through his nose. "Elvaston seems to know his stuff," he said finally. "He's sharp and he was kind to Allyson. Thank you for recommending him," he added, looking at me. I nodded, and he went on. "He says the police don't have enough to arrest Allyson, although they got a warrant for the clothes she was wearing that night. I don't know if he believed her story about looking for the bathroom—probably not—and he suggested to me and Constance that we try to get her to remember a few more details about that night. I took that as his tactful way of saying he thought her story was so much bull hockey." He scrubbed the back of his hand across his mouth.

"Did she tell you anything more?" Maud asked more gently, eyeing her friend with concern.

"Not a word. She won't give me or Constance the time of day. She literally did not say a single word from the time she came out of the interview room until we got back to the Columbine. She went straight upstairs and locked herself in. That's where Constance is now—trying to talk sense into her, although it's damn hard to have to do it through a locked door in a public inn." Looking around for the server, he raised his mug to signal for a refill.

"You know," I said, "it's possible that Allyson might have seen something that would point to the real killer. What time did she say she was in the office?"

"I don't know," Merle said. "Must have been before Van Allen got killed, though, because I don't think she'd have stepped over his body to pilfer the place." The bitterness of an oft-disappointed parent made his voice harsh. I'd had a high school friend who was an alcoholic, and Merle sounded just like his parents had after numerous cycles of drying out and relapsing, of AA and rehab and DUI arrests.

Maud laid her hand over his where it rested on the table, and he didn't pull away. "We'll have to search her room," he said, "so we can return whatever she's stolen since we've been here. I thought she was getting better, that the new therapist was having a positive effect. . . ."

When his second beer arrived, Derek's highly popular Exorcise Your Demons IPA, he became downright loquacious, giving us chapter and verse on Allyson's history of theft, therapy, expulsion, and treatments. I listened to "fluoxetine," "trazodone," and "sertraline" with half an ear, trying to figure out what Allyson's presence in Wallace's office the night of the murder might mean. For the moment, I was discounting the theory that she had murdered Van Allen. There was no hint of a connection between them, and I could see why she hadn't owned up to being in the office if she had been there to steal. I assumed that if she'd witnessed the actual murder, she'd have come forward, but maybe she saw something else. Wasn't it possible that she had seen someone headed toward the office when she was leaving it? Or overheard something?

"We need to talk to Allyson," Maud and I said in unison. I looked at her, startled, wondering if she'd been reading my mind.

"Great minds think alike," she said. "What do you think, Merle?"

"You're welcome to try." He shrugged. He hefted his glass like he was going to take a swig, looked at the golden liquid left in it, and set it down. Pushing the mug away, he slid out of the booth, and threw two twenties onto the table. "No time like the present."

We caravanned to the Columbine, arriving shortly after two thirty. I was conscious of the time, knowing I needed to be back at the Club no later than five to make sure preparations for tonight's birthday event were proceeding smoothly. I trusted Wallace and his staff, but I wanted to run an eye over everything before the guests arrived. Trust, but verify. That could have been my motto. Merle drove around to the guest lot in the back and Maud and I parked on the street. We walked into the inn to find Merle and Constance arguing outside the small parlor where Sandy served cocktails.

"—not making restitution this time," Constance was saying in an angry whisper. "She's an adult, and she simply must start taking responsibility for her actions."

"I agree," Merle said.

"You do?" Surprise rang in Constance's voice. She recovered after a second, adding a waspish, "Well, it's about time." Spotting Maud and me, she said, "What do you want?"

"They're here to talk to Allyson," Merle said, laying a hand on Constance's arm when she moved as if to block the stairs. "Let them. It can't hurt, and maybe it will help."

For a moment it looked like she would shake off her husband, but she tightened her lips and said, "Oh, go on, then. Second door on the left. The Alpenglow Room."

Maud and I climbed the wide stairs before Constance could change her mind and hesitated outside a door with a ceramic sign hanging by a ribbon. "Alpenglow" was painted on the sign, above a rendering of mountains topped with sunshine. The other doors along the hall, all closed, had similar signs with mountainy-sounding names: Peakview, Aspen Glade, Whistling Marmot. "What now?" I whispered.

"We improvise," Maud said. She threw back her shoulders and rapped on the door.

When Allyson didn't respond, I said, "Allyson, it's Amy-Faye Johnson and Maud Bell. We know you didn't have anything to do with what happened last Saturday, but you might be able to help us figure out who did. You don't want the murderer getting away with it, do you?"

"I don't care." The words were muffled by congestion, and I had a vision of Allyson in there crying.

"Of course you do," Maud said briskly. "You're not the kind of girl who wants a murderer running around. Open up so we can chat. We won't take long."

I thought I heard a click, like a door opening, but when I looked over my shoulder, all the doors were still closed. Someone who didn't want to get in the middle of a disturbance, I suspected. If Constance had been up there trying to coax Allyson into opening up for the last hour, the guests were probably heartily sick of the drama.

I turned back around to see that Allyson had opened the door. "You might as well come in," she said. She spoke through a handful of tissues she was using to dry her eyes and streaming nose. Maud and I stepped into the dim room, and she closed the door again. The room was small, but beautifully appointed, with an antique bed and dresser, a rocking chair, and apricot-painted walls that evoked the alpenglow that painted the mountaintops just before sunrise. The four-poster bed was covered with a crocheted spread, considerably mussed, as if Allyson had flung herself onto the bed to cry her eyes out.

"What did you mean about me helping to catch a murderer?" she asked, sniffing. Her mouse brown hair was rumpled, sticking up in the back, and her red-rimmed eyes reminded me of my fourth-grade class's white rabbit, Bunnykins. She had Constance's strong chin, though, and her mouth was set in a resolute line.

"You were in the manager's office Saturday night," Maud said. "Did you see anyone, coming or going?"

Allyson was shaking her head, limp hair flopping, before Maud finished asking the question. "The police already asked me that. I didn't see anyone."

"What about sounds? Did you hear any voices?" I asked. "Or anything from the parking lot—a car's engine, a door closing, anything?"

She wrinkled her brow, trying to remember. "I wasn't concentrating on noises from outside. I've been stealing for a long time now, it seems like my whole life"—she said it casually, as if it was a fact of existence like allergies or dandruff—"and I'm good at listening, but I listen for certain things. You know, footsteps, doors opening, sounds that mean someone might catch me. I tune out everything else. I'm sorry."

"What made you go in there in the first place?" I asked.

She twisted her hands together. "It was the stress. I steal when I'm stressed. It's like . . . like an outlet. When I'm with my mom for any length of time—well, you've seen her. She treats me like I'm twelve, not twenty-two, and she tells every group she talks to about how she's had a bestseller every year except the year I was born. How do you think that makes me feel?" She sniffed hard. "She drives me crazy. Anyway, Saturday night, she was going on and on about how my costume wasn't appropriate, how I should have come as a character from one of her stupid books, and I just . . . I just needed . . ." She stopped and dragged in a ragged breath. "There wasn't anything in the public areas worth lifting, so I just kind of wandered. I came to that hall with all the trophies and the artwork, and I . . . browsed. The office door wasn't locked, so I went in, just to see."

She stilled and her eyes fixed on a spot on the wall behind me. I could tell she wasn't seeing us, that she was reliving her time in Wallace's office. It was a little eerie, frankly.

Her voice grew softer, more monotone. "I never know what I'm going to want in advance. Sometimes an object speaks to me. Like the crystal paperweight at the inn. I'd been in and out past it a couple of dozen times before I just needed to have it. I stood in the doorway a moment, making sure no one was coming. A man came out of the restroom and went toward the party. He didn't see me."

I glanced at Maud with raised eyebrows, and she shrugged. The timing was wrong for the restroom visitor to be the killer. The man probably only needed to relieve himself of a couple of beers or martinis.

"What did he look like?" I asked anyway.

As if she'd forgotten we were in the room, Allyson started. "Oh! Uh, I'm not sure. I only saw his back. Tallish—maybe six feet? Short hair. Just a guy."

"So then what happened?" Maud prompted.

Allyson blinked twice, slowly, and continued. "I went in—it was dim. The only light was from a desk lamp. Heavy furniture, kind of ugly. I wandered toward the desk. Computer, printer, iPod dock—not interested. I never want anything big or bulky. A trophy—shiny and gold. I picked it up. It was a golfer, a man—it had a plaque. It felt awkward, heavier at the base than at the top. I put it back. Framed photos—nothing special. They didn't speak to me. There were display cases on the far wall. I went to them. Indian jewelry—turquoise and silver, beads. Pretty, delicate. A beaded bracelet that I couldn't take my eyes off. Intricate designs in green and black and yellow, a silver clasp. I tried to open the glass lid, but it was locked. Damn. I started toward the desk to look for the key, but I wasn't watching where I was going, and I bumped into a table. A stack of books came tumbling down—so loud!" For the first time since starting her recital, Allyson made eye contact with me, her eyes wide, her mouth slightly open. "Too loud. I was sure someone had heard. Someone would come. My mom would be so mad. I didn't even bother to pick up the books. I ran out of there and down the hall and back to the party." Her gaze went from me to Maud. "I told you I couldn't help."

"Thanks, anyway," Maud said. "If you think of anything else—"

"I don't want to steal, you know," Allyson said, her fingers scratching at a spot on her neck below her right ear. "Like right now, I don't want to steal. I don't go around all day looking for things to lift. But then sometimes, I *have* to steal. This itchy feeling will come over me, sort of a cross between a tingle and hives, and I have to steal something. I just have to."

She didn't say it as if she were trying to get us to understand. Something in her voice told me she'd given up on making anyone understand her compulsion. She was explaining, nothing more. I felt sad for her and for Constance and Merle. I felt like telling her to go for a hike, or to the gym, when she needed an outlet for stress, but I had to suppose a therapist or three had already tried to help her find more acceptable ways of relieving stress. I was no psychologist and I wondered how common kleptomania was.

"Sometimes I give stuff back," she offered with a tremulous smile. "When I can remember where I got it, and if I can do it without getting caught."

I caught a glimpse of the bedside clock and realized I needed to beat feet if I was going to shower and change, and still get to the Club on time to set up for the birthday party. I signaled to Maud and we said our good-byes to Allyson. She stood in the middle of the floor, unmoving, as we left.

"That is one mixed-up young woman," Maud said in a low voice as we descended the stairs. "I'm going to read up on kleptomania."

Constance and Merle were hovering at the foot of the stairs, and Constance took one look at us and plunged up them without a word. Merle looked at Maud. "How'd it go?"

"How long has it been going on?" Maud asked.

"The stealing?" He tugged at beard hairs. "Since she was five. It started shortly after she entered kindergarten. She has a form of kleptomania called sporadic, where there are brief episodes of stealing interspersed with longer remission periods. Every time, we think she won't go back to stealing, and every time, well, here we are again."

I thought about what Allyson had said about stress. I was grateful I turned to chocolate for stress relief, rather than theft or something equally destructive. I surreptitiously patted my derriere, for once not minding the extra padding. A few extra pounds were little enough to carry around compared with the weight of guilt and frustration Allyson and her whole family carried.

"I can't even imagine," Maud said quietly as we crossed the hall to the front door.

I knew she was talking about Allyson's compulsion.

"Nope, me neither."

Faint knocking and indistinct voices drifted from the second floor, and I paused with my hand on the knob. I realized someone was going door-to-door upstairs. Doors opened and closed, and footsteps shuffled. I turned and looked up to see Constance and Allyson standing on the landing at the top of the stairs. The Stewarts, Cosmo Zeller, and Francesca Bugle, all looking curious, gaggled behind them. Constance and Allyson started down, with Allyson carrying a wicker basket.

"Wait," Constance told me and Maud. "Allyson has a few things she wants to return." Constance gripped the banister so hard the bones of her hand stood out white against the thin flesh.

I wondered how many times she'd played out some version of this same scene.

"Merle," she said, surging into the breakfast room, "get Sandy and Dave. I think that's everybody, right, Allyson?"

Without looking up, Allyson nodded. We all trooped into the cheery room, bright with sunlight streaming through the side window. Allyson set the wicker basket on the nearest breakfast table, and then shuffled back a few steps, as if to dissociate herself from its contents.

"What did you say this is about again?" Lucas Stewart asked. He wore a raggedy T-shirt, flannel pajama bottoms, and flip-flops, and his hair was damp. I figured he'd just gotten out of the shower. He looked unbearably hot, but his hotness didn't affect me nearly so much now that I knew how he and Mary had conned Eloise Hufnagle. It was almost as if the knowledge had smudged the sharp lines of his cheekbones, dulled the blue of his eyes, or softened the muscular planes of his chest. Impossible of course, but he definitely didn't seem as handsome as he had when I'd first seen him at Book Bliss.

Mary approached the table and rattled the basket. "What's in here?" She started poking through the contents as Merle returned, bringing Sandy Milliken and her husband, Dave. A big man, Dave was clearly still suffering from his cold, honking his nose loudly into a tissue as he entered.

Several "bless yous" welcomed him.

"I've got an important conference call with the studio," Cosmo said impatiently. "What's this all about?" He sat in a chair pulled out from a table, ankle resting on his knee, foot jiggling.

Allyson gave her mother a pleading look, but Constance shook her head resolutely. Merle, plucking at his beard, said, "You can do it, baby."

With a fleeting smile for her father, Allyson straightened her shoulders and said, "I've, uh, collected a few things here that, uh, might belong to some of you. I, uh, wanted to make sure you got them back." Without further explanation, she gestured limply toward the wicker basket.

I saw Maud whispering to Sandy by the door. Sandy at first looked taken aback, then nodded slowly. She walked toward the table as everyone else hung back. Peering into the basket, she shifted a couple of items and then lifted a snow globe. She shook it vigorously so the "snow" became a blizzard obscuring the pagoda inside. "My paperweight," she said. "I'm so glad you found it for me, Allyson." She leaned over to hug the girl.

Allyson stiffened, her eyes wide with surprise, and then returned Sandy's hug awkwardly. I shot a look at Maud, who had her arms crossed over her chest and a satisfied smile on her face. I didn't know what she'd said to Sandy, but it had apparently convinced the B and B owner to be charitable. "And, look, Dave," Sandy said, returning to the basket and rooting through it again. "Here's that ugly shot glass you've been looking for, the one from that bar in Texas. I was hoping it was lost for good."

Dave greeted the return of his shot glass with a massive sneeze. The glass tumbled out of his paw and bounced across the carpet toward me. I picked it up, noting the grinning skull etched in the glass above the words "Dead Man's Saloon," and the tarnished silver rim. "Is it broken?" Sandy asked hopefully.

I shook my head, and she heaved an exaggerated sigh.

Dave, mumbling something about "more Sudafed," bore his prize away in the direction of the kitchen and their living quarters.

Mary Stewart looked into the basket next, and pulled out a silver bangle bracelet and a travel alarm clock with an iridescent face. "I thought I'd forgotten to bring my clock," she exclaimed. "And my bracelet." Her long, narrow eyes took in Allyson's discomfort. "I could swear I never even took this out of my suitcase, so I can't imagine how you came to find it. I *simply* can't imagine." She faced Constance as she said it, rather than Allyson, and I could tell she was wondering how she could use the situation to her benefit. I figured she'd be hitting Constance up for a quote for her next book, or another joint signing, before the day was over.

Whatever Constance might have said was preempted by Lucas's exclamation. "My Super Tool!" He pulled out each of the blades and gadgets from a lethal-looking Swiss Army–type knife, as if to assure himself they were all there. He polished the longest blade with the hem of his shirt, rubbing at something sticky. "Where did you get this?" His gaze skewered Allyson.

The girl seemed to shrink in on herself. "I—I sometimes—I never remember exactly. . . ." She trailed off. Lucas looked like he would pursue it, but Mary, perhaps taking her cue from Sandy, put a hand on his arm and shook her head.

Curious myself, I walked to the table, and looked into the basket. I was surprised to see something I recognized. "Hey, my sunglasses." I plucked them out, and slid them atop my head. "I've been looking for these—couldn't imagine where I left them."

Maud approached and looked over my shoulder. "Nope, nothing of mine," she said. I wasn't surprised; Maud secured her glasses, pens, and whatnot in the multiple pockets of her cargo pants, and rarely misplaced anything.

Francesca Bugle, looking more casual than I'd yet seen her in a pair of stiff jeans topped with a Blackhawks sweatshirt, strode forward. Without the ubiquitous hats, her hair was a solid dark brown, devoid of highlights or grays, that hinted at a home dye job. Without ceremony, she examined the basket's contents, and pulled out a silver-framed three-by-five photo with a little gasp. Before she clasped it to her bosom, I caught a glimpse of a grinning young man leaning against a highly polished car of 1980s vintage. "My brother," Francesca said. "I didn't even miss this until this morning."

Newly suspicious of "brothers" and "sisters" because of the Stewarts, I cocked a doubtful brow, but when she held the photo out to show everyone, I could see the young man looked enough like her to be her twin. Clutching the frame in one hand, Francesca moved toward Allyson. The young woman looked nervously up through her lashes at the older woman's approach.

"You're a klepto, I take it," Francesca said.

The word jolted all of us, I think, but there was no judgment or condemnation in her voice.

Still as a mouse facing a cat, Allyson slid her eyes sideways, looking to her mother for guidance. Constance looked like she was going to leap to her daughter's defense, but Merle stopped her with a hand on her arm.

"That's got to be miserable, and if you don't want to talk about it, I understand," Francesca said, either unaware of or ignoring the family byplay. "But I'd love to talk to you about it before I leave. I've just realized that making my protagonist's best friend a kleptomaniac in the follow-on to *Barbary Close* would open up all sorts of plot possibilities. I don't know why I didn't think of it before. I was debating whether to make her an alcoholic or give her a gambling addiction, but those are so overdone." Enthusiasm made her talk faster. "Is kleptomania considered an illness like alcoholism? When did you come down with it? No, that's probably not the way to phrase it, is it?" She laughed heartily at herself. "When did you first know? What are the treatments? Obviously, they don't always work."

Constance drew herself up, prepared to be offended, but Francesca was so clearly following a train of thought and not meaning to offend that Constance deflated without saying anything.

"How has it affected your life, your relationships?" Francesca stopped herself with another laugh. "I have dozens of questions, but you probably don't want to talk about it here." She gestured to those of us staring with varying degrees of incredulity or surprise. "Can we talk in your room? When you're done here?"

Allyson gave a tiny nod, apparently never having met with quite this enthusiastic reaction to her disorder. "Ten minutes?" she whispered.

"Perfect." Carrying her brother's photo, Francesca sailed from the room, thumbing her smartphone as she went, undoubtedly looking up "kleptomania."

Sandy, anxious to move things along, turned to Cosmo Zeller. "Mr. Zeller, want to have a look?"

"I'm not missing anything," he said, a hint of distaste in his voice for the process. "But okay." He unfolded himself from the chair, and crossed to the table. "Nothing left in here but a set of keys," he said, upending the basket so the key ring jangled to the table. He nudged the keys with a forefinger. "Not mine." He skidded the basket across the table's polished top. "This has been entertaining, but I've got that phone call." Already pulling his cell phone from a pocket, he was punching a number in as he headed out of the room and out the front door. It closed heavily behind him.

Closest to the table, I picked up the keys and shook them, looking inquiringly at the people left in the room. Everyone shook their heads. Lucas said, "I've got to get dressed," and walked toward the stairs. Mary followed him a moment later. Merle and Constance, clearly relieved that no one was going to press charges against Allyson this time, drifted out, herding Allyson ahead of them. Sandy, probably also relieved that no one was going to sue the inn for the thefts, came forward to take the keys from me. She hefted them in one hand, puzzled.

"I don't think I know anyone who drives a Volkswagen," she said after inspecting them.

The word hit me like a gust of cold air. "A Volkswagen? Are you sure?"

"Of course. Look." Sandy held one key out, and I saw the distinctive V over the W logo. "What's so exciting about a VW?" she asked, apparently picking up on something in my expression.

Maud had come up to us and she explained, "The man who was killed last Saturday drove a VW station wagon. His keys weren't found."

"You think these are them?" Sandy was so surprised she dropped the key ring.

I pulled a pen from my purse and hooked it through the ring, a case of too little, too late, since Sandy, Cosmo, and I had all handled the keys. Allyson, too, undoubtedly.

Maud fished her cell phone from a side pocket of her cargo pants. "I should put the HPD on speed dial," she said, calling the police.

Already so late that I was going to have to sacrifice my shower, I left Maud to talk to the police, and broke a speed limit or two on my way home. At my house, I shucked my clothes, slicked on more deodorant in lieu of a shower, twisted my copper hair into a high bun, threw on the not-quite-knee-length black dress that was my fallback for many events, flicked on mascara, and dashed out the door again, headed for the

Club. I was in and out of the house in four minutes flat. Thank goodness I'd had the sense not to adopt Misty or any other pet. If everything was in order, which I believed it would be, I might have a few minutes to look for the mysterious package before the event kicked off. I put my pedal to the metal.

Chapter 22

Unfortunately, everything was not as shipshape as usual at the Club. Wallace Pinnecoose was out with the flu, and his new deputy was in charge. The young man was a recent graduate from the school of hospitality at the University of Denver, and he was smart and hardworking, but not very experienced. As a result, the staff had started setting up the tables in the Club's smaller party room too late, and half of them were still not finished when Al and I arrived. We took in the situation at a glance, and began to flap tablecloths over bare tables and slap silverware down. The centerpieces, delivered by a local florist, had been left in a sunny spot on the loading dock, and were sadly wilted. I commandeered two busboys and a dishwasher and put them to work reviving the arrangements with a trick Lola had taught me. We pulled the flowers from the vases, trimmed the stems with sharp knives, added cold water and three teaspoons of sugar to each vase, and reinserted the flowers. Luckily, there were only ten tables' worth of centerpieces to do. My dress was water-splotched (which is why I usually wear black or navy to events) and my fingers were pricked and bleeding in several spots from rose thorns by the time we finished.

We had barely set the last vase onto the last table when the honoree and his family arrived. I greeted them, went over the schedule of events with them (receiving line, toasts from preselected relatives and friends, slide show of the honoree from infanthood to the present day, dinner, opening of gag gifts, birthday cake, dancing), and gave Al a few last-minute instructions.

"I am not doing this when I turn fifty," Al said. He looked absurdly young in his black suit with the smiley face suspenders and bow tie. "I'll have all my friends over to the house—I'll own one by then, with any luck—throw some steaks on the grill, and tell them to help themselves to some brews from the cooler. Then maybe we'll play the mid-twenty-first-century version of World of Warcraft. This is too"—he searched for a word—"formal."

"Fusty."

"Stiff."

"Prim and proper."

Our vocabulary game was interrupted by a waiter as he banged through the swinging door near where we stood, and almost let a tray loaded with Caesar salads fall. After helping him right the tray, I told Al, "Hold down the fort for a few, would you? I'm going to take a look around."

Al perked up, his curiosity aroused. "What for?"

"I don't know exactly," I admitted. "Treasure."

"Buried?"

"I hope not." Without waiting for more questions, I strolled away. *Could* Van Allen have buried whatever it was, in a sand trap maybe? No, that was ludicrous.

Too hard, too risky. No, if the package was here, it was inside the Club, somewhere the casual visitor or staff member wouldn't trip over it, somewhere a guest could plausibly be, somewhere easy to access. When I added up those three requirements in my head, it left only a handful of places to search. Trying to be nonchalant, I lifted the cushions on the sofas and chairs in the lobby; asked Wallace's deputy if there was anything unclaimed in the lost and found and sorted through the box of sunglasses, golf visors, expensive pens, swim goggles, iPods, orphan earrings, and miscellaneous other detritus (none of which seemed to fit the bill); asked Danny at the main bar if he'd stumbled across anything; twitched aside the heavy drapes to see if they hid anything; and admitted defeat as dinner was winding up and the staff rolled the cake in on a trolley, fifty candles blazing. I was forced to admit that I'd been wrong: Van Allen had not hidden the package he'd mailed to Sharla in the Club, or if he had, he'd retrieved it before meeting the killer and it was gone for good. My spirits slumped and I wished I could ditch the rest of this shindig and go to Hart's place right now.

The birthday boy almost missed the opportunity to huff and puff and blow out the candles; he came strolling in as the staff parked the trolley at the front of the room, and his wife looked around for him. Wiping his hands down the sides of his legs, he trotted toward the front, taking bets on whether he could extinguish all the candles in one breath. I smiled, tickled that he'd almost missed his big moment because he'd been in the men's room.

Wham! It hit me like a charging moose. The men's room. Allyson had seen a man come out of the bathroom near Wallace's office. Her description had been generic, but it could fit Trent Van Allen. I knew where he'd hidden the package. Taking a quick look around the room to ensure everything was going smoothly, I slipped out the door. Once outside the party room, I dashed for the bathroom.

It was only when I was standing in front of the men's room that I realized I might have been smart to bring Al with me. I mean—*men's* room. I stared at the door with its masculine silhouette for a moment, nerving myself. In the end, my need to know *now* trumped my nerves. I pushed the swinging door inward two inches and called out, "Hello?"

When there was no answer, I looked up and down the hall again, and slipped through the door. The men's room was an attractive facility, with large gray stone tiles on the floor and smaller blue and gray tiles on the walls to waist height. Strong lighting illuminated the three stalls, five urinals, and three sinks with a long mirror over them. It smelled of lavender cleaning products and something mustier that I couldn't identify. At first glance, there didn't appear to be much of anyplace to hide a nine-by-twelve-inch item. The plumbing beneath the sinks was exposed—no cabinets to hide anything. The paper towel holders looked most promising and I broke a fingernail before I figured out how to prize off the top of the metal containers. Nothing in the first one but half an inch of paper towels. I moved to the second one and had just lifted the lid off when the door swung open with a *whoosh*.

Startled, I dropped the metal top and it clanged against the sink and then rattled loudly on the floor. The astonished gentleman at the door, zipper half-undone, met my gaze and stuttered, "Must have the wrong—so sorry—"

"No, I'm sorry," I said. "I'm, uh, restocking the paper towels. I can come back in a minute—"

"No need. I'll use the bathroom by the pro shop." He fled before I could apologize again or get out of his way.

Feeling embarrassed and guilty, I peeked into the top of the second paper towel container. Nothing visible. I lifted up a handful of towels to reveal . . . more towels. With a discouraged sigh, I retrieved the lid from where it had skittered into a stall and replaced it. Hands on my hips, I surveyed the room an inch at a time. No janitorial closet, no lockers, everything in plain sight. Except . . . I stepped into the first stall and stared at the tank. Cops on TV shows and in books were always finding hidden drugs in toilet tanks. It was worth a look.

The toilet and the floor around it gleamed, but I still wished I had rubber gloves as I shifted the heavy porcelain top and looked into the tank. Nada. Feeling a little silly, and trying to hurry, I walked into the second stall. The door closed most of the way behind me, leaving a two-inch-wide gap. Leaning over the toilet, I dragged the lid aside with a scraping sound. Something caught on the lip of the tank and I had to lift the lid higher to free it. A piece of gray duct tape dangled down, cleanly sliced.

I caught my breath and bent my head to examine the inside of the tank. To my disappointment, there was nothing there. I flipped the lid over and rested it upside down atop the tank. In addition to the piece of duct tape I'd already spotted, there were gummy spots inside the lid that suggested more tape had been removed. Given how sticky they still were, I didn't think it had been there too long, certainly not weeks or months. I reached for the duct tape, intending to peel it off, then hesitated. What if I was right? What if Van Allen had stashed his package here, had come prepared with duct tape and secured whatever it was inside the tank? If so, where was it now? Had Van Allen removed it prior to his meeting with the killer, or had the killer gone through the same thought process I had and found it after stabbing Van Allen? I shivered. If the latter, then the duct tape might have the killer's fingerprints on it.

I was so lost in thought, I must have missed the restroom door opening, because the next sound I heard was a tuneful whistling and a zipper whizzing down. Oh, no! Panicked, I eased the stall door closed and slid the lock home silently. Then, I sat on the toilet and pulled my feet up so the man wouldn't see my very un-male shoes. The man must have heard me, though, because he said, over the sound of urine splashing into the urinal, "Quite a party, hey? Hard to believe Bob's fifty. I'll be going over that hill next May. My doctor's already talking about colonoscopies and prostate exams." He laughed and zipped up.

I quickly flushed the toilet, hoping he'd think I hadn't heard him. The whistling resumed and the restroom door whooshed as he left without washing his hands. Letting out a squeaky sigh, I replaced the tank lid, figuring the duct tape was secure enough for the moment, dashed out of the men's room and into the adjacent women's room to wash my hands, and then called Hart. He thought I was calling to tell him I was on my way over, but he snapped to attention when I told him what I'd found.

"Can you keep people out of that bathroom until I get there?"

I told him I would and hung up to go in search of Wallace's deputy, who located a cone with a CLOSED FOR CLEANING sign attached. With that in place, I hurried back to the party room, where I discovered that everything was going beautifully with Al in charge. The DJ was playing "Y.M.C.A." and almost all the guests, including the birthday boy's octogenarian parents, were boogying on the dance floor.

"Everything okay, boss?" Al asked when I came up to him.

"Ducky," I replied. Then, prompted by the excitement buzzing through me at the thought of a breakthrough in the case, I added, "I think I found a piece of evidence related to the murder. In the men's room."

"I'm not even going to ask," Al said, shaking his head. "Only you, boss, only you."

* * *

Later that night, I watched Hart mix up a late-night snack of waffles. I sat on a stool pulled up to the counter at his place, chin on my hands, and admired his economy of motion as he moved around the kitchen, cracked eggs one-handed, and added cinnamon and vanilla without measuring. The drapes were drawn against the dark, and a fire flickered in the gas fireplace. I was tired, but still buzzed from my discovery in the men's room and the end of my event, which had dissolved into disaster when the birthday boy informed his wife, in front of everyone, that he wanted a divorce. He'd been seeing a twenty-six-year-old and planned to marry her. Talk about your midlife crisis. Luckily, by that time, Hart and a crime scene officer were working on the evidence in the bathroom, and they'd managed to separate the warring couple after the spurned wife leaped on her husband, trying to beat his brains out with the foot-tall, ceramic Viagra pill a guest had brought as a gag gift. Despite the disruption, Al and I had sent each guest home with a wrapped-up piece of birthday cake, as previously planned.

Hart and I had talked briefly about the case, standing outside the Club, watching the stragglers pull out of the parking lot. The wind had died down, having delivered a cold front with frigid temps and clear skies. The stars stood out against the cloudless black, each one a twinkly jewel, seemingly within touching distance. If only I could reach high enough . . . Hart brought me back to earth by saying they'd know about fingerprints on the duct tape or the toilet tank lid in a couple of days, but he wasn't counting on anything useful.

"In all probability, Van Allen hid the package in the men's room and came back for it. If not, if he told the murderer where to find it, or he got lucky and stumbled across it like you did—"

"I didn't stumble," I protested. "I applied my analytical abilities, came up with a reasonable hypothesis, and tested it." I felt Lola, the scientist, would have been proud of me.

Hart slanted a grin. "Regardless, this murderer's been pretty savvy so far. I doubt we'll pick up his prints."

"What about on the keys that Allyson had?" I asked.

"Only partials. I talked to her and she can't remember where she got them, says that her therapist tells her that she dissociates from the act of stealing. The idea is that she finds it abhorrent—her word, not mine—to the point that she doesn't have clear memories of what she stole from where, which is partly why she doesn't return more of the stuff she steals. Mumbo jumbo," he said, "but she seems to believe it and either truly doesn't remember where she picked up the VW keys or has convinced herself she doesn't remember."

"What are the chances of the murderer believing that?" I asked, suddenly fearful for Allyson.

"I'd say pretty good at this point. In all probability, the murderer was in the room when Allyson returned her loot. When Allyson didn't confront him or her, or try to return the keys to anyone in particular, it probably set his or her mind at ease."

I hugged my arms around myself against the near

freezing temps as the woman who'd organized the party, the wife of the honoree, staggered out of the Club, spectacularly drunk. Her sister had an arm around her waist and was guiding her to the passenger side of a Volvo. The wife began to retch and her sister shoved her toward some shrubbery, saying, "For goodness' sake, Jan, not in the car. Get it out of your system now." Jan was thoroughly and loudly sick into a clump of lavender. I winced. I had a feeling she was going to balk at paying the rest of what she owed me. Clients did that sometimes—took it out on the event planner when their parties or functions didn't live up to their expectations, even when that was due to something—a cheating, inconsiderate louse of a husband, for example—over which the planner had zero control.

"Ready to go?" Hart asked, touching my shoulder.

"More than ready."

Now, in the warmth of his kitchen, Hart informed me, "This is an old family tradition." He ladled the batter onto the waffle iron. "I'm not sure where it started, but it was a postgame ritual and definitely an after-prom thing. After football games on Friday nights, me and a few buddies from the team would come over and Dad would make waffles. We'd eat two or three each, load up on milk or soda, and rehash each down. Or"—he grinned—"talk about girls. After prom, we'd bring our dates and a couple of friends over after the dance at midnight, and Dad would have the batter already made."

A heavenly aroma was rising from the waffle iron. "That's a nice tradition," I said. "The PTA sponsored an after-prom get-together at the high school here, with lots of gift card giveaways and games and food. That's where everyone went. I like your folks' idea better."

"I know they only started it to keep us from partying somewhere, or getting in cars with drunk friends, but I have to admit, I liked it, even if it was dorky." Using a fork, he pried the first waffle from the iron, split it in two halves, and plated them. He slid a plate in front of me, and passed a tub of butter and bottle of syrup.

"Who'd you go to prom with?" I asked.

Ladling more batter onto the waffle maker, he got a reminiscent smile on his face. "Junior year, I went with my girlfriend, Isabella Chavez. We'd been dating for two months. She wore a mint green dress, one of the kind that are shorter in the front than in the back—?" He looked at me questioningly.

"Hi-low," I supplied around a mouthful of waffle.

"I had a matching bow tie and cummerbund. Can you imagine me in mint green?" He laughed at the memory. "We had a great time, and she broke up with me the next day." He shrugged.

"Bitch," I said.

Hart laughed so hard he dribbled syrup across the counter. "That's exactly what my sister said, and exactly how she said it." Still chuckling, he wiped up the syrup, picked up a quarter waffle, and took a big bite. His next words were muffled. "Senior year I went with Abby Delaney. She was one of my good friends, a real brainiac, went to college at RPI. We went out to dinner at Chick-fil-A beforehand, with a bunch of friends, and we all hung out together, dancing in a big pack, playing some air guitar." He demonstrated by strumming the air. "When I got up about one the next afternoon, my folks told me we ate forty-six waffles and six pounds of bacon."

"Sounds like fun," I said, mopping up the last of the syrup with a waffle chunk.

"How about you?" He freed the second waffle from the maker and looked a question at me. I shook my head; I was full. Switching off the appliance, he came to sit beside me.

"I went with my boyfriend, Doug, both years," I said. "We started dating as sophomores. It took a lot of the angst out of the prom thing, not having to wonder if I'd have a date. The first year, he asked me over the PA system during the morning announcements." I still flushed at the memory—it had been so embarrassing, but in a good way. "I always thought prom itself was kind of a letdown, that the real fun was getting ready with Brooke and another friend or two, painting our nails, doing each other's makeup, dress shopping together."

"Yeah, that's what guys like best about prom, too," Hart said mock-seriously. "Bonding while we pick out corsages together."

I slapped at him. "Don't make fun of my sacred high school rituals."

He stood, drew me off the stool, and put his arms around me. "I wouldn't dare." He kissed me. It started out light, but got more intense very quickly. I felt drugged with passion by the time he lifted his lips a millimeter from mine, said, "We can clean up in the morning," and walked me backward toward his bedroom, kissing me the whole way.

Chapter 23

I slipped out of Hart's condo early the next morning, taking half a cold waffle from the plate in the kitchen. Hart volunteered to make hot ones, but I was running late for church, and feeling guilty that I'd skipped last week's service, so I told him I'd take a rain check, kissed him, and left. I stopped at my bungalow to change out of last night's black dress, and scooted onto the pew beside my mother at St. Luke's Lutheran four seconds before the organist launched into the intro for the opening hymn. Mom smiled and patted my hand before turning her attention to the service. I sat there, letting the familiar rhythms of the liturgy wash over me, alternately tuning into the sermon and reliving parts of last night. A happy haze enveloped me. I managed to be present mentally while taking Communion and during the final prayer.

After the service, I drifted into the parish hall with my folks for coffee, cookies, and socializing. When I was younger, the church used to have donuts during the coffee hour, but I guess budget cutbacks had led to the less-enticing store-bought cookies. I took one anyway and nibbled it. There were probably forty people hanging around, and I spotted a couple who'd been at last night's party, the pastor (who had been three years ahead of me in high school and whom Lola had gone out with a few times), and Cletis Perry, getting around better with his crutches. I waved when our gazes met and he winked at me.

"How's it going at the pub?" I asked Mom. Dad had hugged me and then beelined for his cronies, and was deep into a conversation that revolved around great poker hands, huge fish landed, or amazing golf shots. A mathematician by day, he was one of the guys in his off time, as capable of discussing lures and club lofts as he was of explaining theorems and formulas. A caftanlike garment swathed Mom's bulk, its stand-up mandarin collar lost in the folds of her multiple chins. Its royal blue color was dramatic against her pale magnolia-petal complexion, the envy of every woman north of forty in the entire town. Her naturally curly hair was pinned up, as usual for church. Sheena at Sheena's Hair Jungle was responsible for dyeing it back to its original chestnut every month or so. Her eyes were hazel, like mine, and she had a wide mouth slicked with a coral lipstick. I had fond memories of helping her pick out lipstick at the drugstore when I was younger. She'd always gone for bright colors, saying a smile was one's best accessory.

Mom shifted from foot to foot. I knew her feet had been bothering her lately and wondered if Dad had talked her into a doctor's appointment like he'd promised. Her face lit up. "I am having more fun at the pub, Amy-Faye, than I've had in years. Even though I'm sorry for Derek that Gordon's death made things so difficult financially, I can't help but be glad. Working at Elysium has been just what I needed. I hadn't realized how much I missed the library since I retired, how much I missed *people*. It has cut down on my reading time and the number of reviews I can do, but it's been worth it."

Mom was always a voracious reader, but since retiring from the library, she'd taken to reading a dozen or more books a week and posting reviews online.

"Well, you and Dad have saved Derek's bacon. I hope he appreciates it." Long history with my brother suggested that he would take it for granted. I didn't know if that level of ingratitude was standard for youngest kids, but I suspected Derek took his sense of entitlement to new heights. I'd filled in as temp bartender for him on numerous occasions, and he never even said thanks, unless I counted the occasional free beer or bison burger as "Thank you, sister dear, for saving my ass by playing bar wench when my flaky employees don't show up."

Mom smiled, not one whit disturbed. "I know he appreciates it," she said comfortably. "He might not express it, but I know he's glad to have your dad and me taking care of the books and the day-to-day management. He likes being left alone to get creative with his brewing." She chuckled, the sound almost lost in the rising hubbub of conversations around us.

"Well, I'm grateful to you," I said, kissing her cheek. "I've got a lot of money invested in Elysium, and it's nice to know it's not going down the drain."

She waved to an acquaintance, and then asked, "What are you and the gals reading this month?"

"We read *Rebecca*."

"Du Maurier was a genius," Mom said, "a genius. I was always sorry she didn't write more books. I loved the way she made Manderley come to life, made it a character in the novel. It was grand and unsettling all at the same time. Were you glad or sorry when it burned at the end?"

I hadn't thought about it. "Glad, I think. It gave the unnamed wife and de Winter a chance to start over, to make a life without the shadow of Rebecca flitting around." I raised my arms and wiggled my fingers, making like a ghost.

"I felt the same way. My feet hurt—I'm going to sit down. Would you mind getting me more coffee if you're getting a refill?" Taking my agreement for granted, she began a slow shuffle toward the handful of chairs set up near the wall.

I wasn't planning on more coffee, but I was happy to take my mom's foam cup and refill it at the coffee urn, chatting with acquaintances while I stirred in the two packets of sugar she insisted on. When I crossed the room to where she now sat, I found her laughing at something Cletis Perry had said. He sat in a folding chair drawn up near hers, his crutches resting against the wall.

"How are you doing, Cletis?" I asked, handing Mom the steaming cup. She took it with a "Thank you," and began chatting with old Mrs. Chintala, who had dod-dered over, clutching her old-fashioned purse between both hands as if afraid a mugger would leap out from a poster advertising the past summer's Vacation Bible School.

"I'll be running marathons as fast as I ever did in another week or two," Cletis said, slapping the cast lightly.

"I didn't know you ran marathons," I said, surprised and impressed.

"I don't." He let loose a laugh that made everyone within earshot smile. "So, I'll be as fast as I ever was."

I smiled. "Got a lot of work on your plate? I might have another event in mid-October for you. The Chamber of Commerce is trying to settle on a date for a 'slave auction' fund-raiser where people bid on the Chamber's members and put them to work cleaning their houses or fertilizing their yards—whatever chores they need done."

"Is that right?" Cletis looked thoughtful. "I'll have to buy Big Al Farraday and put him to work mucking out my goat pens. That'll teach him. Give me a call at the office and I'll check my calendar."

I didn't know why Big Al needed "teaching," and I didn't pursue it. I was about to make my excuses and leave when Cletis asked, "Did you ever find out who played that trick on that writer fellow?"

I wrinkled my brow, unsure what he meant.

"You know," he said impatiently, in response to my confusion, "that guy whose manuscript ended up on the sale table at the auction for the gothic shindig, the one that lady with the hat bought." He bunched his fingers over his head, as if to indicate the flowers on Francesca Bugle's hat.

"Ah," I said, enlightenment dawning. "That was her own manuscript. We never did figure out who mixed it in with the sale items."

He shook his head, wispy yellow-white hair dancing. "No, it was a guy, a Frank something." He concentrated for a moment and then jerked his head up. "Bugg," he said. "I knew it would come to me. I'm not ready for the Alzheimer's ward yet. Bugg. Frank Bugg. It said, 'Shades of Passion,' and on the next line, 'by Frank Bugg.'" He nodded his sharp chin triumphantly.

I didn't insult him by asking if he was sure. I didn't know what to say. I stood still as a fence post, trying to understand the ramifications. Cletis's wife came over, greeted me, handed her husband his crutches, and told him it was time to head for brunch at their daughter Annie's. My mom's voice came from far away.

"Are you okay, Amy-Faye?"

I looked down into her concerned eyes. "Fine, Mom. Well, maybe a little tired. It's been a couple of late nights in a row." I didn't explain that my lack of sleep had more to do with Hart than with events. Thinking about it warmed my cheeks and I smiled through my worry.

"LuAnn Sealander told me about what Jeffrey Hovey did to Jan last night," she said, making a *tsk*ing noise. "He should be ashamed of himself. LuAnn said it was a lovely party, right up until Jeffrey went off the deep end. LuAnn said he dove right into his midlife crisis like a hog into muck. You won't have any trouble getting paid, will you?"

Trust Mom to home in on the important stuff. Maybe if she got tired of drawing beers at the pub, she'd come work for me. She could do my billing and collecting, the part of the business I liked least. "I'll handle it," I said. "Look, Mom, I've got to run. Say bye to Dad for me, okay?" Not giving her a chance to ask more questions, I kissed her cheek and took off across the room.

I wasn't sure where I was going at first. Too many ideas were swimming around in my head, colliding and then separating. Francesca had clearly claimed the auction manuscript as her own. She'd almost had a seizure when Cletis started to read out the author's name, I remembered now. Frank Bugg. Who the heck was he? The name was too similar to "Francesca Bugle" to be a coincidence. I wanted to talk to Lola, try to sort it out, but I knew she'd be at church. Ditto for Brooke, who dutifully accompanied her husband and in-laws to the late service at an Episcopal church in Grand Junction. Troy Sr. had had a falling-out with the priest at St. Joseph's Episcopal here in Heaven and made the switch to the Grand Junction church six or seven years ago. Maud had mentioned an early-morning fishing trip and I didn't think she'd be back yet. That left Kerry. I phoned her from the van and got an immediate, "Come on over."

I pulled up in front of Kerry's place ten minutes later. It was a ramshackle two-story gabled house she'd inherited from her parents. To hear her tell it, her entire

mayoral salary went to maintaining the place, to "bubble gum and baling wire," as she put it. She and her
son, Roman, were in the front yard, raking up the
leaves deposited by yesterday's winds. Roman had on
headphones and was swaying to a beat as he raked
near the house. Wearing ratty sweats and work gloves,
with a kerchief securing her short hair, Kerry met me
at the curb and thrust a forty-gallon yard bag into my
hands.

"You hold—I'll rake. I think this is the last of them."
She gestured upward at the two cottonwood trees, one
oak, and two aspens that sat on her property. Blue sky
showed through their mostly bare limbs. "I swear I'm
going to chop them down one of these days."

I took that with a grain of salt. Kerry said the same
thing every fall, and changed her mind every spring
when the trees leafed out and provided gorgeous shade
for her house and yard all summer. She tromped across
the yard to a large pile of crisp leaves. I dutifully held
the mouth of the bag open as she stuffed leaves in.
While we worked, I told her about what Cletis had said,
and also filled her in on finding the duct tape on the
tank lid last night. She listened, her brow slightly cor-
rugated.

When I'd finished, she said, "Well, I think we can
say that Francesca Bugle is at the center of this whole
mess, one way or another. I mean, Frank Bugg? C'mon,
there's got to be a tie to Francesca Bugle. And the way
she bid for that manuscript—what, five thousand
bucks?—she was desperate to keep anyone else from
getting their hands on it. And I don't care what she said

about her publisher being pissed if the manuscript got out. That kind of money means something bigger is at stake."

"Like a whole writing career," I said, straightening and arching my back. I put a foot into the bag and compacted the leaves. They crackled. Kerry heaved more leaves in, trapping them against the tines of the rake, and angling the rake into the bag. Half her load dribbled back onto the grass, and individual leaves, goosed by the breeze, spun up and away, making a bid for freedom.

"Drat," she said. She picked the leaves up in fistfuls and stuffed them in the bag. When she was done, I pulled the plastic drawstring closed and knotted it.

"I did an Internet search on the name before coming over here," I said, "but I got four hundred seventy thousand hits. Who'da thunk there were that many Frank Buggs running around? Without more info, there's no way to tell which one is the one we want."

"I know a foolproof way to find out who he is," Kerry said, planting the rake's handle firmly on the ground, and setting the other hand on her hip.

"How?"

"Ask Francesca Bugle about him."

I chewed on my lower lip. "Or we could tell Hart— the police—and let them look into it."

"Like the police are going to be interested in hearing that Cletis Perry thinks he saw the name Frank Bugg on a manuscript that Francesca Bugle bought. Even if they believe what he says, where's the crime? Where's the tie-in to the Van Allen case? Nowhere, that's where.

Face it: Chances are, there isn't a connection. The whole Frank Bugg thing will turn out to be unrelated." Kerry shrugged in a "there you have it" way.

She made a lot of sense. "Okay," I said, convinced. "Let's do it. We'd better hurry—they're all probably checking out of the inn as we speak."

"I can't go looking like this," Kerry said, gesturing to her dirty, leaf-speckled attire. "Give me ten to shower and change."

"I'll meet you at the Columbine," I said, anxious to catch Francesca before she headed home. I had a feeling that once all the suspects left Heaven, the chances of solving the Van Allen murder would plummet dramatically. Someone would get away with murder and, having gotten away with it once, might kill again when it seemed like a solution to his or her problems. Waving good-bye to Roman, even though I'm not sure he'd ever noticed my presence, I returned to the van and headed for the B and B.

Chapter 24

A white Ford Fusion was pulling out of the Columbine's driveway as I drove up. I caught no more
than a glimpse of what seemed to be a hat atop the
driver's head, and instinctively maneuvered the van
across the driveway's entrance. If it wasn't Francesca
driving the car, I would simply apologize and back up.
The car door opened. Francesca got out and marched
toward me, face flushed with irritation.

I got out to meet her. She wore a plum-colored pants
suit over a gray blouse with a floppy bow tie. I'd worn
something like that blouse to a 1980s-themed party in
college. The poppies on her hat bobbed with each step.

"Don't get out," she greeted me impatiently. "You've
got to move. Can't you see you're blocking the driveway?
I need to get to DIA to catch my flight, so hustle up." She
turned around, confident I would do as she asked, I
guessed.

She was halfway back to the rental before I asked,
"Who is Frank Bugg?"

She froze. I waited.

After thirty seconds of immobility and silence, she
pivoted slowly. Tension made her stiff as a robot, and

made the tendons in her neck stand out like rigid cables. "Why do you ask?"

She knew him! I gave a mental fist pump. Keeping the elation I felt off my face, I said, "Because that name was on the manuscript you bought at the auction." I watched her closely, seeing her consider and discard several lies before the tendons in her neck relaxed and she said, "He's my father."

"Your father?" I parroted. "Then why—?" I couldn't think why her manuscript would have her father's name as the author, but I also couldn't see why that was such a secret. Had she stolen a manuscript from him like the Stewarts had from Eloise Hufnagle? Surely not.

"It's a long story," she said.

"Then the sooner you start telling it, the better your chances of catching your plane," I said, crossing my arms over my chest.

"I don't want to do this in the driveway. You'd better come in." Giving in to the inevitable, Francesca plodded up the six stone steps to the Columbine and pushed through the door.

Sandy was in the foyer, polishing the woodwork with lemon oil. She looked up in surprise. "I thought you'd gone," she said. "Forget something?"

"Do you think I could have a glass of water?" Francesca asked.

Clearly sensing that something was amiss, Sandy nodded. When she had disappeared down the hall leading to the kitchen, Francesca started to walk into the small parlor, but I was leery of being behind closed doors with her. My experience with the Stewarts the other day was too fresh. "This is good," I said, plumping myself into one of the two lyre-backed chairs in the foyer. Francesca ignored the other chair and looked out the narrow window on one side of the double doors. She spoke without facing me and I had to scoot the chair closer to hear her.

"I don't know where to start," she said. "I've never told anyone this story, although I knew this day would come, that we couldn't keep the secret forever."

Impatience and curiosity fizzed through me. "What secret?"

Francesca wasn't willing to be rushed. Still not looking at me, she said, "I've wanted to be a writer always. Always. I can remember lying in bed, covers pulled up to my chin, listening while my mother or father read bedtime stories. We had almost no money, so they couldn't buy books, but my mother had a collection of fairy tales with beautiful illustrations from when she was a girl, and we had the Bible, so I grew up with the swan princess and Noah, Cinderella and the Good Samaritan. I can remember thinking when I was no more than four or five that I wanted to write stories like that. I wrote my first story when I was six and I haven't stopped from that day to this." She twiddled the blinds wand, letting stripes of sun in, shutting them out.

"I wrote all through high school and won awards for my stories, including a partial scholarship to the community college. I worked as a waitress and a housecleaner to put myself through school. When I graduated, I kept waitressing and cleaning, making enough to support myself, barely, while I wrote. I sent manuscripts off to agents, but never landed one. Lots of agents liked my writing style, but I couldn't seem to hit on an idea that wasn't hackneyed and trite. Yes, both those words came up in my rejection letters. By the time I was thirty, I had given up on making a living as a writer, and gotten a 'real' job." She sneered the word "real."

I shifted on the uncomfortable chair. The needlepoint pad had looked comfy enough, but the padding had wadded into pea-sized lumps over the decades. I heard a rustling noise behind me, but I didn't take my eyes off Francesca Bugle to look around.

"I became an office manager at an over-the-road trucking company. I was good at it, and it wasn't miserable, but it wasn't writing. I did that for over ten years. Then—" Francesca took in a deep breath that swelled her back. "Then, my father went to prison."

I stifled a gasp.

"He was sixty. With all that time on his hands, he took up writing. I visited him at least twice a month, and one day he handed me a three-inch stack of paper and asked me to read it. I took it home to humor him, and read it that night. The whole thing. The grammar was iffy and the characters lame, but the story and pacing gripped me, kept me turning the pages, even though I had work the next day. I thought about that book all the next day, while I was doing accounts receivable, counseling an employee, ordering supplies. By the time I got home, I knew what I was going to do. I might not have been able to come up with a good

274 / Laura DiSilverio

story idea of my own, but I recognized one, a hook that would grab readers, when I saw it."

"You sent it off to a publisher," I said, unable to stand the suspense of her drawn-out story.

"Not yet." She opened and closed the blinds a few more times; if anyone from across the street was watching, he probably thought she was sending Morse code messages. No, only Maud would leap to that conclusion. "I rewrote it, gave it my stamp. Then, I talked to my father and he agreed that I could send it out. We compromised on a pen name, Francesca Bugle. I'm really Patty Bugg. Doesn't have quite the same ring, does it?" She gave a bitter laugh, her breath fogging the window momentarily.

"That book went to auction and was an immediate success. The next one hit the *New York Times* extended list, and the third one debuted in the top twenty. I quit my job. Now *Barbary Close* is going to be next summer's blockbuster. It's funny how things work out, isn't it?" She let go of the wand, which swung against the blinds with a muted tink, and began playing with the cord that raised and lowered them, wrapping it around her index finger.

I leaned sideways, trying to read her profile. Sadness and resignation chased across her features. The unforgiving sun deepened the grooves around her mouth and made her complexion slightly sallow.

"I was finally a bestselling author, but it didn't feel the way I thought it would." Her index finger was swollen and purple at the tip. It must have throbbed, because she unwrapped the cord tourniquet.

She was silent so long, I finally prompted, "So where does Van Allen fit in?"

She jerked the blinds cord so hard the metal slats jangled. "He was my father's cellmate."

A gasp sounded from behind us, and Francesca whirled so quickly she stumbled. Still holding the blinds cord, she pitched toward the floor and the blinds ripped from their valance and clattered down. I had hopped up, and turned to look, too, and I discovered that we had an audience in the balcony, as it were; both the Stewarts and all three of the Aldringhams stood on the upstairs landing, peering over the banister like they were watching a play. All they were missing was Playbills and opera glasses. Sandy stood in the shadow of the hallway, holding a glass of water. They'd all clearly been listening for quite a while.

I reached a hand down to help Francesca up, but she ignored it, disentangling herself from the blinds and using her hands on her thighs to push herself upright. She glared at the audience, her face first flushing a plummy red that matched her outfit, and then blanching white. I thought she might cry, pass out, or possibly explode, but then she started laughing. It was a weak, wheezy sound at first, but it grew into her usual ribald guffaw tinged with a hysterical edge. "Oh, my God," she said when she could catch her breath. "I guess the secret's out in a big way, huh?"

A nervous titter and some chuckling came from the others and the tension dissipated. I figured it would ratchet up again when everyone realized, as I did, that Francesca was a murderer. Van Allen had obviously been trying to blackmail her with his knowledge of her faux authorship. If her father's prison was coed, she might end up in the cell next to him.

"What was your father in for?" Lucas Stewart asked. Mary tried to shush him, but he shook off her hand and leaned farther over the banister.

"Well, that's the kicker, isn't it?" Francesca said. She widened her stance and pulled her shoulders back as if bracing herself. "He's a sex offender. I really don't want to go into details."

"Oh, my," Constance breathed.

Everyone else was silent.

"You can see," Francesca went on with an effort, "why it would be damaging to sales if word got out."

I could indeed see. If Francesca wrote thrillers, or caper novels, the details of her father's imprisonment might not matter so much. But she wrote gothic romance verging on erotica. No buyer or reader in the world was going to be able to read her more passionate passages again if word got around about the true author's proclivities. I gulped. It made a dandy motive for murder. And Van Allen's death was in vain, since now more than half a dozen people knew the truth.

"How did Van Allen track you down? What did he say?" I asked.

"Shortly before he was due to be released, he stole a completed manuscript from my father and smuggled it out of the prison somehow."

"He mailed it to his girlfriend," I supplied.

Francesca cocked her head in acknowledgment. "Then Van Allen looked up my schedule on my Web site and followed me here. He approached me after the panel at the bookstore, and said he had a manuscript he thought I might be interested in. I thought he was one of those wannabe authors who wanted me to read his great American novel and pass it along to my agent or editor—people ask me to do things like that sometimes."

"The nerve of some people, right?" Mary chimed in. "That happens to me at least twice a month, too."

Constance nodded to indicate she'd been approached like that before, as well.

Francesca continued. "I refused to meet with him; in fact, I was pretty dismissive. To prove his point or to get back at me, he snuck part of the manuscript into the auction. I about had a heart attack when the auctioneer read off the title and almost blurted out my father's name. Well, I knew Van Allen was telling the truth, so I got a message to my father—said there was a family emergency—and he called me. He was livid, almost incoherent with fury, mostly because he felt betrayed, I think. If he'd been able to get his hands on Van Allen, he'd have strangled him."

"Frankie *Bugg*—Frankie the Cockroach!" I exclaimed, as enlightenment dawned. Noticing everyone's puzzled expressions, I said, "Sharla—Van Allen's girlfriend—said something about 'Frankie the Cockroach' being pissed off. She meant your dad, right?"

Francesca nodded. "That's what they call him. Frankie the Cockroach."

I thought I heard someone mutter something about sex offenders being worse than cockroaches, but Francesca didn't seem to hear. Before she could go on, the front door opened and Kerry came in. "Sorry I'm late," she said. She stopped just inside the door, registering the unexpected crowd. "I didn't realize we were having a party."

"Francesca was telling us about how Van Allen was trying to blackmail her," I said. I knew Kerry had more questions, but I wanted to keep Francesca talking, so I turned to her. "How much did he want?"

"Half a million," she said. "He slipped a note under my door here, his way of telling me he could get to me at any time, I think. I should have paid it and been done with this. Instead . . ."

"Instead, you met him at the Club and killed him," I finished.

More gasps and a "got what he deserved" filtered from the upstairs landing. I didn't look up to see who had said it. I kept my eyes fixed on Francesca.

Francesca reared back as if I'd slapped her. "What? Hell, no. He told me he'd meet me at the costume ball, that he'd have the manuscript and I should have the money. His note said to hang loose and he'd make contact. I was like a cat on hot coals the whole evening, practically hyperventilating anytime someone came up behind me. I saw him a couple of times from a distance at the party, but he never approached me. By the time I decided I should make a move and seek him out, there was that brouhaha with the fake blood and then I heard someone had found a body. When I learned it was Van Allen, I didn't know what to think. I was scared, relieved, skeptical."

"That's simply implausible," Constance announced. Francesca and I looked up at her. Her cream-colored pashmina was trailing over the banister. "No reader would buy that. There's simply no chance that your antagonist was randomly killed by someone else. You'd get a raft of one-star Amazon reviews for that, my dear." She pulled up the trailing end of her pashmina and flipped it over her shoulder.

"This isn't a book, Connie. This is real life," Francesca said through gritted teeth. "Van Allen was a crook and a lowlife and I'm glad he's dead, but I didn't kill him. End of story."

She pivoted her head and tried to make eye contact with everyone in the room. Most of them refused to meet her eyes. They all thought she was guilty of Van Allen's murder—I could tell. I was beginning to have doubts, though. She seemed so open about it all. But, I reminded myself, she'd lived a lie for almost a decade, pretending to be the author of books her father had written.

"What about the manuscript? Did you get that back?" Of course Mary Stewart asked that question. She knew more than most about stolen manuscripts.

"No. I have no idea where it is. I expected the police to find it and connect it to me, eventually, but I haven't heard from them. It's still out there—it feels like a ticking time bomb set to go off when I least expect it." Francesca collapsed into the lyre-back chair I had vacated, as if she'd suddenly run out of energy and gumption and hope. Her hat went askew, the poppies now bobbing to brow level, like too-long bangs.

"Did you tell the police all this?" Kerry asked. She had closed the door and stood blocking it, and I wondered if that was on purpose, to make it harder for Francesca to make a run for it.

Francesca gave her a withering look from behind the poppies. "Or course not. I knew how it'd look." With a sudden angry motion, she yanked the poppies off the hat and crushed them in her fist.

"You must have told someone," Allyson Aldringham said in a soft voice.

"The only person I told was . . . Cosmo." Francesca's voice was little more than a whisper. "I thought he needed to know because of the movie. I couldn't let him get blindsided if Van Allen carried through on his threats and went to a reporter with the manuscript and my father's story."

Something about her delivery felt rehearsed, and as I scanned her face, I became convinced that she had suspected Cosmo Zeller all along, but had kept quiet in order to protect her secret. Now that her secret was out, there was no need for her to keep mum about Cosmo. The longer I stared at her, the more I wondered if she hadn't orchestrated the whole thing. She knew Cosmo was in desperate financial straits and was depending on the success of the movie to set himself up again. He was probably the only person in the world with as much to lose as she did, or more, if Van Allen talked to the media. Despite her squat figure and middle-aged face, I began to see her as a modern-day Rebecca, manipulating Cosmo into killing Trent Van Allen the way Rebecca manipulated Max de Winter into killing her.

I shook my head to clear it of such fancies. Wasn't it more likely that Francesca and Cosmo planned the murder together and that he carried it out? Maud would like that: a conspiracy.

Kerry, ever the practical one, asked, "Where is Cosmo?"

Everyone looked around, as if surprised to realize Cosmo wasn't part of the group listening to Francesca's revelations. She spoke up. "He left for the airport half an hour ago, headed back to L.A."

"Denver International?" Kerry asked.

Francesca shook her head. "No, someplace local. He had a pilot lined up to fly him to DIA in one of those little prop jobs. He offered me a lift, but I don't get into any plane smaller than my car." She shuddered.

"He's got to be leaving from that airstrip out by Brummel's farm. We can still stop him," Kerry said, throwing open the door. Sunlight and chilly air flooded in.

"I'm in," said Lucas Stewart, bounding down the stairs, his face alight at the prospect of action.

As if the gates had been opened for the Pamplona running of the bulls, everyone on the landing thundered down the stairs and swept me along with them as they poured through the door. I was trying to call Hart, but I kept getting bumped and fumbling the phone. Without any discussion, the group converged on my van as the only vehicle in sight large enough to hold all of us. I flipped the keys to Kerry. "You drive. I've got to tell Hart."

She caught the keys and climbed into the driver's seat. I got in on the passenger side, while everyone else piled into the back, seating themselves on the floor.

Constance grumbled at the rustic nature of the transportation, but when Merle suggested she stay, she said, "Don't be a fool," and lowered herself to the floor with as much dignity as possible. The van lurched as Kerry tried to go from zero to sixty in less than the van's usual minute and a half.

"Sorry," she said to the passengers as they straightened themselves, grumbling.

As Kerry flipped an illegal U-turn and drove toward Heaven's airstrip, I finally got through to Hart. When I gave him a succinct recap of Francesca's story, he said, "Damn. A tractor-trailer overturned on Paradise Boulevard and both the on-duty patrol officers are coping with that. We're all on the other side of the semi crash— it's got the road blocked. It's going to take me too long to get to the airfield going on the back roads."

I gave him directions for getting to the airstrip a slightly faster way—not for nothing had I lived my whole life in this town.

"Do not confront Zeller," he said. "If what you suspect is true, we'll work up some evidence and have him picked up in L.A."

I hung up and relayed Hart's message.

"He'll hire a lawyer and never set foot back in Colorado," Merle predicted.

"Maybe we can find some way to delay him without confronting him," I suggested lamely, torn between wanting to make sure Cosmo Zeller didn't get away and not wanting to piss off Hart.

Someone in the back snorted. I suspected Lucas.

Kerry, gripping the steering wheel tightly at the ten and two positions, trod on the accelerator as she turned onto the two-lane road leading to Brummel's farm, site of the grass airstrip that Heaven's handful of private pilots used. Bare-limbed trees flashed past the windows, and I held my breath as Kerry pulled out to overtake an RV lumbering along in front of us. She zipped in front of it mere seconds before we would have smashed into the pickup in the oncoming lane. He went past us with a long blast of his horn, echoed by a toot from the RV's driver.

We flew down the road for another two miles, before I spied the opening to the airstrip. Kerry barely feathered the brakes as she made the left turn, rocking all of us against the van's side. For a breathless moment, I thought the van was going to tip, but it stabilized and we sped down the gravel road toward the hangar that housed four or five private planes. Two planes were tied down outside the hangar and someone was clambering over the wing of the blue-and-silver plane closest to us. Gravel pinged loudly against the van's underside. Black-and-white cows grazed in the field, unfazed by our passing. The airstrip, parallel to the narrow lane, was too small for an air traffic controller, and the pilots that flew out of there coordinated with one another via radio. An orange wind sock fluffed and sagged, fluffed and sagged in the fitful wind. With no side windows in the back of the van, several of the passengers were hanging over the front seat, eager to be the first to spot Cosmo Zeller.

"Do you see—?" Mary Stewart started.

She was close enough that I felt her moist breath on my ear. Ick. I inched to my right.

"There!" Constance's arm came down practically on Kerry's shoulder as she pointed a bony finger toward the small plane bumping its way to the end of the taxiway. It was red and white, with a propeller on the nose, and looked like it would hold four people. As we watched, it executed a turn and lined up for takeoff.

"He's going to get away," Allyson said.

"Not if I can help it." Kerry leaned over the steering wheel, her mouth set in a determined line and her jaw jutting forward aggressively. "Here goes nothing."

She swung the steering wheel to the left so we bounced off the lane and into the pasture, headed straight for the airstrip. A phlegmatic cow lifted its head briefly to watch the van pass, and then lowered it again to keep eating.

"Ow!" someone yelped as we jounced over the rough ground.

The small plane began to move, gathering speed as it trundled down the runway. The van nose-dived into a shallow ditch and I pitched toward the dash. The seat belt bit into my shoulder. Grabbing the dash with both hands, I managed to keep from breaking my nose. "Kerry—!"

"Sorry," Kerry muttered. The van surmounted the small rise and we were at the edge of the runway. The plane was speeding toward us.

It was close enough that I saw the pilot's eyes widen

as Kerry stomped on the accelerator and the van—my poor van—surged onto the runway.

"Hold on," Lucas shouted.

"We're going to die!" Allyson said, sounding more excited than depressed.

For a moment it seemed like she was right and I squeezed my eyes shut tight as we crossed the plane's path. They flew open a moment later; I couldn't stand not seeing what was going on. The pilot must have stomped on his brakes and wrenched his steering wheel, or yoke, or whatever pilots call their steering gadget, because the plane slewed around until it was sideways toward us, its wheels leaving ruts in the runway. I glimpsed Cosmo Zeller's terrified face as the plane slid off the side of the runway and came to a stop not far from a trio of cows, who scattered only after the plane had stopped moving.

"Everyone okay?" Kerry asked in a breathless voice. She released the steering wheel, and held up her hands, her fingers still crooked as if curved around the wheel. She straightened them slowly.

A siren sounded in the distance, getting louder. I craned my head to see out the side window and spotted Hart's Chevy Tahoe racing toward us, lights strobing. A patrol car followed more sedately. Thank goodness. I slumped against my seat, letting out a long whoosh of air.

"There," Kerry said triumphantly as Hart skidded to a stop beside the stalled plane and jumped out of the SUV. "No confrontation. Happy?"

I slid her an "Are you kidding me?" look, but then began to laugh, shakily at first, but with increasing strength. Mary Stewart joined in with a girlish giggle. The whole van was bubbling over with merriment by the time Hart approached us. I opened my door and tumbled out when he was a step away.

His expression was rigid, but it softened a touch when he saw me unharmed. I resisted the urge to throw myself into his arms, knowing he wouldn't like it while he was being official, and simply stood there, beaming at him.

After a moment, his lips quirked up at the corner. He said, "I'm taking Zeller back to the station for questioning. I'll talk to you later, after the pilot's done with you." He jerked his head toward the pilot, who was striding toward us with a stiff-legged gait, anger vibrating off him. "And I think the farmer who owns this airstrip might have something to say, too." He nodded in the other direction, where an ATV was eating up the ground as it cut across the pasture in our direction.

Sardonic satisfaction glinted in Hart's eyes, and I knew he had no intention of interceding on our behalf. Fair enough.

"Where's Francesca Bugle?" he asked. "I'll need her statement."

I turned to watch as the bruised passengers lowered themselves gingerly from the van, Constance sighing as her foot hit terra firma. Merle seemed to be the last one out, because he slammed the door closed when he exited. My brow creased. "Where's Francesca?" I called.

Everyone looked at one another and shrugged. Kerry

opened the door and peered inside, as if Francesca might still be in the van. She turned around and shook her head. The truth dawned on us all simultaneously: Francesca hadn't come with us. In the rush to pursue Cosmo, no one had noticed that Francesca had stayed behind. Hart, absorbing this, put on his grim face again.

For no reason, an image of Francesca at the costume party flashed into my mind. "She was wearing gloves," I said, "at the gala. She wore full Victorian dress, complete with gloves." That memory made me doubt her accusation of Cosmo. She could have found Lola's lost stake, met Van Allen in Wallace's office . . .

Without commenting, Hart turned away, crossed to his SUV, and used the radio. I imagined he was putting out an APB on Francesca. Cosmo Zeller, gripping a small padded briefcase as if glued to it, glasses askew, Officer Hardaway holding his arm tightly, was yelping about his lawyer and his plans to sue the HPD, the town of Heaven, and possibly the state of Colorado. His beige linen slacks and jacket, and tobacco brown silk T-shirt and matching loafers, looked ludicrously out of place in the middle of a cow pasture. What a muddle!

My gaze fell to his case and I started across the grass toward him, an idea blossoming. The VW keys had had Cosmo's prints on them, but not Francesca's. He'd poked at them when Allyson was returning the things she'd stolen, so that was an innocent explanation for his prints; however . . . what if he was smart enough and quick enough to recognize the danger, and he'd deliberately handled the keys when they'd fallen out of the box? Another memory hit me and I quickened my pace. The flat tire! Cosmo had actually been on the road leading to the lot where we found Van Allen's car. What if he had been searching for it like we had? I envisioned him taking the VW keys off Van Allen's body, and looking in the Club parking lot for the car they fit. He'd have been frustrated when he didn't find it and couldn't locate the manuscript. He could have done the same thing we did—searched the nearby streets and lots, looked at a map to judge distances.

I stopped in front of him and Officer Hardaway gave me a curious look. "I know a good lawyer," I told Cosmo.

Hs sucked in two noisy breaths. "Thanks, but I'll be calling my own lawyer. You will not get away with this," he told Officer Hardaway, who regarded him indifferently. "By the time I'm done with you, the Heaven Police Department won't have enough left to buy a box of donuts."

"You know, Cosmo," I said, gaze dropping to the case in his hands, "I figured out where the manuscript was, too. The men's room. You shouldn't have left that piece of duct tape on the lid." I stopped short of telling him the police had found his fingerprints on it, in case he'd worn gloves and would know I was lying.

A tic jumped at the corner of his eye. "I have no idea what you're talking about," he said, making an effort to keep his voice level. His knuckles whitened on the briefcase handle.

"Really?" I said pleasantly. "What's in your briefcase? I'm betting the manuscript is in there. It would have been smarter to burn it or shred it, but I think you hung on to it, planning to use it as leverage against Francesca, maybe to get her to give up some of her rights related to the movie. You must truly be desperate for money."

He made an inarticulate strangling sound and tried to slide the briefcase behind his legs. "This is my private property. You have no right to look in it. I demand to be allowed to call my lawyer immediately." His voice was squeakier than usual.

I managed not to give a celebratory fist pump, convinced by his reaction that I was right. Thank goodness!

"We'll see about your phone call and a warrant when we get you to the station," Hart said from over my shoulder. I looked around, and he met my eye, giving me the slightest hint of a congratulatory wink.

"I may have to put you on the payroll as an honorary deputy," he whispered while Officer Hardaway led Cosmo toward the patrol car and stuffed him into the back.

"Ooh, would I get a badge?" I asked.

"Not a chance."

His smile was as good as a kiss—okay, almost—and I looked after him with a goofy grin as he strode to the Tahoe and got in, giving a brief toot of the horn as he took off after the patrol car. When he was out of sight, I took a deep breath and joined Kerry where she was being harangued by the irate pilot and the landowner.

Chapter 25

Monday night the Readaholics gathered as planned at Brooke's place to watch the 1940 Alfred Hitchcock version of *Rebecca*. Brooke and Troy had recently converted one room of their spacious basement into a theater room, complete with raked seating (deep leather chairs with cup holders), a huge screen, and surround sound. The soundproofed walls were decorated with murals of scenes from famous movies done in gray tones. A popcorn machine in the back of the room let out a buttery aroma, and the wet bar was convenient for drinks. Holding a Diet Pepsi, I settled into a comfy chair between Maud and Lola.

"This is better than going to the movies," Kerry announced from the row behind me.

Brooke seemed semi-embarrassed by the luxury of it. "Troy's been wanting a theater room for ages," she said, seating herself next to Kerry. "I don't know why when he's not that into movies. He likes playing his video games in here, though." She pushed a button on her remote to dim the lights, and the opening sequence filled the screen. We watched mostly in silence as Laurence Olivier and Joan Fontaine worked their magic.

After the scene where Mrs. Danvers tries to trick the

nameless heroine into committing suicide, Brooke declared it was time for a potty break and brought the lights up. Brooke and Kerry left, but Lola and Maud remained. Lola shifted in her wide chair to face me, bringing one leg up so it rested on the chair's broad arm. Behind her glasses, her brown eyes betrayed a hint of anxiety. "Mabel Appleman told my gran that the police arrested Cosmo Zeller for the murder. Is it true?"

I nodded. "Yep. Hart stopped by last night and filled me in." I felt my face warm as I dwelled on what had followed our conversation. "He said Cosmo crumbled as soon as they were able to search his briefcase and found the manuscript, still wrapped in plastic and with duct tape stuck to it. He tried to put all the blame on Francesca, but Hart says they don't have any concrete evidence against her, so there won't be any charges, even though she might have put Cosmo up to it, one way or another."

"It was a conspiracy," Maud said darkly from my other side. She leaned forward to see past me to Lola. "They were both in on it."

"Maybe, maybe not," I said. "The police found the costume Cosmo wore to the party—it was in the B and B's Dumpster—and examined it. It tested positive for blood and Hart's convinced it will turn out to be Van Allen's. When he confronted Cosmo with that info, he tried to say it was an accident, that he'd gone to reason with Van Allen in Francesca's place about the blackmail, and Van Allen attacked him. He happened to be holding Lola's stake, which he'd picked up, planning to turn it in to the Club's lost and found—"

"Yeah, right," Maud said, rolling her eyes.

"—and he killed Van Allen in self-defense."

Lola's expression turned somber. "So that poor man might still be alive if I hadn't brought that stake to the party."

I put a hand on her arm. "I don't think so, Lo. The police also found a gun in Cosmo's luggage, and traces of some sort of cleaning oil from the gun in the pocket of his costume. He had the gun with him Saturday night, which Hart says speaks to premeditation. He was planning to kill Van Allen one way or another. He also tried to kill Cletis Perry by running him down, after Francesca showed him the manuscript she bought at the auction, the one that said 'by Frank Bugg' on it, the copy Van Allen slipped onto the selling table to up the pressure on her to pay up. Cosmo saw Cletis as a potential threat, and tried to silence him. Luckily, he missed. The dent and Cletis's blood on his rental car may help convict him of attempted murder, though, or at least aggravated assault, Hart says. He was clearly willing to use any weapon that came to hand—guns, cars, metal stakes. Probably any handy blunt object would have done, as well—golf trophies, whatever." I desperately wanted to alleviate Lola's sense of guilt.

Lola was silent for a moment, and then her lips curved into a small smile. "I guess that makes me feel a little bit better. You better believe that the next time I'm invited to a costume party, though, I'm going as Baymax from *Big Hero Six* or Casper the Friendly Ghost—something soft and cuddly. Definitely no weapons!"

We laughed as Kerry and Brooke returned. "What's so funny?" Kerry asked.

"That photo of you in the paper this morning," Maud said with a malicious grin. "Going nose to nose with the airstrip guy, Brummel, and giving him that line about 'I'm the mayor.'"

Looking slightly self-conscious, Kerry said, "Well, he was talking all sorts of nonsense about making the town pay to replace his whole airstrip, which was flat-out ridiculous since there were just a couple of ruts that Roman and two of his buddies could have filled in and smoothed out in forty-five minutes. He was looking to take advantage, so I let him know that as mayor I had some say in zoning and construction approvals, and he backed right down. I could shoot that photographer from the paper, though," she grumbled. "He must have deliberately picked the least flattering photo—I don't really have five chins."

"Everyone does when they turtle their neck back like that." Maud demonstrated, pulling her chin toward her chest. We all tried it, and ended up laughing.

"I saw in the paper this morning that the police caught up with Francesca at the Denver airport," Lola said. "Was she trying to run away? The police weren't planning to arrest her, were they? I didn't think there was any evidence of her involvement."

"Flavia Dunbarton interviewed me for that *Gabbler* article," Kerry said, "and she had already talked to Francesca at the Columbine. I'm not sure how she got to her so quickly." A line appeared between her brows as

she pondered. "Anyway, Francesca told her she was trying to get home to Illinois, to visit her father in the pen
and fill him in on everything, so they could get their
ducks in a row. She agreed to come back here when the
police asked her to, to 'help them with their inquiries.'
Doesn't that sound like something straight out of one of
Ngaio Marsh's Roderick Alleyn mysteries?"

"Hart never said anything like that in his life," I
said, trying on the phrase with a British accent. Everyone chuckled.

"That's probably just Francesca, trying to make herself sound important," Kerry agreed. "Anyway, Flavia
said Francesca was booked on a flight out of Denver
this afternoon. She's headed to New York, though, not
Illinois, to do the rounds of the morning talk shows."
Kerry shook her head, disgusted. "From something
Flavia said, it sounded like big-time publishers have
been approaching Francesca and her father about doing a tell-all memoir. There's even talk of a TV movie,
Flavia said."

"That's one book I won't be nominating for us to
read," Maud said.

"Amen," Lola said softly.

"It'll probably make more money than all her novels
combined," I said. "Who was it that said you can't un-
derestimate the taste of the American public, or something like that?"

Brooke helped herself to sparkling water from the
minifridge, and took a swallow. "It's funny how it
turned out to be all about identity, isn't it, like we were
talking about with *Rebecca*?" She used the green bottle

to gesture at the screen, where Olivier and Fontaine were frozen. "Francesca Bugle doesn't really exist—she's just a persona that Patty Bugg put on to sell books. She invented a name and a history. Maybe what du Maurier's saying is that not having a name is the most honest way to be, that it forces us to be our true selves."

"It would sure make it awkward to communicate, though," Kerry put in, always focusing on the practical.

"I think it's interesting how knowing that the author is a perv changes readers' experience with the text," I said, harking back to my English major days. "I mean, Francesca Bugle's books are still word for word what they always were, but knowing that a sex offender wrote those sex scenes makes them unreadable."

"They were always unreadable," Maud snorted.

We all laughed at that and Brooke pointed the remote so the lights dimmed and the movie resumed. We watched in silence until the flames consumed Manderley. When Brooke brought the lights up again, I blinked several times, and stretched my arms over my head.

"I think the fire was Maxim de Winter's punishment," Lola said, taking off her glasses and polishing the lenses with the hem of her shirt. Her eyes without the glasses seemed bigger, her curly lashes longer. "He did commit murder after all, and even if Rebecca was evil and goaded him to it, it's not right that he would walk away scot-free."

"Karma," Brooke said.

"Cosmo Zeller won't get away with it," Maud said. She stood and looked around at all of us. A smile crept over her lips. "Did you see the other photo in the *Heaven*

Herald? Not the front-page ones of Cosmo in handcuffs and our honorable mayor having it out with Brummel, but the one at the top of page three?"

"You mean the one of Mary Stewart in a clinch with her 'brother,'" I said, putting air quotes around "brother." The photo had clearly been taken from a tree outside the Columbine's dining room, and it showed Mary Stewart sitting on a table, her legs wrapped around Lucas's waist, kissing him like there was no tomorrow. Which there probably wouldn't be now for her writing career.

Maud's grin grew broader. "That's the one. Talk about karmic justice. What are the chances that Eloise Hufnagle missed that?"

"Slim and none," Kerry said. She eyed Maud narrowly. "You wouldn't have had anything to do with that photo, would you?"

"Moi?" Maud assumed an air of innocence. "Why would you think that? Just because my lover's a world-class photographer, and I thought Eloise was owed a little payback for the way the Stewarts treated her, and I knew they could barely keep their hands off each other . . . I tore my favorite shirt getting out of that dang tree. I just hope Hufnagle's lawyer can use the photo to win her case. It sure links Lucas and Mary in a way that will make it much harder for her to claim she had no connection to Eloise." Her grin was pure Cheshire cat.

"What do you think will happen to Allyson?" Lola asked, plucking popcorn bits from her chair and dropping them into the metal bowl. They dinged as they hit bottom.

"I don't think the police here have any interest in

her," I said. "I mean, no one from the Columbine pressed charges. I guess she'll go back to California with Merle and Constance."

"I hope she'll get the help she needs," Lola said.

"What she needs," Maud said with asperity, "is to move away from Constance. I think Merle gets that now. Her condition is aggravated or activated by stress, and it's clear that being around her mother sends her stress levels through the stratosphere. Merle's going to help her get set up in an apartment in San Leandro, where she's got a job offer. She'll keep on with the counseling and meds, too."

I studied her face, but saw no trace of melancholy or regret. Merle might have been important to her once upon a time, but no longer.

We all trooped upstairs, emerging into Brooke's gourmet kitchen in time to hear the garage door go up.

"Troy's back," Brooke said with a smile.

"We haven't picked a book for next time," Kerry reminded us. "Maud, it's your turn."

"I'll e-mail you," Maud said. "I'm thinking something with a little action, maybe a spy or two, some straightforward skulduggery after the lurking menace of Manderley and its inhabitants. I'm thinking something by Helen MacInnes or Alistair MacLean. I'll let you know."

Brooke pulled open the front door. "Hey, it snowed."

We crowded around the opening, looking out on a landscape made magical by a two-inch carpet of white snow. Big flakes were still falling, and they sparkled in the yellow glare from Brooke's porch light.

"First snow angel of the year," I said with delight,

and dashed to the center of Brooke's snow-covered yard. Cold snow wedged its way down my collar as I lay on my back. I shivered. I began to fan my legs and arms. Snow scrunched between my legs and under my armpits. Brooke, Lola, and Maud joined me, while Kerry remained on the stoop, hands on her hips, shaking her head back and forth slowly.

"Not me," she said. "I'm not an eight-year-old."

"You don't outgrow snow angels," I said, getting up and dusting snow off my backside.

"Oh, what the hell." Kerry joined us, lowering herself stiffly to her knees, and then rolling onto her back. "Damn, it's cold. Roman will wonder what happened to me when I walk in soaking wet."

"He's a teenage boy—he wouldn't notice if you walked in on fire," Maud said.

"True," Kerry laughed. "I'm going to make another one." She shifted to a smooth patch of snow.

"Me, too." I found an un-angeled spot and flopped down again. I let the cold embrace me and looked straight up, letting the snow sift gently onto my face, and wondered if Brooke was thinking about teaching her baby to make snow angels in a year or two, or if Hart had ever made a snow angel. He came from Georgia, so maybe not. With a smile, I thought what a joy it was to have friends to make snow angels with on the first snowfall of the season.